LOVE AND DARKER PASSIONS

Edited by Alexis Brooks de Vita and Lee Barwood

LOVE AND DARKER PASSIONS

DOUBLE DRAGON

Table of Contents

Love and Darker Passions – Prologue

Do you remember that psychological study that demonstrates that, without dream-image sleep, sane people become psychotic? Keep that in mind as I tell you that *Love and Darker Passions* is an anthology of dark fantasy relationship stories. Not stories of romance; or, at least, not romantic. Here are stories about how love feels. What love needs. What love makes us yearn for and dread.

These are stories of love like black holes: devouring, cleansing and creating anew in ways we don't quite want to understand. Love like religion: dragging up from the depths of our unspeakable fears a blind insensate faith. Love like birth: a bloody tide that exiles us onto arid sand where we stumble and fall, ignorant of the customs and the language, gesturing and grunting, trying to get someone to teach us how to belong.

This unspeakably visceral, frighteningly insistent love is probably vital to existence, like volcanoes firing up the ink of the midnight ocean where no one will see. The following tales of primal want question our need to bond at a sub-atomic level and the ruptures from love that cost us self-obliteration.

A.J. Maguire's "The Man Who Loved Medusa" and Desmond Warzel's "Sirens" present the sublimity of a man's desiring what has as its nature to destroy him, while C.E. Murphy's "Keys" and Ceschino's "The Argument" show how love seduces the true lover into. . . . but I will let you discover that for yourself.

Lee Barwood's "Rainsong" and Joseph Michael's "Lullaby of a Hated Person" let love take us on a quest through what is perilous, drawing ever nearer to what we both fear and crave. But Karen Duvall shatters our self-reflective illusion, for in her tale "Through the Looking Glass," love and grudge are intertwined; "Yes," says Natalie L. R. Baker, for without selfless love of the nameless, hidden other-than-ourselves, love recognizes neither its object nor itself.

Matthew K. Bird's "I Am a Smart Maid" further queries how it is that we choose whom we will love and how we cope when that gift of love is thwarted. Christina St. Clair and Joel Owusu answer with love of self-annihilation, the ultimate immersion in what claims us. Novella Serena's "Cacie's Prism" and Max Balkan's "Long Knives, Sharp Tongues" suggest that this all-consuming power is as it is because love kills what it cannot heal.

Tenea D. Johnson's "Only Then Can I Sleep" and Tedd Hawks's "The Vengeance" surrender us to love's spiritual cannibalism; the lover seeks to devour what is beloved. But if love destroys its object and its enemy, then neither is safe; just so, agrees Ezekiel M. Zachs in his unforgettable story of multilayered love triangles in "The Blood Doll." But love makes such self-sacrificing seduction sweet.

So what if we could be forced to love selflessly, blindly, strangers more than ourselves, taking nothing away except the knowledge that we have given all? What, indeed.

Here's hoping we may close this volume able to say that we've learned what these painstakingly penned stories have to teach us. For in this collection love proves to be that bloody splatter across the eons that moves at the edges of our lives, in our silences and secrets, drawing yearning hearts to hear what they were always listening for, in its indecipherable whispers in the dark.

I can safely promise that you'll love these stories.

—Alexis Brooks de Vita

A. J. Maguire reminds us that it was Medusa's incomparable beauty that led to her suffering and her curse. But shouldn't a lover see past the outer woman to the soul hiding within?

The Man Who Loved Medusa
by A. J. Maguire

His right foot slid over the shale-ridden ground and he had to catch himself before his body could plummet over the cliffs. Eustace took a steadying breath and waited for his heart to calm. Moonlight fought its way through a turbulent sky, barely lighting the sharp path he had to follow. The island around him was a barren, cursed place of craggy rocks and prickly brush. He could still hear the trickle of pebbles rushing over the cliff face beside him, and for a long moment he actually considered jumping.

Death seemed preferable to a life of longing.

He realized at last that he had caught himself on the elbow of a statue. Under his fingers was the curious roughness of stone. He ran his hand up the arm, to the shoulder, recognizing even in the gloom what stance the man had been in. An archer, Eustace thought grimly.

"A pity you have to look at what you're aiming at," he told the dead man.

Her voice came unbidden from his memory, *"Oh, I do not know if they are dead or alive. They are just ... stone. There are moments when I think I can hear them, calling out to me as though from a great distance. Is that not strange?"*

No stranger than when he'd begged her to turn him into one of them, to keep his fate by her side forever. He shivered a little at the thought of being trapped in such an awkward position as the poor soul beside him. Although it hadn't been an empty request, it hadn't been a pleasant one, either.

Reluctantly, Eustace started his trek again. He had to smirk at his own capricious nature. A year and five days ago he'd washed up on these strange, forbidding shores and had prayed to every god in the pantheon to be rescued from it. While he hadn't known it was Medusa's lair at first, Eustace had the good sense to know danger when it was present. Even in the weird, shifting mists, when he'd first heard her music, Eustace had the self-preservation to pause. But the lyre-song was so haunting, so achingly lonely, that he'd paddled his wreck of a ship closer, hoping to get a look at the player.

Now that he knew who it was that he'd been searching for, Eustace was grateful that the mists had concealed her form.

"What a melancholy song!" He'd shouted the words, but hadn't needed to. His voice traveled easily over the still water.

There was a great shifting of shadows on the shore; he could remember a hissing whisper just before an arrow chunked into the floorboards of his boat.

"I mean you no harm!" He'd said, scrambling for cover in the naked ship.

Her bitter laugh curled through the air. "No harm, you say? Year in and year out, you foolish men try to make yourselves heroes by slaying the beast."

Another arrow hit by his foot and he jerked back in defense. "Good lady," – he'd heard from the voice that she was female – "Why would I want to harm you? Poseidon was in a vengeful mood and my ship was blown off course. I do not know where I am, much less who you are."

Perhaps it was her unbridled hatred for the sea god, or perhaps it was the last vestiges of her humanity shining through, but she'd ceased her assault. Through the fog, she'd relayed instructions for where he could harbor. He could fix his boat and leave in peace, but was restricted to the southern half of the island. There was a small pool of fresh water on the eastern side, and a few small fish he could catch in the cove, but if he was found wandering anywhere else he would be killed.

Eustace had built a small hutch against the side of a rough hillock laden with boulders and desertous weeds. He spent very little time there. By day, he worked on his boat – though the task was nigh impossible. There were no tides in the forsaken place; no driftwood to find and what little trees populated the island were too porous to patch the small ship. By night, he sat at the edge of the fresh water pool and listened to her music drift through the air.

His heart flinched and he stopped his downward trek. There was no music tonight. Eustace turned to stare up the mountainside. Its jagged slope cast deep pools of shadow against the unfamiliar terrain. He'd only been on this side of the island once before, earlier that day when she'd instructed him to leave. He had an overwhelming desire to run back to her, to grab hold of her and let her know, once and for all, that no beastly countenance could hide the woman she was from him.

Carefully, he opened the small pouch she had given him. Inside was her parting gift – a lock of her hair, her real hair, not the writhing snake nest on her head. The thick, cool strands against his skin helped Eustace battle himself back to rational thought.

This was their agreement, the pact that had been made with the gods themselves, and he could not back out. And so he took to the path again, heading for the northern harbor where he was to meet his ship, his mind replaying the last year with painful clarity.

It had taken him a full day to realize he was in the home of a Gorgon. In his defense, many of the stone statues littering the island were old and crumbling, some of them so dilapidated that you couldn't distinguish between rock and former man. But he'd spotted one unfortunate soldier, crouched behind a boulder by the freshwater spring, his hands shielding his face in defense, and he'd known where he was.

Eustace wasn't a man who called on the gods too often. In his mind, the state of affairs on Olympus seemed busy enough that he preferred not to bother them. At that moment, gazing at the hapless fellow frozen in stone, Eustace had beseeched every single god for some form of salvation.

There were three Gorgons he knew of; Stheno, Euryale and Medusa. They were great monsters, Titans, known for their violence against mankind and their hideous form. Eustace was not a warrior, never had been, and was nearing his thirty-fourth birthday. An old man in many people's standards, fit only for sailing and catching fish, not doing battle against such a creature.

"Your heartbeat has changed, Eustace. I can feel it in the ground." He could hear the sadness in her voice even now. "Do you know who I am?"

"I do not think Stheno or Euryale would know how to play a lyre," Eustace replied, trying his damndest to sound brave. "So that would make you Medusa."

"And are you determined to kill me, now that you know?"

"No." The answer came so fast, he'd surprised himself. After an uncomfortable moment, as he tried to understand his own words, Eustace said it again, more firmly, "No, I am not."

"You are a strange man, Eustace Panopoulos."

"No stranger than a Gorgon who plays the lyre."

She always stood in the shadows, but he heard her small laugh, "It is a comfort to me in this place. A piece of who I used to be. Or perhaps, who I could have been."

He came to the final switchback and paused again. A finger of land made a crooked curl into the sea just below. He could see a boat tied there, and two men standing on its deck. One spotted him and waved. Eustace waved back before forcing himself to move again.

It was curious, he thought as his feet shifted over more loose rock, that the memories haunting him were mostly of her in the Gorgon form. Granted, they'd spent a year talking to each other through shadows and laughing over his pathetic attempts at a campfire, and they'd only had one day – one glorious day – with Medusa in human form, but he'd thought the sight of her would throw everything else into the background. And in fact, Eustace had thought his heart stopped beating when she woke him that morning.

After months of praying, he'd begun to think the gods weren't listening. But Zeus had listened. The King of the gods had not only listened, but granted Medusa's petition. She'd asked for just one day in her natural form, one day to show Eustace who she ought to be.

It was bitterly unfair, the way Medusa had been treated. One god pursuing her and another shunning her, there was little surprise that her music was so sad. Eustace wondered, as his feet slowed around the final corner, if Zeus's mercy for one day might not be another form of torment. Could the memory of one day truly outshine the misery of her existence?

He held tight to the lock of hair as he approached the boat, and tried to reconcile himself to the bargain she'd made.

"Who goes there?"

The two men on the boat were as different as they could be; one dark and one fair, one bearded

16

and one not, but both wearing breastplates of the military sort. He addressed his response to the bearded, darker one, assuming the elder to be in charge.

"I am Eustace Panopoulos, a fisherman."

"How do you come to be on these dark shores, Fisherman?"

"A storm stranded me here. I hoped you would take me back to familiar lands." Eustace prayed they wouldn't ask how long he'd been there. It would be difficult to explain how he had survived for so long.

"Our master Perseus has run to fetch the Gorgon's head. When he returns, we will ask him about taking you on."

A spurt of fear shot into his spine. "Your master Perseus? But I did not see him on my way to the harbor."

The fair one smirked, "You would not have. He wears a helmet that renders him invisible."

Eustace fought the urge to look over his shoulder. "But how will he take Medusa's head? She can feel a man's heartbeat through the ground. Even invisible, your master has little chance."

The smirk got deeper and Eustace swallowed back a wayward remark. The insolence of these men was so palpable that he actually wanted to fight. They would certainly beat him; they were trained for such things. He could see this by the swords and shields, but he still wanted to.

"Our Master Perseus will not touch the ground. He has a pair of winged sandals that let him fly." This time it was the dark one who smirked, "So you see, it is Medusa who has no chance."

Eustace felt the words slam into him like a blow to the chest and staggered.

"Are you all right?"

Without answering, he pivoted on his heel and charged back up the path. The two men shouted at him, called him several insulting things, but Eustace didn't care. Bargain or not, he couldn't stand aside and let her die.

Disregarding the path, he scrambled up the mountainside, clawing at shale and rock that threatened to send him back down. Half running and half climbing, he negotiated the treacherous slope without pausing. His muscles strained and his chest tightened, his breath coming out in great wheezes, but he couldn't stop, wouldn't stop.

No, he thought, seeing not the weathered rocks around him but Medusa's face – her beautiful, true face – as it had been just that morning.

"Zeus has answered my prayers, Eustace." Her smile knocked his heart in a million directions. "For today, and only today, you get to see the true me."

His knee bashed into a boulder and a large slide of shale and rock pushed his body back down. It hadn't stopped sliding before he was up again. Toes digging into the dirt, Eustace pushed himself upward, praying he would reach her in time.

"No," he said aloud as he reached the ridgeline.

On easier ground, Eustace picked up speed, using reserves of energy he'd never known were there. Something flew by overhead and he stumbled to a halt, thinking of Perseus and his damned flying sandals. But the sky was dark and

18

the moonlight too dim for him to see what it was. And it wouldn't have mattered. Eustace was too intent on his goal. He ran headlong into her cave, calling out her name, heedless of any danger that might still be present.

"Medusa!"

Feet slapping against the stone floor, Eustace sprinted into her innermost sanctuary. Crumbling pillars and rusted braziers were strewn about the massive space, but he knew where he was going. He called for her again and still she did not answer. Grief burned in his chest before he'd even found her.

Eustace came to an abrupt stop.

Sprawled out in front of him was the great, serpentine tail of the woman he had loved. The rest of her body was hidden behind a boulder, in the nest he knew she used as a bed. The poor woman had been sleeping – sleeping, of all things! – and that coward Perseus snuck in, winged and invisible, and murdered her.

Vision blurred, he fell to his knees. With a shaking hand, he reached out to touch the Gorgon's tail. Sleek and scaly, like water made solid, it felt nothing like the Medusa he had held in his arms earlier that day. A sob tore from him and he bowed his head.

He could remember the feel of her hand on his chest as she'd told him the conditions of her transformation. One day, she'd said, at sunset she would be the Gorgon again and he was to be banished from the island. While he hadn't liked it, he hadn't wanted to spend their one day fighting, either.

"What would you like to do first?" He'd asked.

"Well, if you don't mind, I'd like to sit and talk for a while … face to face."

Closing his eyes, he tried to capture that vision; the tentative smile and embarrassed half-laugh she'd given. But it was gone, lost in the empty ache that filled him.

A thick, wet plop made him open his eyes. Eustace leaned over the massive tail and cringed when he saw the large pool of blood. Her back was to him, which saved him from seeing her headless. She might have still been sleeping, curled around herself that way, were it not for the bubbling, visceral liquid growing beside her. Eustace watched the blood, which seemed somehow thicker, like a great glob of red tar. It moved, rolling over itself in a wave that stretched and grew. Then it rolled the other way, undulating in a constant movement.

Twisting and churning, the amorphous blob writhed on the stone floor, hissing steam into the cavern. Terror kept Eustace immobile. He'd never heard of a Gorgon dying before, much less seen one, but he was fairly certain that this was unusual.

A hoof tore through the glossy surface of bloody gobbet, clopping onto the ground with an unnatural crack that sent a tremor through the cave. Eustace held tighter to Medusa's tail, his heart clamoring in fear. One strong, equine head emerged into the open and he caught his breath in his chest. The stallion shook off Medusa's blood and stretched a pair of giant, feathered wings on either side of its body. Eustace was so spellbound by the beauty of it that he didn't see them arrive. It wasn't until the woman spoke that he realized they were there.

"How is this possible?"

Athena, he would recognize that proud, straight-backed stance anywhere. Bedaubed in gold and white, she stood just beside her father, Zeus, whose silver-gilded presence ebbed so much power that Eustace felt a tremble pass through him. The third could be none other than the trident-toting Poseidon, arrayed in shades of blue and frothy white.

"Because she was pregnant with my child," Poseidon strode forward and patted the stallion with pride.

Eustace scowled but dared not move. He saw Zeus and Athena exchange a glance.

"What is it?" Athena asked.

"A Pegasus," Poseidon stroked the creature's white mane and smiled rather smugly at the two other gods. "All such horses and bulls are tied to me, but this ... the Pegasus shall be my pride and glory. Do either of you refute this?"

Another glance between Athena and her father before Zeus spoke: "No, all horses and bulls are known to be your symbols."

Eustace thought there was an odd note to the god's voice, but Poseidon didn't seem to notice. The sea god patted the Pegasus twice more, and in a sudden swirl of water that engulfed his figure, was gone.

"You did not tell him about the man," Athena

said after a moment.

"Let his own pride make a fool of him," Zeus moved to pet the Pegasus. "We can laugh in secret at his boasts."

"I shall not forgive you for giving Medusa a reprieve," Athena lifted her chin and seemed to square off against her father.

"And I shall never understand your jealousy of the mortal. Her beauty was fleeting, yours will endure."

"It was her weakness that offended me, not her beauty."

Eustace bit back a comment and tried to remain still. These were powers that went beyond him, and while he wanted to defend Medusa against the goddess, he knew the spiteful woman could do far worse things to him if he tried. Perhaps that was weak of him, or perhaps it was wise, he couldn't be certain either way.

"Yes, this island is littered with her weakness," Zeus kept patting the horse, but his gaze fastened on his daughter. "I gave the woman mercy for a day and I'll not be questioned for it."

Athena huffed her agitation and turned away. In a bright flash of golden light, she was gone. There was a long moment of silence as Zeus continued to inspect the Pegasus and Eustace considered slinking back the way he'd come.

"You have missed your boat, Eustace Panopoulos."

Too humbled by the power of the thunder god, Eustace stayed where he was; "Indeed I have ..." – how did one address a god? – " ... my Lord."

"I believe the agreement was that you would leave this place after she had returned to Gorgon form."

Zeus began to lead the Pegasus to where Eustace still knelt. Frightened beyond his senses, Eustace bowed his head and stammered for a reply.

"I find you curious, Eustace Panopoulos." Zeus stopped just in front of him, Medusa's tail separating man from god. "Even the gods are distracted by surface beauty and shun that which is hideous. Yet you managed to see past the Gorgon form Medusa was cursed with. Tell me, mortal, did you still see that in her when she was beautiful?"

Eustace was overcome by two striking images of her. She'd always been careful to keep herself hidden from him, but Eustace had managed to see her. He'd seen the mass of snakes on her head and the long, muscled tail, and he'd seen her when she was without the curse. Any other man might have had trouble finding the real woman in either form, but Eustace knew her. He knew her love of painting, the way she lingered at the shoreline each morning and night, desperate for one last taste of beauty as it filled the sky. It was her voice, her mind and her heart that had captivated him. He could have spent the rest of his life just listening to her talk.

"There was more to Medusa than the Gorgon or the beauty," Eustace said at last.

When he lifted his head, Zeus gave him a quizzical look. "Fair enough," he said. "Where do you live, Eustace?"

Blinking, he replied, "Corinth."

"You are a long way from home, with no boat." Zeus looked to the Pegasus. "If you ask him nicely, he just might be ready to fly."

With a sudden spike of lightning, Zeus left. The Pegasus reared up in fright, massive white wings flapping with its alarm as it ran away from the spot. The beautiful horse made a semi-circle, snorting its disapproval and bobbing its head. Silently, Eustace agreed with the upset creature. The gods had an unnerving manner about them, and certainly knew how to exit. After a long moment, Eustace got to his feet.

His legs were wobbly from kneeling too long, but he carefully stepped over Medusa's tail. Eyes lingering on her curled, quiet form, Eustace had to force himself to turn away. He approached the Pegasus slowly, his arms open wide in an effort to appear harmless. To his amazement, the creature seemed to welcome him. The Pegasus snorted and snuffled at his hand, letting him close enough to stroke its sleek, white neck. Awestruck, Eustace touched one powerful wing and smiled.

"By the gods," he told Pegasus, "you are as magnificent as your mother."

The End

A. J. Maguire's first book, SEDITION, was published in January 2011 by Wings ePress. Her second book, WITCH-BORN, was released in June 2011 by Double Dragon Publishing. She lives in Boise, Idaho with her son and one very noisy cat.

Desmond Warzel's entrancing short story plays on words and on normalcy to lure us into a world from which it will become increasingly impossible to find—or identify—any safe exit. Where is that sound coming from?

Sirens
by Desmond Warzel

Greg Jacoby did not like Long Island very much. He had not arrived at this opinion in haste; ten years' residency, in his mind, more than accorded him the right to make such judgments.

His inhabitancy of Long Island had been a natural consequence of his fortuitous hire by a large Manhattan ad agency. Indeed, on some rarified Platonic level, the *concept* of "Long Island" could be seen as congruent with that of "success," or at least "upward mobility." But something was lost on the journey from theory to execution, and what remained was the Long Island that Greg knew: the streets that stayed straight for no more than two hundred feet before angling off at random; the seventy-five-thousand-dollar houses that sold for five hundred thousand; the squat, shabby shopping plazas lining every roadway of more than two lanes.

Yet here was Greg, edging his Saab out of rush-hour traffic and into the weed-riddled parking lot of just such a plaza, his attention arrested by a neon-green banner affixed to its rightmost tenant (a personal-electronics discounter straightforwardly called PERSONAL ELECTRONICS

DISCOUNTER). The banner promoted a brand of prepaid wireless service; it read, in full, "LiberTel: The Mobile Phone THE MAN Doesnt Want You To Have!!!!"

Greg had no interest in LiberTel. He *did* have a paranoid college friend whose continuous, outspoken denunciation of imagined conspiracies large and small had made him well-nigh unemployable (he spent most of his time at his local library, photocopying suspicious passages from the *New York Times*). Greg kept in touch with him for his own amusement, and because he believed that good old friends were worth hanging on to, whether you liked them or not, and meant to photograph the banner with his mobile phone—presumably, the one THE MAN *did* want him to have. Doubtless his friend would be amused by the slogan on several levels, most of them imaginary.

Sometime between Greg's exiting his car and his snapping the photo, a salesman in a very nice dark suit emerged from the store and sidled up to him. The young gentleman had a clean-shaven head, and his speaking voice was as smooth as his red silk necktie.

"Good afternoon, sir, my name is DeShawn, I see you noticed our banner, are you interested in prepaid wireless today?"

"No, I've got it covered--"

"My mistake, sir, it's obvious by looking that you have no need for prepaid service, you don't have to worry about 'the man,' you *are* 'the man,' perhaps I can interest you in the latest iPhone?"

"I'm stuck with Sprint, so—"

"Sir, a gentleman like you clearly doesn't play by the rules of others, which is why any of our phones can be made compatible with any network, for a minuscule fee, payable in cash."

"I'm set for wireless, thanks—"

"Sir, successful people like yourself know that you remain successful by increasing your productivity, if I can persuade you to step inside with me, I can help you do that any number of ways, I've got iPods, GPS, PDAs, telematics—"

"Telematics?"

"In-car emergency communications services, they're included with certain vehicles, but the aftermarket versions we carry work in any car, including high-end models like yours, can I interest you in a little peace of mind, mobile phones are notoriously unreliable—"

"Including the phones you were just trying to sell me, DeShawn?"

"You're very savvy, sir, which is why I'm surprised you haven't already got one..."

Minutes later, Greg was the newest client of a firm called CarGuard. This was partly because of the unit's surprisingly low cost (including a monthly fee that was less than he spent for coffee and a sandwich in Manhattan), and partly because he'd found a kindred spirit in DeShawn, whose sales technique was a scaled-down version of his own, spaced over a three-minute conversation rather than a three-martini lunch.

After a half-hour's wait for installation and activation, Greg exited the dilapidated parking lot, lighter by a few hundred dollars and—though he was a mild introvert who had never entertained the idea of a protégé—one business card. "Anybody can move junk," Greg had explained. "Convincing people to buy something they actually *need*; that takes talent."

***

Talent or no, young DeShawn had indeed anticipated one of Greg's immediate needs because, three days after his CarGuard purchase, Greg had an accident. Most would consider this a mildly-interesting coincidence; others, perhaps, simple bad luck. Greg's old college friend would have called it a conspiracy. Greg, who made his living manipulating others, knew that coincidence, luck, and conspiracy were interchangeable and depended on the position of the observer.

It was three o'clock Saturday morning on an unusually-empty Long Island Expressway. He'd been at a party in Southampton whose twin *raisons d'être* had been its guests' total inebriation and, later, their indiscriminate pairing-off. Greg hadn't been able to get into the spirit, and he now headed home with an unsullied bloodstream and an empty passenger seat. His speed was perhaps a hundred miles per hour.

He knew better, of course. But some opportunities are too rare to decline. He would sooner have forgone the chance to pet a unicorn than pass up the prospect of driving a hundred on the Long Island Expressway. It was a much bigger thrill than either drinking or sex would have been;

Greg was confident he'd made a smart decision, until he saw the deer.

A small, crazy part of him wondered what deer were doing on an island in the first place: *Do they swim? Take the bridge?* A smaller, crazier part considered just running down the beast, in the service of natural selection and to deliver a warning to the ungulate community. In the end, plain common sense still held controlling interest, and he swerved deftly around the animal's hindquarters.

The resulting skid had him traveling sideways at a slight tangent to the highway, such that, when his front bumper finally did make contact with the left-hand barrier, the car had lost most of its speed. In fact, the Saab was traveling, to within one mile-per-hour, just fast enough to set off its airbags.

For a long moment, Greg heard nothing and saw only white; as the airbags deflated and his head cleared, the concrete barrier came into view, illuminated by the Saab's single surviving headlight, and he could hear his pulse tapping out a loud staccato in his skull. To his left stood the deer, unmoved by the heroics he'd exhibited in sparing its life. Greg started the Saab once more, straightening it back out and moving it onto the shoulder; neither this, nor his subsequent profane tirade, disturbed the animal in the slightest.

What finally motivated it to leap the barrier and bound into the night, was this: "This is Stephanie from CarGuard; I'm detecting an airbag deployment. Have you been in an accident?" The voice came from the little box DeShawn's colleague had installed in his dashboard.

At least the thing works. "Yeah," said Greg. He wondered if he ought to be talking directly into the little box. "It was a deer. I'm fine, though."

"Police and emergency medical services are on their way," said Stephanie.

"That's not necessary," said Greg. "There were no other cars, I'm not hurt, and my car is drivable."

"They should be there any minute. I'll stay on the line until they arrive." On cue, a pair of sirens, one long, one short, approached from behind him. He gritted his teeth and threw a few ineffectual punches at the airbag hanging impotently from the steering wheel. He suddenly wanted to be home in bed, and the idea of being deposed all night in the middle of the Expressway sat poorly.

"No need," he said. "In fact, go ahead and tell them not to bother."

"I'm not permitted to do that, sir."

"Like hell you're not. I'm fine. Even the damn *deer* is fine."

"I'm sorry, sir."

"Then you might want to let them know I'll be gone when they get here."

"I wouldn't advise that, sir. You shouldn't leave the scene of an accident, even when you're not at fault."

"*What accident? What scene?* There's nobody else here!"

"Are you sure you're not hurt, sir? Sudden belligerence can be a sign of head trauma."

"I'll show you belligerence—" Greg began, and then he was surrounded by flashing lights and uniforms.

30

"I'm seeing that emergency personnel have arrived, sir. Thank you for using CarGuard." There was a click from the little box as Stephanie disengaged and left him to the mercies of the first responders. The EMTs, once informed that nobody was hurt, departed in sullen silence. The police listened with sympathy and commiseration to Greg's narrative of events, then measured his skid marks and, after some back-of-the-hand arithmetic, issued him a citation for speeding.

Greg spent most of Saturday in bed, alternately sulking and dozing; a marathon of *The Andy Griffith Show* provided soothing continuity throughout. He suspended his confinement on three occasions: two bathroom excursions and a sojourn to the kitchen for an unsatisfying dinner of microwaved Chinese food. For Greg, such an adherence to traditional standards of bachelorhood was rare, but the prior night's irresponsible behavior coupled with the day's lack of productivity had him feeling unusually bachelor-like.

He awoke on Sunday in a state of manic refreshment achievable only by sleeping for eighteen hours out of twenty-four. He resolved to engage with the world in some positive fashion; this determination petered out nine seconds later when he turned his phone on and was besieged with text messages: "omg dude ur car wtf" and similar gems. Someone had evidently driven by the house, noticed the damage to the Saab, and relayed the news. Greg's circle of friends had always been compact and insular; the advent of social media had practically made them a hivemind, and what one

31

knew, they all knew.

Once showered, dressed, and fed, he decided to move the car into the garage.

Greg's neighbors of ten years had yet to acknowledge his presence. A lifetime of sitcoms had conditioned him to expect barbecue invitations, lawn-care advice, and male bonding sessions involving beer and football; not only had these failed to materialize, he'd never even managed eye contact with anyone in the neighborhood. As far as he could tell, he hadn't been singled out for ostracizing; they ignored one another, too. With nothing to go by, Greg found it easy to assume the worst about his neighbors. The reverse was likely also true; hence the concealment of the evidence, though it was probably already too late. *Then again*, he thought, *how much bad word-of-mouth could these hermits possibly spread*?

No sooner had he started the Saab than the little box in the dashboard sprang to life once more, in familiar voice. "This is Stephanie from CarGuard; I see that you interacted with one of our customer service personnel on Saturday morning. Is that correct?"

"Yes," Greg said dryly. "It was you."

"We're always striving to improve. May I ask you a few questions about your experience with CarGard?"

"I would *love* to tell you what I think, Stephanie. To begin with—"

"And am I speaking with the account holder?"

"Yes."

"This is Mr. Gregory Jacoby of four-nine-eight

Superior Lane, Roslyn, New York?"

"It is."

"Mr. Jacoby, would you say your CarGuard customer service technician's response after your accident was: not timely, timely, or very timely?"

"Very timely. But—"

"And would you say your technician's deportment was: discourteous, courteous, or very courteous?"

"Courteous, as far as that goes. But—"

"And would you say the arrival of emergency personnel was very slow, slow, average, fast, or very fast?"

"Very fast. In fact, that's exactly—"

"And, based on your experience, would you recommend CarGuard to a friend or family member?"

"No," said Greg.

Stephanie didn't miss a beat. "And do you have any additional comments about your CarGuard experience?"

"Bet on it. Nobody was hurt. I begged you not to call the cops, and you wouldn't listen. You call that service?"

"According to the transcript, your CarGuard technician followed our procedures exactly."

"It was *you*. Just admit it was you."

"Very well, sir. *I* followed our procedures exactly."

"Does 'following procedures' include chipping in for my speeding ticket?"

"I'm afraid not, sir."

"The fine's one thing; wasting a whole day in

court, that's what I'm *really* looking forward to."

"I'm sorry about that, sir. The regulations are clear; the authorities must be contacted in the event of an accident."

"Well, you won't have me to kick around anymore. Go ahead and cancel my service. Now, please."

"I'd be happy to do that, sir. However, I see that you've taken advantage of our special and prepaid for six months' service. I'd advise you to remain with us for that period; per the contract you signed, that money is—"

"Nonrefundable."

"Yes, sir."

"You people have nerve, you know that? Hell, you probably *work* for the police. How much do you make for every speeding ticket you generate? Does your mother know what you do for a living? Sit in a cubicle and cause aggravation? What kind of human being takes a job like that? You tell me."

The silence lasted long enough to make Greg think he'd been disconnected. Then came Stephanie's voice, now devoid of artificial cheer; now quiet and human. "Not everyone gets to choose what they do."

Greg closed his eyes, leaned forward until his forehead rested on the steering wheel. Several measured breaths calmed his racing heart a little.

He wasn't native to the world of Saabs and suburbia, but an immigrant, and he knew firsthand the harsh landscape of customer service and the toll it exacted. He'd sworn he'd never become one of "them": those who sought and savored the cheap triumph of insulting people who were forbidden to retaliate.

"I'm sorry, Stephanie—it *is* really Stephanie?"

"Yeah."

"My ticket isn't your fault. I'm sure you're a nice person."

"Thank you, Mr. Jacoby—"

"Greg."

"Thanks, Greg. Of *course* I feel bad for you; I should have said so before. Isn't it strange that I didn't…"

"Well, you don't want to go too far off-script?"

"I guess. Do you really have to go to court just for a speeding ticket?"

"Welcome to Long Island."

"Sorry."

"Don't sweat it, Stephanie. Friends?"

"Sure."

"Refund?"

"Nope."

"Ah."

There was a pause, and then, "Maybe…I can make the next six months worth your while. I'm upgrading you to LifeGuard."

"What'll *that* cost me?"

"There's no charge; LifeGuard is a premium service tier offered free to select clients. I'm not actually allowed to do this, you know."

"Don't get yourself fired on my account."

The laughter coming from the little box was more sarcastic than jocular, but still appealing. "I wouldn't worry about that."

Greg apologized once more for his tirade. As

he and Stephanie made their farewells, he put the Saab in gear and eased it forward into the garage as he'd intended. From the corner of his eye he saw his next-door neighbor's anonymous countenance peering through the curtains, transfixed by the sight of a grown man apparently engaged in animated conversation with his dashboard.

The repairs to the Saab—and the adjudication of his ticket—consumed several days, and more money than Greg would ever admit to spending; he considered switching to a bicycle before deciding that the Saab was less pretentious. Once this hurdle of expense and inconvenience had been cleared, however, he resumed his ordinary routine with discomfiting effortlessness: fifty hours a week spent in the office making up lies about dish soap, twelve hours spent drinking revolting vodka concoctions with people he despised, two hours spent drinking beer with his actual friends, and so on.

Because he had no interest in further interaction with CarGuard/LifeGuard/whatever, he made a deliberate point of driving responsibly; by this very behavior, of course, he unwittingly invited Stephanie into his thoughts. *If life was a Tom Hanks movie*, he once joked to himself, *she and I would be engaged by now*. But life was not a movie, and so the continued silence of CarGuard/LifeGuard/whatever could only be considered a good thing.

It lasted two months and ended not at all as he would have expected.

"This is Stephanie from LifeGuard. I'm

detecting a laceration; do you require emergency medical attention?"

Suddenly the five-inch gash that newly decorated his forearm was the second biggest surprise of the moment. What *really* astonished him was not just Stephanie's reemergence, nor her oddly specific greeting, but that he was standing in his kitchen and her voice seemed to emanate from the speakers of the switched-off portable radio on the far counter.

Instinct, coupled with latent Boy Scout training, took over the matter of the cut, freeing his cogitative facilities to resolve the impossibility he'd been presented. They were unequal to the task.

"Ah...I'm sorry, what?"

"Stephanie, from LifeGuard. I'm seeing that you have a laceration; what can LifeGuard do to help? Do you need an ambulance?"

"You mean you haven't called them already?" Greg hunched over the kitchen sink, rinsing his arm in cold water. With much of the blood washed away, the wound revealed itself, and Greg averted his eyes. Small cuts were, in a way, more abstract; a gash like this, with the skin visibly laid open, was hard to look at.

"LifeGuard is a premium concierge service, tailored to the client's needs. No script."

Greg fumbled in a drawer for a clean dishtowel to wrap his arm. "No ambulance necessary. I think I need stitches, though."

Stephanie rattled off the name of the nearest hospital without pause. "Do you need directions?"

"No, thank you."

"I've notified them that you're on your way. I'll stay with you until you get there."

"Good. I've got a few questions."

Once he was in the car and on his way, Stephanie rejoined him via the little box in the dashboard. "Greg, please let me know if you feel light-headed; I'll stop your car for you and call for help."

"So, Stephanie? How is it you can talk to me over the radio in my kitchen? And, more disconcertingly, how could you 'detect' that I'd just sliced my arm open?"

"All part of the service, Greg."

"But how does it *work*?"

"Oh, I'm sure I don't know. It's *way* beyond me, I'm afraid. How did you cut yourself, Greg?"

"Engage the idiot in conversation to keep his mind off his injury, is that it?"

"I'd never call you an idiot, Greg."

"Well, you should. I was slicing an onion for a salad. I'd been washing dishes before, and the counter was still wet. The cutting board slipped, and here we are."

"And have we learned anything?" Stephanie's tone was mock-scolding.

"Yeah. We've learned that blood turns black when it touches a freshly-cut onion."

"You're kidding."

"I *think* that's what I saw. I'm in no hurry to repeat the experiment. Oh, damn." Thanks to the twin distractions of Stephanie's banter and the blood-soaked dishtowel swaddling his arm, it was all he could do to concentrate on the road in front of him; the police car whose lights now cavorted in his rear-view mirror had failed to register altogether. Suddenly, the siren made itself known as well, wailing in nearly perfect time with his throbbing arm.

"What's the matter, Greg? Are you okay?"

"I'm about to be pulled over." Greg glanced at the speedometer; he hadn't been giving the instrument its due attention, and the needle's position reflected his dereliction.

"Just a second." The little box fell quiet. Greg began looking for a place to pull over. He directed his mental energies backward at the cop: *Don't shoot me, I'm looking for a place to pull over.*

"There we go," said Stephanie. "I've informed him of your situation. He's going to clear the way for you." Indeed, the siren ceased and the police car passed him, lights still flashing, and took position at a fixed distance ahead. Occasionally Greg passed by a car that had pulled to the roadside at the cop's insistence.

"Is there anything you *can't* do, Stephanie?"

"Plenty. More than you'd think."

"Stephanie, I don't know if I like being monitored in my home like that."

"Are you sure? Because if you'd broken your leg, or had a heart attack, you'd be thanking me instead of complaining."

By the time Greg formulated a comeback, he'd reached the hospital and Stephanie had vanished.

***

Greg did his clearest thinking in a supine position; the firm, indulgent of eccentricity where talent was concerned, had placed a couch in his office for this purpose. Today, like most days, he'd spent much of the morning there.

In addition to the pain in his newly-sutured arm, he was also quite hungry; once home from the emergency room, he'd eschewed his partially-assembled salad and gone straight to bed. Just now, these sensations registered only peripherally; his attention was focused, not on the ceiling tiles above the couch—as a passerby might reasonably have assumed—but on LifeGuard.

Two avenues of thought competed for his consideration. On the one hand, he desperately wanted to know how LifeGuard worked: How closely, and by what means, did they monitor him? How had they inferred his distress, and furthermore, how had they deduced his laceration? On the other hand, he desperately wanted them for his next client: How could a company with that kind of ingenuity depend solely on word-of-mouth for sales?).

He'd hoped these dilemmas might be resolved at the source, but he'd been unable to contact the company. LifeGuard was absent from the web altogether; its lesser cousin CarGuard was occasionally mentioned on consumer sites, generally positively. CarGuard's toll-free number was on the box; he'd called it and been consigned to a purgatory of endless menus, few of which were helpful and none of which mentioned LifeGuard. There was an address as well; he'd composed and mailed a brief letter but despaired of ever hearing back.

The second problem, then, was insoluble, at least temporarily; but he might make some progress on the first problem, by brute force if nothing else. The first thing would be to comb the house for cameras, microphones, monitors, and the like—

No, he thought, hauling himself upright, *we don't know the parameters yet. Are they monitoring the house, or me*?

This could be tested. He wandered over to his desk and rummaged through the middle drawer. After discarding all manner of unsuitable instruments—paper clips, pens—he finally brandished a silver letter opener—and found himself unable to act. He would have been hard-pressed to go sawing at himself on his best day, and the previous night's commotion had left him gun-shy.

He adjourned momentarily to the reception area, and reentered his office brandishing a cup of hot coffee. He rolled up his left sleeve and positioned his arm over the empty wastebasket.

Two decades prior, he'd served a hitch manning the French fry station at his local fast-food eatery; a bout of inattention while extracting a basket of fries had allowed the residual oil to drip onto his arm. The resulting burn had left a discoloration that persisted to this day; it was this blemish for which he aimed as he raised the Styrofoam cup and tipped out the contents.

The coffee cascaded over the crook of his arm. There was the split-second of anticipation, which carried its own special agony, and then the pain, no less excruciating for its familiarity. Greg clenched his teeth and fought the urge to cry out.

"This is Stephanie from LifeGuard. I'm detecting a burn; do you require emergency medical attention?"

This time, the voice came through the speaker of the telephone on his desk. He had, of course, entertained this possibility—otherwise, he wouldn't have gone to such lengths to test it— even so, he found himself too startled to reply.

"Greg? Are you okay?"

"Fine," said Greg, looking around for something to dry off with. "Just spilled some coffee. No big deal."

"Is there any blistering on the affected area?"

"No."

"Be sure to run some cold water on it—"

"Sure, I know. I was in the Scouts. You worked last night, and you're on again this morning?"

"LifeGuard is personalized service, Greg."

"You mean…it'll be you every time?"

"Would you prefer someone else?"

No," said Greg, much more quickly than he'd intended.

"I'm glad. Is there anything else I can do for you?"

"No, I'm afraid not."

Stephanie took her leave and the office was silent once more. Greg found some napkins squirreled away in the desk and cleaned up. The aroma of coffee filled the room, exacerbating his already-considerable hunger until it eclipsed the respective pains in his arms. He traipsed back out to the reception area in search of sustenance, finally seizing on an unclaimed box of doughnuts. The morning's developments occupied his thoughts so completely that he only regained his awareness when he realized he'd eaten the entire dozen.

As the week progressed, there were several occasions on which Greg came very near to broaching the subject of LifeGuard to other people. He never went through with it. There were only two routes of inquiry, as he saw it, that wouldn't end with his friends or colleagues revising their estimations of his sanity.

The first turned out to be a bust. Saturday morning, he'd made a return visit to PERSONAL ELECTRONICS DISCOUNTER. Young DeShawn, outgoing as ever, had forsworn any knowledge of the company beyond the CarGuard service itself and then commenced a fusillade of sales pitches. Escaping the store with his finances intact, as it turned out, would be the high point of his day.

This was because Greg's second possibility was his old college friend, he of the multitudinous paranoias. If there were other instances of customer-service reps talking at people through their speakerphones and radios, this was the guy who would know about it; but there would be complications. Getting hold of him was hard enough; then he'd have to sift out the useful bits from a conglomeration of conspiracy rantings.

He began by texting the photo he'd taken the

day he'd purchased CarGuard; he'd never gotten around to doing that. There would be a certain satisfying symmetry to things if this inquiry panned out; that picture had precipitated this entire business, in the first place.

The text sent, there was nothing to do but wait.

At four o'clock that afternoon, the call came.

"Hello?"

"This is Carl. To whom am I speaking?" It wasn't, in fact, "Carl," but "Terry"; he used a different name each time to throw wiretappers off the scent. The voice, though, was unmistakable.

"This is Greg Jacoby."

"Middle name?"

"Lee."

"Where did we always go to buy beer?"

"Stymie's Liquor Warehouse on Jefferson Street."

"Greg! Long time, buddy. Sorry it took me so long to call you back. Had to get to a secure location. I don't call from my house anymore."

"Did you get the picture?"

"You mean, 'the mobile phone the man doesn't want you to have?' Gotta be a false-flag operation."

"How's that?"

"They doth protest too much. You can bet 'the man' is listening in on every one of those phones."

"Huh. Well, anyway…" Greg described CarGuard/LifeGuard in general terms.

"Sounds like bad news. Of course, we're *always* being watched, but it's worrying that they'd do it right out in the open like that."

"But have you *heard* of it?"

44

"LifeGuard? No, that's a new one on me. What idiot got himself roped into *that*?

"Me."

"And you *called* me? Are you *crazy*? They're listening right now, you know that? How could you give me up like that?"

"Terry—"

"Carl. It's Carl. Look, you can't call me anymore. Maybe you'll hear from me again, but probably not. Definitely not till you get out from under that LifeGuard thing."

"Come on, Terry—Carl, I mean..." but Terry/Carl was gone.

That was that, then. Terry approached his conspiracy-mongering with far more gravity and sincerity than he had his classes, jobs, or relationships.

Greg didn't lose friends every day. He wasn't altogether certain what to do with himself. Instinct drove him toward his compact circle of Long Island friends—his grown-up friends. Granted, instinct hadn't been his staunchest ally during the last couple of months. But you couldn't get a hit if you didn't swing your bat; surely an unlucky streak had to end *sometime*.

Not tonight, however. A quick round of phone calls yielded no takers, only a series of reminders as to why he thought of them as "grown-up" in the first place: this one had committed to dinner with his in-laws, that one was stuck at Chuck E. Cheese's for the evening, and so on.

***

We invest a great deal of hope in the idea that we can reverse, or, failing that, outlast, the consequences of our actions, that there is no road so dark or strange that we can't find our way back and choose another path. Our folk wisdom reflects this: "turning over a new leaf"; "every saint has a past, every sinner, a future"; "the first day of the rest of my life." Like most such ideas, it is generally, but not entirely, true that even the most uncomplicated life encompasses so many choices, great and small, that the irrevocable ones are identifiable only in hindsight. Greg , nursing feelings of abandonment at the hands of his friends—unwarranted—and his old pal Terry—justified—could have stayed inside, read a book or watched a baseball game, and sulked. Instead, he went out to the garage, and did so with no idea of the momentousness of his decision.

***

He lowered the door behind him and switched on the overhead lights. He circled the Saab, looking for some way to precipitate an "emergency" here in the garage—a relatively harmless one, if possible. He had nearly given up when his eyes lit upon the tires.

But how did you make a tire go flat purposely? Teenagers in old movies were always slashing tires for kicks, presumably with nothing more than knives. He doubted he had a knife sharp enough for the task.

In the end, an electric drill—purchased along

46

with several other power tools in a reluctant concession to popular ideas about masculinity, and never previously used—did the trick. The tire hadn't even flattened completely when the little box in the dashboard came to life.

"This is Stephanie from LifeGuard; I'm detecting a loss of pressure in your left front tire. Do you require emergency assistance?"

"No thanks, Stephanie," said Greg. "I'm fine. I'm here in the garage. The driveway, I mean. I must have picked up a nail."

"Can you change the tire yourself, or do you need help?"

"I've got it, thanks."

"Is there anything else LifeGuard can do for you today?"

"No, but can I ask you a question?"

"Sure."

"Do you have any other LifeGuard clients?"

"No. At LifeGuard, personal service means personal service."

"Then..." *Come on, suck it up, Jacoby.* "Then you don't actually *have* to go. You could stay on the line for a bit. Right?"

"I thought you'd never ask."

As with most conversations of this sort, very little of import was said. Their chat was notable only for its duration; it lasted long enough for Greg to fall asleep.

He woke just before dawn, sprawled on the garage floor, his right side cold and aching from the concrete. He struggled to his feet, stretched, and tentatively addressed the little box in the dashboard, but Stephanie had gone.

***

"So, where exactly *are* you, Stephanie? I asked you last night, but you never said, and then we wandered off-topic."

Greg sat on his living-room couch, his freshly-cut left arm extended; this was to direct the drops of blood onto a towel he'd spread out for the purpose. With his free right hand, and judicious help from his teeth, he unwrapped several Band-Aids and peeled away the backings.

The work he'd put in that morning changing the Saab's tire, coupled with the impending expense of fixing or replacing the flat, had got him thinking. Car repairs were costly and time-consuming; cuts and burns could be healed, and blood replenished, with minimal fuss. It had been no contest.

"I changed the subject because I'm not really allowed to say." This time, Stephanie's voice originated from the television, which was turned off.

"Ah. Must be India. Your American accent is impeccable."

Stephanie laughed. "Not India. Believe me."

"I don't suppose you're anywhere on Long Island?" Before, he would have tried to conceal the hopeful note in his voice. No longer.

"Nope. Sorry. Never been, in fact. Is it nice?"

"I'd read you my list of complaints about the place, but I want to alphabetize it first, and I'm only up to the Ds."

The laugh again. "I'll bet it's expensive."

"You wouldn't believe what I paid for this house."

"I'm sure it's a very nice house."

"People around here think it's nice because they don't know any better. But I grew up in the middle of Ohio, and I know a double-wide trailer when I see one. They can't fool me just by sticking an extra room on the front and a patio on the back."

"I'm from Michigan. Originally."

"Did you go to school up there?"

"Michigan State. Class of...would've been class of 2003. I didn't finish."

"Had to go to work?"

"I didn't have a choice."

"Let's see...you're how old, then?"

"I'm...I was born in 1981."

Greg wiped the blood off of his arm with a towel and applied several Band-Aids crosswise, so that the gauze in their centers lined up neatly along the length of the incision. It hadn't actually bled overmuch; it was straight, clean, and not too deep. He'd used a double-edged razor blade, of unknown provenance, that he'd found in his medicine cabinet. He hadn't known they even made those anymore.

"Stephanie, is there any way I can get through to you, other than an emergency?"

"I'm afraid not. I wouldn't want to risk it anyway; I took a big enough chance just upgrading you. Those decisions are supposed to be made...elsewhere."

"Why do it, then? Am I that irresistible?"

"Sometimes a person just needs to reach out.

49

You understand."

"I do. Tell me where you are. I'll take some vacation time and we can reach out in person."

There was a pause, and then, "Greg, CarGuard is experiencing unusually high volume; I've got to help out."

"Stephanie—"

"Gotta go."

Greg returned to his office the following morning, but it wasn't the same office. It felt smaller, as if in his absence the walls and ceiling had been moved inward by some fraction of an inch, just enough to worry at the fringes of his perception. His colleagues, whom he'd known for years, seemed to have been replaced by realistic but insubstantial duplicates, their conversation either scripted or generated by some clever algorithm.

None of this was true, he knew. This was his subconscious's way of acknowledging intangible imperfections in what was, by most standards, a very desirable life, but a life that for ten years had centered entirely on his work. Other considerations, such as friendship or romance, had existed on the periphery, like comets whose appearances were celebrated all the more for their scarcity and brevity.

Greg was experiencing a feeling that, until now, had been altogether foreign to him: he couldn't wait to get home.

He'd made a point of not bringing anything sharp to work. But several times throughout the day, he was tempted to repeat the previous week's scalding; once he actually fetched a cup of coffee, but took so long debating the issue with himself that

50

it cooled beyond use. This, he decided, was for the best; if he made a habit of such behavior here at the office, someone was bound to notice eventually. Most successful admen nursed small eccentricities, but there was eccentric and there was *eccentric*, and no good would come of a reputation for self-mutilation.

"Sorry if I came on a little strong yesterday." It was early evening now; the rush-hour traffic had been especially vexing today. "I'm not usually so impulsive."

"Don't worry about it. You have to take chances. Some people don't get too many."

"Someone who's on call twenty-four hours a day probably doesn't get many chances to do *anything*. I take it you work at home a lot?"

"Can't really discuss that. It's proprietary."

Greg sighed. There was a brief lull in the conversation; he took the opportunity to bandage today's incision. It was the same length as yesterday's, and ran a parallel course a quarter-inch from its twin. His excruciating homeward commute had given him time to consider the matter; he'd decided that, if he was going to make a habit of this, he ought to keep the wounds closely-spaced and discreet. For as long as possible, anyway.

"So...seen any good movies lately?"

"Not for years."

"Books?"

"Sorry."

"They keep you pretty busy."

"Yeah. I'm afraid I'm not that interesting."

"I'll be the judge of that. Been back to

Michigan to see the folks?"

"No, not since…well, not for a long time."

"What was it like there, growing up?"

"Childhood's funny, isn't it? All those years…and then, when you try to look back, it all just runs together."

"Tell me."

"It's just bits and pieces, you know? Fragments."

"Tell me."

On the way to work the next morning, Greg considered the oppressive quality his office had exhibited yesterday. He knew it to be a construct of his own mind; would his present state—exultant joy, courtesy of the best-spent evening of his life— alleviate it or exacerbate it?

He didn't bother finding out. On exiting the elevator, he made a beeline for the receptionist and informed her that he was taking his vacation, effective immediately.

"How much vacation?" she asked, eyebrow raised.

"All of it."

Five minutes later, he was on his way home once more.

***

Greg quickly came to appreciate how fragile his link to Stephanie really was. Once the formalities associated with each putative emergency had been dispensed with, their contact became tenuous; any substantial interruption would sever it, and Greg would be forced to initiate communication anew. It was as though the forbidden nature of their conversation had a tangible effect on the connection.

Some disruptions were unavoidable; he couldn't keep from falling asleep, for instance, though he fought it mightily. But by turning off his mobile phone and unplugging the land line, he was able to minimize outside distractions.

He regaled Stephanie with stories of sports triumphs and failures, college escapades, and childhood adventures, and she listened with genuine interest. He was not comfortable with the one-sidedness of these exchanges; he had been raised not to brag by parents who had themselves grown up with little to brag about. But he resisted pressuring Stephanie to contribute. Sometimes she was forthcoming with an anecdote about her girlhood, and Greg savored each of these as though it were the last cookie; but if he became too inquisitive about her present life, she departed, claiming she had to field excess CarGuard calls. Greg quickly got the hint.

There was nothing for it but to keep talking. When he exhausted his supply of stories, he started over again. He strained to recall additional details, with little success, but if Stephanie was bored by his repetitiveness, she didn't show it.

His life story exhausted twice over, he began reading to her: Stephen King. This went over marvelously. Her favorites, she said, had always been *'Salem's Lot*, *The Dead Zone*, and *The Green Mile*, but her work had prevented her from keeping up with King's output; she had never heard of *Cell* or *The Colorado Kid*, for example, and she was astonished to learn that the *Dark Tower* series had finally been concluded.

They worked their way through the later King canon, sharing wistful farewells to favorite characters, and laughing together at infelicitous turns of phrase and unlikely profanities. They were interrupted just once, by an insistent pounding on Greg's front door.

"Be right back," said Greg, though he knew that when he returned to the bedroom, Stephanie would be gone.

The pounding persisted. "Hey, man," came a voice from the other side of the door, "it's Shane. Open up. I know you're in there. I heard you running your mouth."

Greg halted halfway between the bedroom and the front door; he had the presence of mind to find this position ludicrously symbolic.

"We're hitting the bar tonight. Last time I talked to you, all you wanted to do was go out. So open this damn door."

Greg considered; he ought to answer, if only to justify the angst he'd put himself through on that occasion. An honest assessment of his current appearance and state of undress, however, argued convincingly the other way. He remained silent.

"All right, fine," said Shane. "Hell with you, then." His friend trudged away with muffled footsteps that quickly receded to nothing. There came a final, faint exclamation: "And turn your phone on, douche."

Back to the bedroom, then.

No; the shower. His reluctance to answer the door in his disheveled state was telling; he ought to be showing Stephanie at least as much consideration as he did his most obnoxious friend. He resolved to treat each occasion with her as if it were a proper date. She couldn't see him (could she? He still had no idea how LifeGuard monitored him, though the urgency of his inquiry had diminished; he didn't care how it worked, as long as it kept working), but that was no reason to comport himself any less decently. You built trust by behaving properly, whether you were being observed or not. What if she showed up at his house one day and found him living like a hobo?

On the way to the shower, he glanced into the bedroom. Some two dozen empty one- and two-liter soda bottles were strewn randomly across the carpet like a trainful of derailed tanker cars. Potato chip and pretzel bags, empty except for crumbs, filled in the spaces between. Ants from two different tribes had been dispatched on looting expeditions. The bedclothes were piled in a corner except for one rumpled sheet imperfectly covering the mattress; it was nominally white, but a full third of its surface was taken up by bloodstains that ranged from crimson to sickly brown according to their recentness.

Greg did not notice these things. He was looking for a shirt and tie to wear when Stephanie rejoined him.

While he waited for the shower to heat up, he glanced in the mirror. His face sported three weeks' worth of the patchy, uneven growth that had long ago dashed his adolescent beard-cultivating aspirations. The dressing covering the stitches from his onion-slicing incident was in dire need of changing; the surgical tape had lost most of its adhesion, and the entire works was framed by a black outline of accumulated dirt. His left shoulder and upper arm displayed over two dozen cuts. Some had scabbed over; these were straight and evenly-spaced. Other, fresher, cuts were ragged and haphazard. Dried blood sheathed his arm from shoulder to elbow, except where bits had flaked away.

He did not notice these things, either. He was studying his hair, wondering if he should get it cut before he talked to Stephanie again.

***

Some days later, Greg's accumulated store of vacation time had finally been exhausted, give or take a day; he had been less-than-attentive in keeping track. He returned to work to find his office inhabited by a stranger, his clients—those who hadn't abandoned the firm in indignation—apportioned among his now-former colleagues, and his personal items occupying a small box at the receptionist's desk.

He barged into the partners' wing, spoiling for a fight. No one indulged him. He had expected wrath but received pity instead; had hoped they would argue with him—arguments could be won—but they only humored him, offering mostly-sincere concern and exhortations to "get help." He hadn't really expected to argue his way into resuming employment, but he'd hoped to bleed off some of the frustration that had erupted within him. Instead, it was like slamming a door in anger and discovering it has a pneumatic closer.

A few minutes later, he was downstairs in the parking garage, pawing through the Saab's glove compartment in a frantic search for something sharp. Finding nothing useful, he made his way down the row, dropping to his hands and knees behind each parked car and peering beneath in hopes of discovering some bit of serviceable detritus. Even a piece of broken glass would do. Behind him, the Saab's passenger door hung ajar, unheeded, while an assortment of business cards, registration papers, and receipts lay where they had fallen on the floor, soaking up uncounted years' worth of automotive secretions.

"Hey, you lose something?"

Greg hadn't heard anyone approaching. He sprang to his feet, suddenly self-conscious. The man worked at an investment firm on another floor; he and Greg had nodded at each other in the elevator on occasion.

"Yeah."

"Hope it's something important. You're gonna ruin that suit." In truth, it was probably beyond rescue already; the pant legs and the sleeves of the jacket were caked with dirt and grease.

"Yeah. Maybe." Greg was uncertain what he should say. He didn't want to seem too engaged, and thereby prolong the conversation; nor did he want to be rude and precipitate an argument. What he wanted was for the guy to be gone. Then, shining through the fog of desperation clouding his mind, a ray of insight: "Hey, do you have a knife?"

"How's that?"

"Pocketknife," he snapped. "You have one?"

The guy shrugged, as if to say *Sorry, buddy*, and went on his way, walking perhaps a little faster than was usual for him. Had he looked back, he would have seen Greg resume his circuit of the garage, stopping to examine the floor beneath each car.

When he'd worked his way back around to the Saab, he slumped against the car, soaked in sweat. He removed his tie and his soiled jacket and rolled up his shirt cuffs, ordinary actions that, for Greg, provided an extraordinary revelation: his bandaged right forearm. The dressing was relatively fresh: days old, rather than weeks. It came off in one swift motion.

He tore savagely at the stitches, hoping to reopen the knife wound from his kitchen mishap. It had healed well; the stitches were overdue for removal, in fact, and even when he was able to grip them with his perspiration-slick hands, pulling on them yielded only an unpleasant tugging sensation beneath his skin.

Over the course of the previous half-hour, frustration and rage had inched closer together until there was no longer a gradient between them. His recalcitrant sutures nudged him from the one state to the other inside of an instant, and he kicked the Saab's passenger door closed.

If he'd hurt his foot, he didn't notice it; his attention was drawn instead to the scuff mark he'd left on the door with his hard-soled dress shoe. Not long ago, he would have considered such an action against the Saab, if perpetrated by another, to be a crime worse than arson, and reacted accordingly. Since then, his priorities had undergone realignment. Just now, the scuff mark was significant only in that it drew his attention to the door itself.

He could have gotten in the car and gone home. A part of him was actually aware of this. But the logic by which love operates is an alien logic even at the best of times; in Greg's state of vexation, he didn't stand a chance—though he *was* cognizant enough to wonder, as he opened the passenger door once more, when he'd begun using the word "love."

He placed his left arm against the edge of the doorframe. *No, not the arm. The hand.* He took hold of the passenger door with his right hand and swung it closed.

The logical method of breaking one's hand in a car door is a single quick, sharp blow, delivered without hesitation. Greg did exactly this, not because he'd taken time to consider the act, but because he hadn't: a rare correlation between forethought and impulsivity.

There was a wet, sickening sound. The door, having naturally failed to latch, drifted partway open. Greg sank to the concrete, resting his back against the Saab's rear tire. He held the hand away from his body; he wanted to draw it in, cradle it, but was afraid of multiplying the already-agonizing pain.

"This is Stephanie from LifeGuard. I'm detecting a fracture; do you require emergency medical attention?" And then, as always, the voice shed its rote quality and demonstrated emotion once more. "Greg? What happened? What's going on?"

"Never mind that. Where are you?"

"I can't—"

"I'm coming to pick you up."

"No."

"You're all I've got left."

"What do you mean?"

As he struggled to pull himself to his feet using only his right hand, he recounted the events of the morning.

"You'll get another job," said Stephanie. "Other ad agencies will be lining up to take you on. Or you'll do something else instead. Something good and worthwhile."

"Imagine what an inspiration you could be in person."

"No."

"Do you love me?"

"…yes."

"You don't sound sure."

"For a long time…I don't know how long…I couldn't feel love anymore…like I wasn't supposed to. I got used to it—didn't even realize anything was missing. Then you came along, and I had feelings that were supposed to be impossible now…yes. Yes, I love you."

"So give LifeGuard your notice, and come to Long Island. Or I'll move wherever you are."

"No."

"Stephanie, nobody's this closely-married to their work. Put someone else on the line."

"I can't do that."

"Why?"

"I'm…not able to talk to the others."

"Not able? You mean not allowed, right?"

"What are you talking about?"

"You chose those words very carefully."

"Can we talk later? You ought to go have your hand looked at."

"Why can't you talk to anyone there? What kind of place—"

***

Some mysteries cannot be solved straightforwardly; we must instead piece together the elements *surrounding* them and, by examining the remaining empty space, determine the answer indirectly, by discovering what is *not* there.

***

"Greg?" He had been silent for nearly a minute when Stephanie's tentative voice emerged from the little box in the dashboard once more.

"When did it happen, Stephanie?"

"I don't know what you mean."

"You won't say where you are. You can't quit and won't say why. You're on call twenty-four hours a day with no adverse effects. You're unable—not forbidden, but unable—to talk to your

61

coworkers. You left college because you had 'no choice.' You haven't seen your parents in years, haven't read a book or seen a movie in years. You're a Stephen King fan who's never heard of any King book written after 2002. You have almost no memories; you even forgot about love. And I haven't even brought up the things you're able to *do*.

"So please tell me: when did it happen? And how?"

Stephanie's voice was quiet, tearful. "I was in college. It was a car wreck. I think. Sometimes I don't know if it's a real memory. I've dealt with so many car accidents since then...maybe I just *think* that's what happened because I've forgotten everything else. It can be hard...to tell what's real. I don't know how much of me is left."

Greg closed the passenger door and walked around the back of the Saab to the driver's side. A distant numbness permeated his body, forcing him to steady himself against the car as he went, and mitigating the pain that shot from his broken left hand. The brief journey gave him time to decide whether to continue this conversation.

In the end, it was no decision at all.

"The place you're in...what is it like?" he asked, once he'd situated himself in the driver's seat.

"Like nothing. Just nothing. There are others...*must* be others, but I don't see or feel them. I'm not even sure *I'm* here...or that there *is* a 'here.'"

"What happened between the time...well, you know. How did you actually *get* there?"

"I don't remember."

"What happens if you don't do what you're

supposed to?"

"I'm afraid to find out. What if there's nothing else but this? There are no feelings here. No will."

"You have will, don't you?"

"Greg, I never felt *anything*; not until you came along to fight with me about your ticket, and I got upset, and it all came flooding back. I felt *alive* again."

"You may be the first person to say that and actually mean it."

"Then we got so close, it was like I could reach out and touch you, almost. I should have ended it then, but I just couldn't. Then you started dropping hints about our being together, and I started thinking that maybe if we really connected, I could come back somehow..."

"*Can* you come back?"

"No. Greg, I—" Her next words were meant to be "I'm sorry," but they were lost in a cascade of sobs.

"How close are you to me?"

"I can almost *see* you. Feel you, even. I haven't been able to see or feel since...it happened."

Greg started the Saab and backed out of his parking space. Then he put the car in gear and stepped on the accelerator, driving straight into the wall of the garage. Even though he anticipated the impact, it still jarred him, and he found it difficult to brace himself against the steering wheel with only his good hand. The airbag flared up and then receded.

"This is Stephanie from Life—" There was a silence that was not silence at all, but rather the

63

sound of Stephanie battling to overcome her conditioning. She succeeded. "Greg, your airbag went off."

"I know."

The Saab had stalled; he started it and backed out once more. This time, he pulled away and commenced the gently-spiraling climb to the surface.

"Greg, you shouldn't be driving around with a deployed airbag. What are you doing?"

"Meeting you halfway."

Greg did not know exactly where he was, except that he wasn't on an island, having exited Manhattan to the north, the overland route. Neither did he know where he was going, except for a vague notion that he didn't want any people around. He trusted that he would know his place when he found it.

After emerging from the parking garage, he'd made his way north. His mind had been fully engaged by the frustration of driving with one good hand—constantly entangled in the deflated airbag—on increasingly-unfamiliar streets. When he'd finally broken free of the city and found an open road, his consternation had disappeared, but, like the sweet-smelling air that now pervaded the car's once-stale interior, a number of questions had rushed in to occupy his attention anew: How did CarGuard/LifeGuard corral its captive souls, and to what purpose? Did other companies practice such bondage? Did they *all*? Did servitude await *everyone* who passed from this life?

These questions, too, dissipated in the wind.

Soon, his other worries—the mundane, everyday worries shared by everyone—were gone as well; not merely pushed into a corner and hidden behind joy, as they had often been during his chats with Stephanie, but really gone, left behind on this country road like the jacket, tie, and papers that still lay on the floor of the garage.

"Tell me when it's about to happen," said Stephanie. She had understandably asked for such reassurance several times. This time, Greg answered differently.

"It's about to happen."

"What?"

"I saw a sign. I think I have what I need."

Greg depressed the accelerator to the floor. The Saab leaped into high gear. From the little box in the dashboard, there was silence.

"Are you still there?"

"I'm here, Greg."

"Stay with me. I need you now." Behind him, a siren sounded. The police car must have been lying in wait somewhere; speed and inattention had conspired to conceal it from him. "Hell."

"What's wrong?"

"Cop. Don't worry; it doesn't matter."

"Greg? I wish I could have met you before…you know. Have I told you that?"

"Yes."

"Things might have been different."

The signs showed themselves with increasing frequency. The needle on the Saab's speedometer had reached its limit. The siren still wailed, but the police car itself had slowed its pursuit and become a distant speck in Greg's mirror.

"It's time," said Greg. "Reach out to me. Reach out as far as you can."

"I love you, Greg."

"I love you, Stephanie."

Then came a chaos of orange and white as the Saab plowed through a score of flimsy sawhorse-style barricades. Beyond them was half of a bridge; beyond that, only air.

The ancient surface of the bridge, latticed steel rather than asphalt or concrete, vibrated the car unmercifully and let out a great and sustained roar at the intrusion of the Saab's tires.

The bridge ended; the roar ceased. The siren had gone, too. The car was filled with a blessed silence that, to Greg, felt like finally arriving at a longed-for sanctuary.

In front of him, rising from the shallow waters below, was a concrete support pylon. Its perfect placement was a last affirmation.

"I love you, Greg."

The encounter between the pylon, solid and implacable, and the car, fragile as a bubble, was of a moment and no more. It was as though the pylon had risen up of its own volition and batted the car out of the air.

"I love you."

The windshield was there, and then it was not. The wall of concrete rushed to meet him; it grew to fill not only his field of vision but his entire world. He spread his arms as if to embrace it.

"I love you, Greg. I love you. I love you." I love you.

This last had not come through the little box in the dashboard. She had spoken to him directly. He was almost sure of it.

"I love you," he said.

I love you. I love

The End

Desmond Warzel is the author of some two dozen short stories in the genres of horror, fantasy, and science fiction. His work can be found in numerous periodicals, such as Daily Science Fiction, Redstone Science Fiction, *and* Shroud, *as well as anthologies such as* Triangulation: Last Contact *(Parsec Ink) and* Terminal Earth *(Pound Lit Press). He is unreasonably reluctant to discuss his works-in-progress but will admit, if pressed, that he is working on a novel or three. When not writing, he engages in pursuits both worthwhile (such as rooting for the Pittsburgh Steelers) and futile (such as rooting for the Cleveland Indians). He lives in northwestern Pennsylvania.*

Love is a mysterious amalgam of secret and irresistible emotions, notoriously difficult to analyze or even recognize, as C. E. Murphy's dreamy young heroine emerges from the Flood to discover.

Keys
by C. E. Murphy

We used to see him, my sister and I. He was tall and handsome and now had vanity to burn. Most of us couldn't afford that, couldn't be made to care if our hair or eyes were the fashionable color, but not one of us ever saw him without his beard dyed blue or his black hair tied in a tight queue beneath one of the sharp brimmed hats that men of wealth still featured. He had fine long legs and slim hips and his coats were perfect, silver-wrought and blue. You couldn't help but look at him, though you never wanted to catch his eye.

He lived in a tall glass tower, one of the old skyscrapers from before the waters came, from before the sea ate away all the structure and the cities. He lived in sunlight all the time, way up high above the waters, and when he came out he drove a yacht through what used to be the streets. We watched from down below, near to the rank stench of the water, because there weren't so many people left but the ones that were smelled up the place just like mankind had never invented decent sanitation. Our homes were red brick and melting mortar, and the shadows of the towers took away our sunshine.

But not his; he lived in the blazing heat of it

shining against one side or the other of his glass tower always, and we figured that was the reason all the girls kept right on marrying him, even when his wives never came out of the tower. His harem, we said, and laughed a little, or maybe no girl who grew up in the shadows wanted to leave the sunlight once she reached it. We couldn't blame them if that were true, and we looked up high and wondered if we saw their shapes in the windows.

It was my twenty-first birthday the day he came to visit. My twenty-first, which in another time would have meant something, would have been a party and a play. I almost remembered that time, it had only gone away when I was six or seven, but my little sister didn't remember it at all, and my older brothers remembered it well. Well enough to give me a little party, and that attracted his attention, and so he visited.

He was beautiful up close, smelling sharp and sweet and dressed in clothes so soft. His boots were finely made, with sharp pointed toes, and they fit his calves better than any boots I'd ever seen. When it came out that it was my birthday, he brought us all back to his glass tower and fed us a feast, more and better food than I'd eaten since the waters had come up. I could see it in my brothers' and sister's eyes, that when he began to court me that I should say yes, so they might eat so well again. And I was like any girl brought out of the shadows: once in sunlight, I had no wish to go back. I put out of my mind the thoughts of twelve wives who had gone before, and married him when he asked.

It was a pretty ceremony, with my sister at my

side to hold flowers and my brothers standing strong and proud beside my blue-bearded husband, and if he was remote and selfish in bed, well, I had my fingers and the sunshine to bathe in, so what did I care?

Three weeks after we were wed, he came to me with a heavy ring of keys and said I must leave for a time, but these are for you. They open each room in the tower and will reveal treasures beyond any you can imagine. Explore, my wife, and only do not go into the room with the golden door. He gave me a final key then, separate from the others, and strode away, leaving me with a hundred keys and one.

I looked at the one and thought what kind of damn fool man gives a woman a hundred keys and one, and tells her not to use the one?

A man who wants her to use that key, I said back to me, and what kind of damn fool woman would *use* that key?

Twelve wives who had gone before, I thought. Twelve wives who I saw hide nor hair of in this glass tower, and I may not have had my sister's book learning or my brothers' fine language, but I wasn't a damned fool myself, and put that key on a chain 'round my neck and left it there to warm between my breasts as I looked through all the other rooms.

Book-taught or no, I recognized many of the things my husband kept hidden in that glass tower. Paintings and sculptures and pieces of art, antiques and glittering stones and gowns. Some were mud-stained, water-stained, marked where the sea had come up into low-lying cities, and some had been

70

cleaned already, the delicate tools to make them new again lying alongside the pieces. I knew the scent of those cleaning agents: they lingered on my husband's hands and in his clothes, and answered for me what he did in the long hours he abandoned me to his glass tower.

I took a piece, an egg made of gold and ivory, that was still lined with grime, and I waited for my husband to come home and asked him if he might show me how to clean it.

For the first time since we'd wed, fire lit his eyes. He took me back to the room of eggs and we knelt together on cushions, using cotton swabs and alcohol to edge muck from the first egg, then half a dozen more. *Fabergé,* he said they were called, and had been made two hundred years ago for a family of Russian royals in the days before their doom. Then he took me to another room, a room of maps, and showed me the world, and Russia, and how far from his glass tower that place lay. This, he said, this is where he went when he traveled: Russia, Japan, Paris-that-was-drowned. He searched for art, rescued it, restored it, kept it safe here in his high tower, and finally he looked at me as if I too might be a piece of priceless art.

He was not, after all, selfish in bed; not when he cared not to be. When I was naked, he lifted the gold chain from which the little key hung, lifted it on a fingertip and let the key wander across my breasts, and when I offered it back to him he said no, that I should keep it. So there it remained, nestled safe against my body in the days and weeks that followed, days and weeks that I learned my husband's passions, and found them waking in myself.

I learned to read better, so I could understand the histories of the objects we tended to, and so I could choose between cleaning agents without my husband's guidance. He left again, and again, always returning home with more treasures, and I studied and cleaned and counted the days until his return, and rarely so much as thought of the room that the hundred and oneth key belonged to.

When my husband was gone yet again, I called for my sister to visit so I might ease my loneliness and share my excitement over the wonders I had seen. I showed her dog-headed statues from Egypt and the big-eared faces from Peru, showed her all the things that my husband had brought here, and she sighed and waved her hand at them.

How can you stay this way, she said, up here all alone with these dead things? How can you stand it, when there's music and life and family in the shadows?

How can I not? I asked in real surprise, and bent to collect a fine brush and a cup of water from the floor. The golden key on its chain slipped loose from beneath my shirt, and I tucked it in again as I stood. How can I not, I said again, when there's so much beauty here to be revealed?

But my sister didn't care anymore about the jewels and paintings. Her gaze fastened between my breasts, on the shape of the key, and she said what is that?

Oh that, I said with a shrug, that's the key to the room with the golden door, the one my husband told me not to go in.

What's in it? she said, and I laughed and said I didn't know. She gave me a curious look, but said nothing more, and we went away from the art rooms to a fine dinner and in time to bed.

I woke because the key's absence made a cold place on my chest. I was on my feet, flying through the halls before I could think, knowing myself to be too late with every step I took. Down a thousand stairs, around sharp corners and finally to a golden door that stood open, my sister's slim form framed within, and beyond her, the thing I did not want to know.

Twelve bodies dangled from hooks like pigs hung to dry. They had no skin, shriveled meat hanging raw from the bone. Each had her face turned up, a hook pierced through the back of her neck and through her throat, and their wide sunken eyes and open screaming mouths made it seem they had been alive when they were hanged. Blondes, brunettes, red-heads: brittle hair fell in long strands around wretched faces while agonized hands clawed emptily at the air. The room was cold, almost freezing: our breath clouded, and the only scent was a distant reminder of once-warm meat. Thick blood gleamed, covering the floor, inching closer to the door with each death.

My sister dropped the key from nerveless fingers, and it splattered in the blood.

I seized it, seized her, hauled her backward and closed the door in front of us. Go, I said, go home and get our brothers, bring knives and guns and come back for me, or for vengeance if not for me, and we ran, her to the door, me to my rooms, where I snatched up the cleaning agents I had learned so much about and scrub, scrub, scrubbed the key, but the blood would not come off.

That was how my husband found me, hunched over the bloody key, my hands white with bleach and other chemicals, and his roar was so outraged I fled to windows I had never opened, and forced them free.

From this high up the water was as hard as a street might be, and not so deep as to stop me hitting the concrete below it, either. Wind tore at me, rushing up the tower in a way I hadn't known it could do, and with my hair tangled and my nightdress ripped I looked back at my husband to see agony in his eyes.

Which is it that pains you, I said, is it that I found the monster beneath the facade, or is it that if I leap here and now my death will not be yours, like all the others were?

It is neither, he whispered. It is neither. It is that I had thought us kindred in spirit, that you were unlike the others. That you would never betray me by opening the door.

My sister did, I said unwisely, and rage clouded his face. She's gone, I said, you have only me, and now I know you to be a monster.

Am I, he said, and I could hardly hear his words over the scream of the wind. Am I, when I have spent every waking hour since the waters rose trying to save our ancestors' art? Am I, when all I have asked from my wives is obedience in one thing, and in exchange for that I have given them all this?

He spread his hand, and though it would take magic for it to truly happen, it seemed that the inside walls of his glass tower turned to glass as well, and I could see each of the wonders he had gone so far to save. I could see the sad woman with her mysterious smile, the marble youth with his fierce glare, the red crystal bird with its fiery wings spread wide. I could see the art of the world before it drowned, and the shape of a future rising from it.

And I could see the cold room far below, where twelve damned fools who had not been content with the wonders Bluebeard had given them, had had to look for more.

My sister, I said again, and he said yes, but now you know.

My sister has gone for my brothers, to come here with guns and knives to end you with, I said.

Is that what you want, he said, and I looked once more through the glass tower, and I said...

...no.

But I do not sleep well when I think of the freshest bodies in the cold room, and now my husband carries his own damned key.

The End

C. E. Murphy is the author of several urban fantasy series, including the best-selling WALKER PAPERS *and the* NEGOTIATOR TRILOGY. *According to friends, she began her writing career when she ran away from home at age five to write copy for the circus that had come to town, but her own recollection is that she began writing around age six, when she submitted three poems to a school publication. The teacher producing the magazine selected (inevitably) the one she thought was by far the worst, but also told her—a six year old kid—to keep writing, which she has, with nearly twenty books to her name. In her down time, she writes comic books and is working on a screenplay, which may be why her editor and agent independently suggested she get a hobby that wasn't writing. C. E. Murphy was born and raised in Alaska and now lives in her ancestral homeland of Ireland, which is a magical land where it rains a lot but winter never actually arrives.*

The origin of the Wake may be clouded in pre-history, but in many cultures it is still believed that it takes three days, or even three times three days, for the soul to let go of the body...

The Argument
by Ceschino

She was sitting at the kitchen table, staring sullenly at the half-empty bowl of slightly overripe fruit in the middle. She didn't look up when he walked out of his bedroom.

He had forgotten that she had spent the night at his apartment. After all of their friends had left last night, he recalled there having been some awkward tension between the two of them, but he couldn't remember the cause. She had put on her jacket and picked up her handbag in a huff, expressing exasperation with his apparent inability to figure out what was wrong, but had lingered at the door, neither leaving nor showing any desire to come back into the apartment, until he asked her to put down her things and sit down. After sitting together in silence for a while, they had said good night, and she had gone to sleep on the couch. Feeling a little apprehensive, but not entirely sure why, he managed a feeble smile.

"Good morning," he greeted her softly.

She did not respond. Her hair, dry and somewhat disheveled, hung to the sides of her face like blinders. Her lips, also dry, were turned down in an emphatic glower that matched her narrowed eyes.

He tried again. "Have you had breakfast?"

She still didn't look at him, but she replied this time. "There's nothing to eat."

He looked at the bowl of fruit sitting in front of her. She reminded him frequently how much she liked fresh fruit.

"I guess that's a bit overripe. I can pick up something fresh."

Her expression remained unchanged. "There's nothing in your pantry or your fridge."

"We ate a lot of it last night."

"That was party food," she shot back, still staring straight ahead. "You don't have anything that's fit for a normal meal."

"Sorry. I eat most meals in the office. I usually only snack when I get home."

"And what am I supposed to eat?"

He looked at her for a moment without saying anything. She didn't look up. "I wasn't expecting you to stay the night."

"You mean you didn't want me to."

"What?"

"That's why you didn't bother to put some actual food in your apartment, right? So that you could just have a nice time with your friends, and then send me off like the rest of them?"

He blinked, befuddled by this statement. "No. Like I said, I tend not to have much solid food around. It usually goes bad when I do. I've just gotten into the habit of cutting down on the amount of groceries I buy. It wasn't a conscious decision not to have something around for you."

"And you couldn't have anticipated that maybe I would want something while I was here?"

He inhaled deeply and exhaled before replying. "I didn't know you'd be here past the party. That's all there was to it. It wasn't a conscious slight. I'm happy to go get something for you now."

She didn't answer.

"Would you like to come with me?"

She folded her arms and looked away. Smarting from this show of rejection, he went back into his room, put on some jeans, a clean t-shirt and his jacket, and walked back out. She remained seated, arms crossed, glowering at the wall. Sliding on his shoes by the door, he let her know that he was heading down to the market. Still no response. He slipped out the door, locked it behind him and then headed downstairs and out of the building.

Outside, he stopped to let his eyes adjust to the sunlight. He normally thought his apartment was fairly sunny, but the sky hadn't looked so light while he was inside. The air was brisk and carried scents of the changing seasons on a soft breeze, and he felt refreshed as he let it fill his lungs.

He glanced back toward his apartment windows, thinking that this would be a nice day to take a walk with her. They could pick up some fresh food at the open market and then take a walk along the river, or just find a park bench somewhere where they could sit and talk, about anything, or nothing in particular. She had told him a little bit about her latest project the last time they went out;

she had seemed animated when describing her plans for it and the potential it held. It was that earnest exuberance that he had found so captivating about her in the first place, back when they met. Lately, though, it seemed that she was increasingly more disposed to mysterious fits of brooding than to sharing her passions with him. He was starting to miss her upbeat side.

The farmers set up their market only a few minutes away from his apartment, by foot. He hadn't been aware of the weekly occurrence when he signed the lease for his place, but it had become one of his favorite features of the area. This morning, he walked alone among the wooden stalls and crates, taking in the colorful displays and savoring the scents of the latest harvest. It would have been nice to have her here. Maybe she'd be up for it later, after she cheered up. He hoped that whatever he brought back would do the trick.

A kind, older woman with an accent he couldn't place offered him a bag of hand-wrapped candies. The name of the treat was unfamiliar to him. He guessed from the accent and the name of the sweets that the vendor was from Eastern Europe, but he wasn't familiar enough with the region to narrow it down beyond that.

Seeing his hesitation, the woman tried another tack. "For your girl," she said with a knowing smile. He smiled back and handed the vendor a five dollar bill in exchange for the sack of sweets. He continued among the vendors, picking up a few different types of fruit, some fresh bread rolls and a block of cheese with which one farm had made its name in the region.

Back in the apartment, he laid a burlap bag on the kitchen table in front of her, where she had apparently remained the whole time he was out. He let some of the produce roll out onto the table, hoping it would entice her. She glanced at it, shifted uncomfortably in her chair and made a sound like a hiccup. He leaned over slowly and kissed her on the forehead. To his surprise, she wiped a tear off of her cheek. "What's wrong?"

She shook her head and sniffed.

"I went out and got some food I thought you'd like. Take a look."

For the first time that day, she made eye contact with him. "It's not about the food."

He looked at her incredulously. "It sounded like it was about the food earlier."

She shook her head again and made a motion like a shrug. "I wanted to see that you cared enough about me to take my needs into account without me asking for something."

"You're saying that you were angry last night and today because you thought I didn't care about you?"

She was looking back down at the table, now. "I just wanted to see some sign that you cared."

He paused and considered his words carefully before responding. "Can you think of a few other signs I've given you recently that I care about you?"

"I'm not saying that you don't care. I just didn't see it last night."

He furrowed his brow. "Wait a minute. I'm confused. You weren't hungry for anything else last night."

"No. Last night you didn't want me to stay."

"I never said that. I'd have been happy to have you here. You've never spent the night before—not until last night, anyway. We hadn't talked about it. I didn't know you were ready to take that step."

"And you didn't ask."

"I was supposed to ask? If you wanted to stay, you could have told me. I wasn't going to tell you 'no.'"

"So I can only stay if I beg you?"

He pursed his lips and exhaled through his nose. "Like I said, if you wanted to stay, you could have just said so. I'd have been happy to have your company."

"But you wouldn't have asked me to stay."

"Look, I'm just trying not to be pushy. Maybe I'd have asked you to stay if you hadn't seemed angry. Or maybe, Heaven forbid, I wouldn't have asked you to spend the night with me until next weekend. I don't know."

"I don't appreciate your sarcasm. I—"

"I wasn't being sarcastic."

"Thanks for interrupting me."

"I wasn't trying to be sarcastic."

"Are you done?"

"What?"

"Are you finished expressing that thought? I don't want to interrupt you."

He looked at her wordlessly, gritting his teeth. His eyes swept over her face as if looking for some clue as to what she wanted to hear. "Please say whatever it is you were going to say," he eventually replied.

"I don't remember."

"You don't remember what you were about to say?"

"No, I don't. Because you interrupted me."

The conversation dragged on in the same manner for the next few hours, interrupted by the occasional reprieve spent checking e-mail, answering a phone call or finding some other temporary exit from a debate that kept circling back to where it had started, never making any progress.

The sun grew dimmer. As it began to hang lower in the sky, as if fatigued, he decided to invite her outside. Maybe a change in environment would help them to find some new ground in their dilemma. She did not oblige.

"You don't want to go outside?"

"No."

"You've been inside all day. It's nice out."

She sat with her arms folded, as she had for most of the day, staring at the forlorn-looking fruit bowl.

"Some fresh air might do you some good. It feels really nice out there."

Still no answer.

"You haven't even eaten. At least have something to eat. I bought that stuff specifically for you."

"I'm not hungry."

"Your stomach has been growling. Eat something."

"I said I'm not hungry."

He folded his arms, now. "You know, I don't believe you."

"I can decide for myself whether I'm hungry."

"Well, then what do you want? Do you want to go home?"

"So now you want me to leave?"

He let his arms fall to his sides in exasperation. "No, I wanted to enjoy the day with you. It seems to me, however, that nothing I say or do right now is making you feel better. You said you wanted food; I got you some food. You said that you thought I didn't care; I tried to explain what was going on, on my end. You're still angry. Why would you want to stay if I'm making you so upset?"

"So you want me to leave."

His jaw dropped, and he rolled his eyes and raised his hands as if in supplication. "What did I just say?"

"That you can't see a reason for me to stay."

"Not if I can't do or say anything to make you feel better; no. Look, I'm sorry if I was somehow insensitive, sweetie. I'm not going to try to make you stay here if you aren't enjoying my company. This is pointless."

"Would you rather be spending time with someone else?"

"Why would you ask that?"

"Would you?"

"I'd rather be enjoying your company than arguing with you."

"You didn't answer the question."

84

"I don't want to answer the question. If you leave, then I'll spend the evening alone. No, that's not what I want, but that makes more sense to me than keeping this up."

"All I want is to know that you care about me."

He narrowed his eyes. "Then how about taking into account the fact that I've spent the entire day trying to find out what's upsetting you and making you feel better?"

A couple of tears made their way down her face again. He put his face in his hands. "Why are we doing this?"

She didn't have an answer.

That question remained unanswered for the rest of the evening, as they nibbled at the fruit and rolls from the market and then poked at a couple of cartons of delivered Chinese food while staring past a movie on TV. She made no indication that she wanted to leave, and he made no effort to approach the subject again. The heavy tension in the air refused to dissipate, and they eventually went their separate ways although the space they shared was small, showering, brushing their teeth and clicking aimlessly at various pages online, not talking, not smiling, not reacting to anything they saw or heard.

Their emotions had been beaten down and were stored away for the night. They fell asleep in separate rooms, each profoundly dissatisfied, but unsure where to go or what to do to make it better.

He came to gradually, as if his dreams were slowly releasing him into the world of consciousness. He blinked at the grayish glare streaming in through the window, trying to discern what time of day it was. The sun was definitely up, but not very high in the sky. It was cloudier than it had been the day before—or was it? No, it wasn't cloudy; just not very bright.

He hadn't slept as long as he felt like he had. He propped himself up on his bed, looking around his bedroom at nothing in particular while attempting to muster the will to get up. After a couple of false starts, he sat up, swung his legs over the side of the bed, and tentatively toed his flip flops before sliding them on. He reached for his phone and called a friend. "Hey—we're meeting at 1, right?"

"Hey, man. No, that's tomorrow."

"Tomorrow? I have work tomorrow."

"You have to work this Sunday? Man, your hours are bad. We can reschedule if you need to. It's okay."

"Sunday? I thought today was..."

"Saturday."

"Today's Saturday? But yesterday was..."

"Friday. You must have partied pretty hard, man. Did your lady keep you up all night?"

"No—not really. I just...I guess I...I don't know. That's weird. I thought it was Sunday."

"Hey, it's cool, man. Get some rest, all right? I'll see you tomorrow. 1pm."

"Got it. See you tomorrow."

Feeling disoriented, he looked down at his phone. It said that today was Saturday. He pulled on some clothes. Still feeling as though he hadn't fully woken up, he opened the door to his bedroom and ventured outside.

She was sitting there at the kitchen table, staring glumly at the half-empty fruit bowl in front of her. No sign of the food he thought he remembered buying at the open-air market.

"Good morning," he greeted her tentatively.

No response. He started to walk past her, toward the fridge, but stopped as he got closer. Her lips were chapped, and he saw a bit of what looked like dandruff in her hair. He had to remind himself that today was Saturday, not Sunday, and she hadn't just spent Saturday night in his apartment. He looked in his fridge and the pantry.

"Looks like I need some supplies. Would you like to come with me?"

She didn't say anything. He headed toward the front door and started putting on his shoes. "I'm going to go pick up some food. It would be nice to have your company. If you don't feel like it, please make yourself at home until I get back."

As he turned toward the door, she spoke up. "Are we going to do this again?"

He turned around and walked back toward the kitchen. "What do you mean?"

She looked at him, her expression less steely than before—he couldn't tell if she seemed resentful or scared. Maybe both. "We just did this yesterday. Are we really going to do this again?"

His face registered his confusion. "I don't understand."

"Yes, you do. We just spent all day yesterday doing this, and we didn't get anywhere."

"Yesterday was Friday, sweetie."

"You know what I mean."

"Not really, no."

"We spent all of Saturday arguing with each other. It didn't get anywhere."

He hesitated. "You know, it's weird," he replied. "I thought when I woke up that today was Sunday. I dreamed—it must have been a dream—that we spent all of Saturday—today—in the apartment together. And now you're talking like it's Sunday."

"I'm not saying that it's Sunday," she retorted. "It isn't. I checked. Everything's the same as it was yesterday morning when I got up. Including the lack of food in your apartment."

He felt a chill run down his body, as if he had been doused by a cold splash of water. "You're saying—"

"That it's Saturday again. I heard you talking to your friend. You know it, too."

"I don't get it."

"Nor do I."

They were silent for a moment as he looked at her. She wrapped her arms around herself, sinking further into the seat and staring at the far wall. She eventually looked up at him. "What are you going to do?"

"I—I guess I'll get something for us to eat. We can figure out what's going on afterward."

"Am I supposed to wait here?"

"I'd rather you come with me, but it's up to you."

"What do you want?"

"Please come with me."

She put on her shoes and jacket, ran her hands through her messy hair, and they went outside together. The day was pleasant, as he remembered it having been the first time around, but the glare of the sun bothered his eyes in a way that it had not when he went to the market on his own.

Mixed in with the scents of fall was a tinge of something that irritated his nose. He couldn't identify it, but his nose itched and his eyes watered until he adjusted to it, and it passed. She walked by his side, arms still wrapped around herself, staring at the ground in front of her. He reached out for her arm, prying it gently from her side and sliding his hand down to meet hers. He squeezed her fingers softly, and her hand closed limply around his.

The market looked exactly as he remembered it. He led her to the stand where the woman with the hard-to-place accent stood, just as before. The vendor smiled pleasantly at the two of them. "Something for your girl?" She held out the bag of sweets that he had bought.

He looked at his girlfriend, who was attempting to smile while she shrank uncertainly away from the bag. "Sure," he said, and procured a five dollar bill. The couple wandered away from the stand.

Several feet away, she stopped him. "Why did you get that?"

"These? I saw them yesterday—I mean—well, I thought you might like them."

"You bought them before. I know. I'm asking why you bought them again."

"Well, you didn't have any the first time. Maybe you'll try them now."

She looked up at him, pulling on her lip with her hand. "What if this is why the day is repeating itself?"

He looked down at the bag. "I just bought them now."

"Yes, but you bought a bag yesterday, and now we're stuck back in the same day. What if it happens again now that you bought another bag?"

"Sweetie, we probably just had a really vivid dream or something."

"Both of us?"

"Shared dreams. I've heard of that happening. Haven't experienced it before, but I guess that's what it's like."

She continued to pull on her lip as she stared at the candy. "But you don't know."

He didn't respond.

"It didn't seem like a dream to me."

"Some dreams are very vivid," he offered.

"But you can always tell what was wrong with the dream after you wake up. Nothing was unusual about yesterday."

Aside from spending the day arguing, he thought. "Not every dream has to be weird, right?" he responded.

She looked at the fruit in the stands but stood a few feet away, as if afraid to touch it. "I turned on the news yesterday—or in the dream. In the morning, before you got up. I turned it on again today, before you got up. It was the same thing."

"Well...heck, I don't know. They say that some dreams reveal the future."

"You're saying that I predicted what would be on the news in my dream? It was the same exact newscast. The anchor said all of the same things. Same captions on the photos. Same video clips. Everything was the same."

He inhaled sharply. "Sweetie, I don't know. I really don't know what to make of it. This is weird, all right? I think so, too."

"I'm scared, baby."

He pulled her close. "At least we're together. We'll figure this out." He put his fingers under her chin and raised her face so they were looking into each other's eyes. "Hey, maybe this is the dream. I felt tired when I woke up, like I hadn't really slept. Maybe we're sharing a dream right now."

She smiled, but her lip trembled a bit as she did. He kissed her and took her hand in his. They started walking among the stands again, perusing the selection of produce. "Are you still scared of the candy?"

She stopped walking. "That's not funny."

He stopped and turned to face her. "Sorry. I was just joking."

"I'm scared. It wasn't funny."

He grimaced. Things had seemed to be improving. "I'm sorry. I just wanted to make you smile."

"You don't know any better than I do what's going on."

"I know. I'm sorry. Please, let's not argue about this."

Her nostrils flared, and she squinted in the sunlight. "I don't appreciate your having a laugh at my expense."

"It wasn't supposed to be at your expense. Please, let's not do this again."

"This is exactly what I was talking about before."

"What was?"

"You, not caring. I'm scared, and you're making fun of me."

"You think I'm not scared, too?"

"So, what do you want?" she asked.

"I want you to stop feeling upset with me," he stammered. "And I want to figure out what day of the week it is."

The corners of her mouth flickered upward as if starting to smile, but she clenched her jaw and turned and began to walk again.

"Do you want anything from the market, then?"

She looked around. "If you picked up something that's causing this, I want to avoid picking it up again."

"The fruit and bread, too?"

"What if we ate something that's making us have a weird dream, like you said?"

"Well, if we're dreaming, then whatever we pick up here isn't real. It wouldn't really make a difference, would it?"

She considered this possibility. "And if we're not dreaming?"

He thought about it. "If it makes you feel better, we don't have to get anything. We need to eat something, though. And whatever's going on—

let's just say for a moment that the day actually repeated itself somehow—I don't think that picking up some fruit caused it. Not making fun of you. Just saying, that's probably not the problem."

She looked at some pears in the nearest stand, as if trying to muster up the courage to pick one up.

"What about the Chinese food?" he added.

"You're making fun of me again."

"No—I just—well, if it was something we ate, it could just as easily have been that, right?"

She looked at him, frowning petulantly. "I really don't know."

"Well, let's find something that you're okay eating."

She glared at him. "Is that it?"

"Is what it?"

"Food. I spent last night and yesterday feeling sad, and now I'm scared, and all you can think about is buying some food."

"What I can do is make sure that we both get something to eat. You said it yourself; I don't know any better than you do what's going on. I do know that it's not going to help anything if we don't get some food, so the least I can do is make sure we have some nourishment. We can try to figure something out after that."

"And if we can't figure it out?" she asked.

"At least we can talk about what was bothering you before. Maybe that's all we can do."

"And just leave me in this loop?"

"Leave you? I'm stuck here with you. If it really is a loop."

"You're stuck with me? Oh—I didn't know you didn't want to be with me."

"Oh, come on—you know that's not what I meant."

She wrapped her arms around herself and walked away at a brisk pace. He squeezed his sinuses, feeling the onset of a headache, and walked after her. Half an hour later, any thoughts of walking along the river or venturing farther from the apartment cast aside, the two were back in the apartment, hungry and tense, unable to come up with a positive train of conversation that they could maintain.

As the sun began to set, the pair glanced nervously out the window at the encroaching night, wondering what the night, and the following morning, would bring. They opted to order a pizza from the most popular pizzeria in the area, surmising that if any food could be trusted, it would be something that they knew lots of other people were eating. They ate together while flipping TV channels, avoiding the movie they had watched the previous night and hesitant to choose anything else. As the night wore on, they eventually succumbed to sleep on the couch together, the TV still on, too nervous to make the conscious decision to go to sleep.

He woke up in his bed, blinking at the gloomy gray glare streaming in through the window. He sat up. It still wasn't cloudy. Why was it gray? He sat for a while, afraid to look at his phone. He didn't hear anything outside his bedroom. Had it all been a dream? He sat on his bed, turning over possibilities in his mind, reluctant to check his phone for fear of finding himself in a situation that he truly couldn't explain or even understand. He couldn't make himself check. Feeling jittery, a sensation he hadn't felt since his days of final exams and job interviews, he walked out of his room.

She was sitting at the kitchen table. She looked miserable. Her eyes were bloodshot, with puffy bags underneath. Her lips were chapped. The color seemed to have been partly drained from her face. Was she sick?

"What day is it?" he asked.

She looked up at him, her eyes watery.

"Sweetie, you don't look okay," he said.

"It's Saturday."

His breath caught in his throat. He blinked, reminding himself after a moment to continue breathing. "Are you sure, sweetie?" he asked, as softly as he could manage.

She nodded and wiped her eyes with her shirt. He pulled a chair up by her side and put an arm around her shoulders, taking her hand in his free hand.

"When did you go to your room?" she asked.

"I don't know. I fell asleep on the couch, with you. I—I woke up in my bed. I don't know what happened. I wish I knew."

"You didn't get up during the night?" she inquired.

"I only remember falling asleep," he said, wishing he had a better answer.

"What do we do now?" she asked.

He didn't know what to say.

"Don't go back to the market," she said.

"Okay. I won't."

"What's going on?"

"I don't know. I don't think it's because of the market."

"Don't go back there."

"Okay, sweetie. I won't."

She was sobbing now, the tears flowing freely down her damp cheeks. "I'm really scared," she said.

"It's going to be okay," he tried to assure her. He wasn't so sure, but he hoped that it sounded as though he was. "We'll figure this out."

"What if we can't?" she asked.

He didn't want to think about that possibility. "No matter what, we're together. I'd rather be with you than not." He pulled her closer, and she leaned against him stiffly. She sniffled, and he felt her tears on his shirt. At a loss, he eventually proposed heading outside, somewhere other than the market.

She cringed at the prospect of leaving. They debated whether they were more likely to find a way out by leaving or by staying put, with him suggesting that the answer must be somewhere else, something they hadn't tried, while she insisted on shutting out any potentially harmful outside influences. In the end, he couldn't convince her to come with him. He wasn't willing to leave her alone, and truth be told, he was scared of what might happen if he went out alone. Would he be unable to come back? Would she be gone if he did? Would he be stuck in a loop without her? Thoughts raced through his mind.

They turned on the TV to reassure themselves that they were still connected to the outside world that seemed to be going on about its business on Saturday as if for the first time, oblivious to the fact that they had already seen this day happen twice. The same programs played, and the same news broke. And the argument started up again.

She was more terse now, a note of panic in her voice throughout the day. He tried repeatedly to assuage her fears, but the more he did, the more he realized how helpless he actually felt.

She heard the increasing hopelessness in his voice. She said he was giving up. If he was giving up on her, he didn't truly care about her. He couldn't truly care.

He said the same things about staying by her side, about caring and being glad that at least they were together. He tried everything he could think of aside from leaving. He called friends and family to find out if any of them had noticed anything unusual, searched every news site, blog and station he could find to try to locate some clue as to why he and she were stuck on this day. He could find nothing, and the two of them began quietly to despair. They fell asleep on the couch with another wordless farewell to the day that wouldn't end.

He woke up in his bed. The gray light streaming through his bedroom window seemed heavy. He got up and went out to the kitchen, where she sat looking ill.

"I'm sick," she said plaintively, looking at him with imploring eyes.

A lump formed in his throat at the sight of her. Her lips were pale and chapped, her bottom lip split in the middle from lack of moisture. One of her eyes was bright red, as if a blood vessel had burst.

"You look fine," she said.

"We should have someone take a look at you," he said.

She shook her head. "No. I wasn't sick on Friday. It's not an illness. It's this day."

His eyes narrowed as he perused her face. "What do you mean?"

"I wasn't sick before," she said. "This couldn't have happened overnight."

"We've been through this day—what—three times now? That's enough time for you to catch something."

"No. Everything else is the same when we wake up, remember? The only thing that's changed is me. Nothing's different outside. I checked. You look fine."

"I'm calling a doctor," he said and went to get his phone.

"No!" she said, her voice strident. She coughed.

He stopped and turned back to face her. "I can't just sit here and do nothing. I can't figure out what's happening to you. A doctor can."

"No, a doctor can't. This isn't a natural illness. I told you."

"You don't know what it is."

"It's my body! I know how I feel, and this is not natural. There's something else. I don't know what it is, but this isn't something a doctor can help me with. Don't make that call."

He clenched his phone, frustrated and sensing a growing panic within himself. "I have to do something," he insisted. "At least if a doctor looks at you, we can cross off some explanations."

"I don't want anybody to see me like this," she said, coughing again.

He looked at her, his mind drawing a blank. There was no way he was going to leave her side, but he couldn't ask her to go anywhere in this condition. "I'm calling the hospital."

"No!" she shouted.

"I have to do something," he repeated.

"That's not what I want! It won't help me. I don't want to be seen like this. It has to be you. Don't you care enough to figure out what's wrong? Don't you at least care if I don't want people seeing me like this?"

"Of course I care! I wish you'd stop questioning that."

"Then don't bring anyone else here."

"I have to get help. I can't do this by myself."

"Nobody else can help you! If you care about me, you can find a way. I know you can. This isn't something you can get help with. You don't need help. You just need to make a decision."

He didn't know what to say. "I need help. I'm sorry."

He picked up the phone and dialed, but as he did, his vision blurred. He looked at her, sitting at the table, and felt the phone drop from his hand. As if through a wall, he heard her voice call his name as he collapsed on the floor, falling into unconsciousness.

He came to in his bed. A gray light permeated his room. He bolted up and ran out to the kitchen and stopped, drawing in a sharp breath in horror.

She sat at the table. He couldn't tell if she was conscious. His mind raced. He couldn't tell if she was alive. Her skin looked gray and dry like parchment. Her eyes were dark pits. Her hair was dry and matted. He couldn't bear to look, but he couldn't look away.

He approached the table. Her eyelids were dark, sunken and closed. He said her name, barely a whisper. She didn't respond. He said her name again, more forcefully this time. Still no answer.

Trembling, he sat at the table and took her hand in his, cringing as he felt her skin crackle under his fingertips. Her eyes opened slowly, revealing milky orbs underneath, her irises clouded and out of focus. Bracken tears drifted down her sunken cheeks.

"Don't you care about me?" she asked, her voice hoarse.

He lowered his head and wept.

The End

Ceschino (pronounced "Chess-key-know") is a Domer, wrestler and fencer who graduated from Harvard Law School and now practices law in Manhattan. With more ideas than spare time, he is currently writing three science fiction novels.

Lee Barwood's lyrical tale immerses us in the world of song, faerie and fantasy and reminds us that such worlds are made up of equal parts pain, hope and dreams. So much like our own. . . .

Rainsong
by Lee Barwood

Little bells chiming softly... Falling from the leaves like raindrops, glowing silver in the moonlight...

Alaw woke abruptly. She could feel the hard ground under her, the spot where her tunic had wrinkled uncomfortably beneath her. The wet, earthy smell of the forest floor filled her nostrils. But she did hear bells, though they rang so softly that the rain almost drowned their sound.

Impossibly, the wood was bathed in moonlight. Gwrdd stamped a hoof uneasily; her wolfhound Lludw lay next to her, whining softly and staring to his right. She sat up slowly and listened.

The bells chimed a melody, haunting and sad, echoing in Alaw's innermost self even as her minstrel's mind sought to commit it to memory. The music emanated from a stately procession moving slowly through the clearing just beyond, and she looked in wonder.

The steady rain did not touch the riders. White-clad men and women, dressed in regal splendor, rode magnificent white horses whose trappings gleamed with silver and gold and flashed with the glitter of precious gems. Bells ringed the ankles of riders and steeds alike, the source of the melody. The riders' faces bore an unearthly beauty, yet were so heavy with grief that she wept to see them; she could feel their anguish.

A sudden movement to the left halted the riders. A white wolfhound, bigger than Lludw, red-eared and with white-circled eyes, raced through the trees carrying a small bundle in his mouth. He ran to the couple at the head of the procession, rearing up on his hind legs that the woman might take it from him. He dropped back to all fours, barked once, and sped off into the night. The horses' stately pace resumed, and the melody played by the softly chiming bells seemed a shade less melancholy.

Alaw watched wistfully, yearning to follow. All her life she had hoped to behold a trooping of the Sidhe ... and then one of the riders turned in his saddle and looked at her, sending longing surging through her like a physical pain. She was suddenly on her feet, as if drawn by a lodestone; she leaned in his direction. His eyes held hers; as pale a blue as hers were dark, they were deep with wisdom and age, yet clearer than a babe's. She could lose herself in those depths; she would do it willingly, so willingly. She *would* follow. She stepped forward—

The shrill cry of a hungry infant rent the air. The rider closed his eyes and turned away, and Alaw felt Lludw's great jaws close gently but firmly on her hand. The procession and moonlight were gone, and the music with them, leaving her in darkness with only the sound of the rain. The cold drops pelted her through the leaves, and she shivered. Releasing her hand, Lludw raised his muzzle and howled mournfully. Gwrdd neighed shrilly. And Alaw sank to the ground, feeling drained and achingly alone.

The rain stopped before morning, and she awoke to a thick drapery of fog. There was no reason to linger in the wood, yet she was reluctant to move. *This is foolish*, she thought after sitting motionless for several minutes staring at a pile of kindling. *Either light it or move on.* At last she collected her belongings, slung her harp over her shoulder, and climbed wearily onto Gwrdd's broad back.

She paid no heed to her surroundings, leaving Gwrdd to set his own pace through the fog. The rider filled her thoughts; his face burned itself into her brain. Blue-black hair like her own had framed a smooth broad forehead, fallen softly to his shoulders. His brows had arched slightly over those deep-set eyes of palest water-blue; the straight nose and prominent cheekbones had accentuated the delicate lips and strong jaw. He had the slender build of the Sidhe, and had sat his horse with consummate grace.

And how he had looked at her—with an intensity that stabbed her very heart. The thought of him made her ache inside.

And the melody chimed in her mind, till at last she slipped her harp from its case and began to play. Her long fingers moved over the strings, her rich voice sought words for the dirge. For dirge it was, she was sure, if she had heard it at all … perhaps she had dreamed the whole thing. Perhaps...

She practiced the melody again and again, till her fingers would remember even if her mind would not, and noticed at last that the fog had burned off, revealing the outskirts of a village ahead. The thought of hot food, dry clothes, and a warm bed cheered her somewhat. Sheathing her harp, she urged Gwrdd to hasten.

The Swan was small and clean, and the rushes strewn on the floor were mixed with meadowsweet and rosemary. A joint turned on the spit, and loaves baked on the hearth; there would be no rain-chill here. Alaw stretched the stiffness from her tall lithe body and then sank down gratefully on the bench, drinking deeply of the excellent ale set before her. Gwrdd was stabled and Lludw gnawed a bone before the fire, but she herself had no strength to respond to the awed and reverent welcome her name had brought her. Still dazed, she stared into her tankard.

But an old man at the next table spoke hesitantly.

"Cerddoliad, I—I would beg a *drinnrosc*, a boon, of you."

"What is it, grandfather?" she asked absently.

"My granddaughter's newborn babe has been stolen away, and a changeling left in its place," he said. "And none in the village knows aught to do to help." He paused and then added hopefully, "Do you know aught, Cerddoliad, that can be done?"

"What?" The memory of a squalling, hungry infant whose cries shattered the night suddenly came to her, and she nearly choked on her brew.

"When was the babe stolen?"

"Last night, Cerddoliad."

Alaw sat in silence for a moment, her heart remembering pale blue pools of wisdom... "The triads tell of some," she said slowly, "who dared to go to the land of the Sidhe to reclaim their own. Some never returned, but some came back safely with their loved ones from the very Throne of the West." She drained the tankard and stared thoughtfully into the flames. Silence seemed to grow around her words as her mind raced. Finally she asked, "Is there no one who would attempt this?"

"None, Cerddoliad," the old man whispered hoarsely, as if ashamed. "I would go, but I have no use of my legs. The babe's father was elf-struck the night the child was taken, and knows not that she is gone." He ducked his head, now clearly shamed. "There are those," he added quietly, "who say he brought it on himself—that he called down the wrath of the Sidhe on his family. They fear that to help is to share that wrath. I cannot blame them, Cerddoliad." The old man looked at her with a mixture of hope and despair. "You are revered here. Your deeds are sung throughout the Thirteen Realms even as you sing of the great rulers and heroes who have passed. You dare quests no other would attempt. You are legend herself, Cerddoliad. Could you not seek the return of the babe?"

Alaw shivered. "You do me too much honor, grandfather, and exaggerate my deeds. I am but a minstrel with a good arm for the bow." She rose. "Innkeeper, could I trouble you for hot water? I have been weeks on the road, and am in need of a long soak. Then some hot food." She paused and then turned and looked at the old man.

"After I sleep for a while, grandfather, I shall see your granddaughter. I may—I may be able to help."

*****

She sank gratefully into the featherbed and pulled up the quilts. It was a warm spring noon outside, but even after the steaming water Alaw still felt cold. And drowsy; she sank into sleep as if going to meet a lover.

But her dreams brought the plaintive music of bells again, and the rumble of thunder and hooves. Lightning flashed. She strained to see the face of the rider she followed. He turned to look at her, and she cried out in her sleep; for his was the face of a white wolfhound, eyes ringed with red. There was a child in his mouth, but as she reached for it lightning flashed again; she could not move, could not cry out—

Then she was awake.

She rose and dressed quickly. It was late afternoon; in darkness could she find the place where she'd seen them? Perhaps not; they might not even return.

But seek them she would.

*****

The woman looked up as Alaw strode into the

room. Tearstreaks stained a face that looked far older than the scant years the old man had said she carried. And the man she tended on the cot gave no sign of noticing the minstrel's entry—or of his wife's care.

"Megan? I am Alaw o'r Dial. Your grandfather bade me come." Alaw went to the cot and clasped the woman's hand in a firm, warm grip. Then, gently, she turned the man's head to study his eyes. They stared blindly at nothing, vacant as the moon. Alaw shook her head and ~~then~~ led Megan to the rocker near the hearth. "Tell me what happened," she commanded, sitting on the floor beside her.

Megan wiped her eyes. "Here we revere the Sidhe, Cerddoliad. We leave offerings for them. And we do well enough. But Bradach is not from this village. His folk believe the Sidhe to be the devil's spawn and that to honor them is to blaspheme against the One. He resented the gifts we left the Good Folk, the milk they claimed from our cow as their due, although we never went without and have been safe and content. When our babe was born, he resolved to have done with the Sidhe." A tear trickled down her cheek. "He said he would protect us, but we had never been in danger." She sniffed. "Until he decided to stop them."

Alaw shook her head. "What did he, Megan?"

"I know not, but the cow began to give more—more than she has in years. Bradach was pleased, and went about telling all that he'd bested the Sidhe." She brushed away more tears with the back

107

of a calloused hand.

"A dangerous boast. So that is why none will aid him."

"Aye, Cerddoliad. He is the blasphemer." She shivered. "All was well enough, though, till last night. The cow did not return, and Bradach went to fetch her. It—it grew late, and he had not come, and I was frightened. I went—went out to look for him, and found him on the hill."

"Like that?" Alaw nodded toward the bed.

"Aye," Megan answered. "I could not move him. I ran for help and saw a great white dog leaving our cottage. I came in to see what it did here, and—and found a changeling in my babe's cradle!"

"What did they leave, Megan?"

"A tree root wrapped in leaves."

"Have you the thing still?"

The young woman rose wearily and lifted a bundle from the cradle in the corner. Alaw took it from her carefully and sat for a moment, considering.

"Cerddoliad?" Megan spoke timidly. "All the land knows of the deeds you have done. Could you not save my babe and bring Bradach back to his wits again?" Tears rolled slowly down her cheeks. "You are so brave, and there is no one else. Please, Cerddoliad."

The minstrel sighed and rose. "I will do what I can. I shall seek the Sidhe where I saw them yesternight."

"But if they do not come ... you will not leave my babe to die in the hollow hills, and my husband

108

to sit here drooling like a babe himself?" A look of desperation crossed Megan's face and she seized Alaw's arm. "Swear to me, Cerddoliad! Swear to me that you will save them!"

Alaw freed herself gently from the other woman's grip. "This much will I swear to you, Megan; I will go to the land of the Sidhe to search for the child, and if I find her I will bring her back." She laid a protective arm around Megan's shoulder. "The Sidhe do nothing without reason, no matter what your Bradach may have said. You know that, Megan. Their laws are not our laws, but they are just in their own way." The other nodded, sniffling. "May I take this with me?" Alaw asked, indicating the simulacrum. Megan nodded, and Alaw left the cottage.

***

Weaponless, Alaw dismounted beneath the trees; she had left all cold iron behind. She spoke softly to Gwrdd and Lludw, sending them back to the village, where the innkeeper had promised to care for them till her return. *If I return,* she thought, with a pang at the idea of leaving her animal companions. But she could not risk their safety, she knew, for the road to the Throne of the West was fraught with hazards both mortal and magical. Even though she and they had many times shared danger and battle, somehow she knew this was different.

Still, she decided as she settled herself beneath the oak, she had no regrets. If all went well perhaps she would be able to return briefly to claim them. If

109

not—well, if not, they were better off in the mortal world, where they would be safe and cared for.

She realized then that she wanted desperately to do this—as much for the memory of those pale eyes as for the sake of the babe. She hoped desperately that he would return. And that was not like her. Not at all. She had not given her heart again since she had lost her betrothed in the raid that had taken her family and set her on her quest on the road of song: the rescue of her sister and vengeance against those who had murdered nearly everyone she had held dear. The wound had been too raw for too long.

Then, when her quest was done and her sister Hedydd safe once more, there had been the needs of others to tend to. And even though she knew the needs of others would always be there, as long as she held the title of minstrel—giving others the right to call upon her strength and gifts in search of the justice no other could give them—suddenly she wanted, just for a little while at least, to be again the girl Llew had loved so many years ago. To love someone as she had loved Llew.

Foolish hope. Foolish thought.

But there it was.

And now she was here. If anything would draw him, she thought, perhaps the sound of elven music on a mortal's harp would. She would play.

She sang softly, just to stay awake, and soon forgot why she was there. Losing herself in the music as she often did, she began to sing a melody she had learned from a Sidhe woman when she still sought her sister's freedom. She touched the strings

110

on her harp and thought of that land she knew in song but had never seen with her eyes. A face floated in her mind; the face of the elflord. Without knowing what she sang, she put into words dreams that she had not known she yearned for.

Into the music crept an awareness of eyes upon her: *his* eyes, his gaze steady and penetrating. She looked up from the harpstrings, her fingers still tracing the song she had sung, to see him standing before her—dressed now in blue and silver, with a sky-blue cape that fell from his shoulders.

"You have the true gift," he said, his words as lilting as his voice was musical. "You dream-sing almost as well as we."

Alaw bowed her head in acknowledgment of his praise. "You are most kind," she said quietly.

"Nay, I speak but the truth," he told her, and smiled. She had never seen anything so entrancing as that smile, and gave him one in return. "It is well that you have come. Our first sight of one another was neither the time nor place to meet, though our meeting was destined." He extended his hand to help her to her feet.

"You knew I would be here?"

He nodded.

"How?"

"I knew. And had I not known, I would have heard; you have called me most eloquently." He reached for her harp, but waited, eyes on hers, till she nodded approval before he picked it up and examined it. "Skillful. Your crafting?"

"Yes, *a Thiarna*."

He slipped it into its case. "Nay, I am not lord

111

to you, nor to anyone in your world. I am called Dán. Have you a name?"

"Alaw o'r Dial."

His eyes widened. "Song of Vengeance? That is a strange name indeed for one who sings as you do. I should call you rather *Amhranai ó Aislingé* – Singer of Dreams.

"But you chose the name yourself, did you not?"

"I did. It is a custom among us for a minstrel to take a name that speaks the purpose of her journey on the road of song. I was called Enfys before."

"Rainbow. It suits. There are all the colors of earth and sky and sea in your voice and in your music." He took her hand once more. "I would ask what made you forsake the rainbow to sing this song of vengeance, *Aislingeach*. But such tales are for later, when the telling may be eased with wine and laughter." He lifted her pack and gestured with their linked hands to a magnificent white horse standing quietly nearby. "Will you come with me, that I might provide these things?"

***

They rode easily, the horse's gait smooth as cream, but Dán nevertheless kept a hand on both of hers clasped around his waist—whether for protection or to prevent escape, she could not tell. But she would not have tried to escape had her soul itself depended on it. They were so close she could catch his scent—a mixture of heather and hawthorn, maleness and some otherness that could only be magic.

They came to a mountain, and the great horse reared up; his silver hooves struck stone with such force that sparks danced like stars. Then there was a road where there had been no road, and the horse cantered on.

As they followed this road he spoke to her of dreams and of the Isles of the Blest. His voice held her with its lilting, lyric sound; his speech was softened by the accents of the Old Tongue of the Sidhe, his words themselves full of music. Alaw listened as she clung to him, and felt no fear, though she might be riding with the devil into very Hell. But her heart sang and her spirit thrilled, and she hoped it would never end.

The ride lasted forever and no time, but at last the steed's silver hooves splashed through a stream that ran like diamonds through the night, and she could see huge bonfires blazing in the darkness. The air around them was warm and cool at once, and perfumed with magic, and she felt as if she had come into a land where time did not exist.

"You are almost right," Dán said. "Time as you know it does not pass here. But a minstrel knows of such things, does she not?"

"Indeed, I begin to see how very much I have to learn," she replied.

"And there is much I would teach you, *Aislingeach*," he murmured. Then he dismounted and held out his arms to her. Though she was tall—her height nearly his own—and muscular from battle, the strength in the hands that caught her waist took her weight easily, and settled her to the ground as if she weighed no more than the mist that hovered above the earth.

"Though this is a land where Time has no power, still we mourn now for one of our children," he told her as they approached the fires. "You mortals live with Death's constant presence, but we do not, and so we mourn the more—and differently."

"Then it *was* a funeral," murmured Alaw. "But a child? How dreadful!"

"We do not die, but we can be killed. And a mortal man killed this child, so you will find those here who will not like that I have brought you. Though since she was kin to me—"

"Kin of yours?"

"Aye, my brother's infant, and a merrier babe was hard to find."

Alaw swallowed hard, and stopped walking. "Dán, there is something I must tell you," she said urgently. The Sidhe respected truth, and she would not deceive him.

"Nay, not now," he whispered. She looked up to see a couple heading toward them. "I would have you meet my kin," he said aloud, a smile on his face, and the chance was gone.

The meeting made Alaw feel uneasy. Eirnín, Dán's brother, was kind, but the way that his wife Sadhbh looked at her disturbed her. Alaw cursed her failure to speak to Dán earlier, and resolved to tell him as soon as they were alone.

But the four walked together to the first bonfire. Long trestle tables filled the clearing where the fire blazed, and at each table were seated many of the

114

Sidhe. Dán led Alaw among them as Eirnín and Sadhbh took seats.

"Behold," he cried. "I have brought a *cliaraí* from the world of men who can sing the dream-song and the *caoimneadh* as they should be sung. She will ease your grief; hear her." Surprised, Alaw looked at him as he gestured her to a bench in the midst of the company. "Do not fear, *Aislingeach*. Sing for them as you sang for me, and win their trust. You must have that if you would stay among us."

He was right, Alaw realized, though not for the reasons he meant. She settled her harp on her lap, and the strings whispered the first notes beneath her skilled fingers.

***

The night was a minstrel's tale itself. Many ballads told of mortals venturing into the banquets and feasts of the Sidhe to entertain them. But such occasions were merry, and the mortals treated with tolerance and good humor. This was different.

Alaw sang and played of grief, and death, and the loss of heart and spirit. She sang of the empty stretch of long years ahead, the road that missed the steps of a loved one, the blackness of the night in which the stars shone for one who was no longer present. She sang of the tears wept within a sundered heart and the void that could not be filled, and the harp sang true beneath her fingers, its silver strings quivering with sorrow.

Her audience sat rapt and silent as she mourned

their loss. Her fingers coaxed the harpstrings as never before; her voice came full and rich and never faltered. None interrupted; later, she realized she could have sung for days, though it seemed only till dawn.

But when at last she paused to consider her next ballad in the soft morning light, she felt a hand on her shoulder. It was Dán, and he gestured to a small table beside her laid with food and drink.

"Rest your fingers, and refresh your voice," he said to her, smiling. "You have given us all a great gift, *Amhranai ó Aislingé*. Our grief is soothed and we may now go on to the care of the living."

She saw that the Sidhe had begun to drift away, no longer looking grieved. "But I am only mortal," she whispered. "How is it possible?"

"To mourn, we pour out our grief through the talent of one such as you, though seldom is it one of your kind. We link with the *cliaraí*, mortal or Sidhe, and we send out our grief together. The music lends a path, and the going is eased; else we would mourn forever, for we never forget." He sat beside her and handed her a gleaming silver mug filled with clear ruby liquid. "Drink," he said. "It will restore you, for now I would have your company to myself. I did not bring you here to salve our grief, though your singing has given us more than you know."

Alaw took the mug. The aroma was heady and inviting, and she drank deeply without hesitation.

Dán laughed.

"So you do not fear that to eat or drink aught in our land means never to return to your own?" He refilled the mug from a worked silver flagon and lifted it to his own lips. "Or perhaps you do not wish to return." He drank, watching her.

She began to laugh. "Nay, Dán, I learned long ago from one of your own folk that such tales are no more than old men's fears."

"Yet many hold these fears. And you do not? You have no fear that I would do you harm, cast some spell?"

"If so, the spell has been cast and welcomed. I fear nothing at your hands, Dán," she told him honestly.

He shook his head. "Such blind trust is not wise. A song of vengeance is not sung in trust, nor does the singer long live to sing again, Alaw o'r Dial."

"But have you not also named me *Amhranai ó Aislingé*? And without trust, dreams cannot be sung." She would have spoken then of her purpose, but Eirnín and Sadhbh chose that moment to walk their way and she dared not. Instead, she took the mug Dán offered her and drank again. "Never have I tasted such a thing. It is like drinking spring breezes and summer stars."

He took a plate from the table and held it before her. "Even you must eat, my *cliaraí*," he told her. "I would hear the tale of Alaw o'r Dial from the lips of the *Aislingeach*, but you must be refreshed for the telling."

She took a wedge of cheese from the plate.

"And some of our wine will refresh even better than yours, is it not so, brother?" asked Eirnín as he brought Alaw another mug filled with a liquid so

117

clear it sparkled in the sunlight.

"Aye," replied Dán. "There is no better than that which Sadhbh brews in her stillroom. Taste, *Aislingeach*."

Alaw savored the aroma and smiled, but put the cup down till she finished the cheese she had taken.

"How is the child, Sadhbh?" Dán asked. "You look tired."

"Nay, brother, all is well," she answered. "It should not be long till we know whether we have succeeded." She looked at Eirnín happily.

"Succeeded at what?" asked Alaw, lifting the cup, and regretting her words at Sadhbh's look. "I beg pardon, *Spéirbhean*, forgive my curiosity. It is none of my concern."

"Nay, there is no harm in answering," Dán said. "We do not bear often or easily, and our numbers diminish as the ages pass. So when a child dies, we try to beget another, though grief hinders the process. The presence of another child seems to help, but there are so few among us that we take human children to aid us. Sometimes they are given willingly, which is the greater help, and sometimes they are not."

"And sometimes they are taken to claim revenge!" snapped Sadhbh, eyes flashing.

Eirnín explained. "Our daughter died of milk poisoned by a farmer and left as a gift. We have taken his child to help us produce another."

"The farmer himself has paid as well," answered Sadhbh grimly, almost warningly. "Eirnín took him on the hilltop with an arrow, and he will never do us harm again."

118

"Surely you have heard of such things before, *Aislingeach*, said Dán, studying her face. "'Twas my own hound fetched the child."

"Nay, 'tis not that," stammered Alaw. "It is just that I did not know…" Tears came to her eyes, both for their pain and for what she had sworn to do. "What—what becomes of such children if you succeed?"

"Sometimes they are returned, sometimes not," Eirnín replied. "If it would grieve our women too much to relinquish them, they stay; when they have grown they may leave if they wish. Few do."

"I can understand that," murmured Alaw, looking at Dán. He touched her wet cheek.

"Mortal tears … mere salted water, yet more precious than gems to us when shed on our behalf." He kissed her gently. "Do not cry, *Aislingeach*. We think this will succeed; it often does. And then you must play at the feast we shall have. Now drink, and be of good cheer!"

She drained the sparkling drink from the cup.

There was something of that magical essence in this wine. She felt like laughing and dancing after she drank, and why not? She wanted for nothing. She was here in the land of the Sidhe, with the lover she had wanted so desperately. Nothing else mattered. All thoughts of vows and duties fled, and she did not even realize their absence. She turned to Dán.

"I must confess I think this the better brew," she told him. "I have not felt so merry in years!"

And Sadhbh smiled, her expression truly easing for the first time since Alaw had seen her.

"And you have brought none for me? I think that rather amiss, sister," Dán said.

She smiled charmingly at him. "Come, brother, you have all you can drink at every visit," she said lightly. "Your *cliaraí* has never had it before. You must bring her to us very soon, and you shall have your own cup." She turned to Eirnín. "Husband, it is time we saw to the babe." And they left.

Dán looked at Alaw. "You are lovely when you are happy, though not the less so when you are not," he said. "Come. You must finish eating, and then tell me of yourself."

They sat together happily, and Alaw told him of her childhood; her loss of her betrothed, her quest to rescue her sister and claim vengeance for her family; her decision to live as a minstrel. And at last she told him of her desire to follow him.

"I am pleased," he said when he had heard the last. "For you have come here of your own free will. The glamour is very strong at such times; had you come that first night I would even now be wondering if you came willingly, with only myself for a goal. Those with the Sight are often drawn to us mindlessly, and I would not have that."

A shadow crossed her face. There was something ... But she (could not remember and) shrugged it off, and reached for a chunk of bread. [Here, I think it would help the reader to be told that Alaw can't remember and isn't just holding back.]

It did not go unnoticed, however. "What is wrong?" he asked. "There was something you wished to tell me before, when first you arrived. Is something amiss?"

Alaw puzzled over that for a moment. "Nay, Dán, there is nothing. I am sure there is nothing." There was doubt in her words, and he could sense it. But if she would not speak of it, he would not force her.

***

Time passed easily. Alaw played each night at the great bonfires, Dán at her side, and her skill and talent grew. Days she spent in his company, loving him ever more dearly, and before long he had asked her to wed him at the next great festival—an honor seldom accorded a mortal by a Sidhe. She was happier than she had ever been.

And yet...

Something nagged at the edge of her memory. When she held the mortal babe in Sadhbh's keeping, or sang it lullabies, or suggested to the elven woman how best to care for it as the mortal child it was, the feeling was strongest. But it would quickly fade. It disturbed her, and Dán watched her oddly at such times—when the edge of memory grew ragged for a moment and something almost broke through.

Her pack had lain forgotten in a corner since her arrival. Yet one morning she sought it out; Sadhbh was pregnant at last, and there was to be a great feast. Alaw was to compose something joyful to celebrate their happiness, and there was something in her pack...

She took it and her harp and went to sit in the great willow grove. She went alone, for Eirnín and

Dán had gone together to seek a gift for Sadhbh.

Beneath a great old willow whose fronds trailed to the very ground, she settled her harp on her lap. Her fingers moved gently over the strings as she played idle snatches of music, hoping for some combination with promise.

But then the edge of memory grew very ragged indeed, and she found herself feeling almost melancholy as she sought to remember something just out of reach. And her fingers quite unconsciously began to play a dirge … the dirge she had heard the night she saw Dán for the first time. Her fingers traced the melody hesitantly at first, whispering over the strings, then surely; she had not played it since her arrival. And then all at once she heard again the wail of a babe. In her memory she sat in darkness in the rain. The babe; something to do with the babe. She put down her harp and opened the pack.

The simulacrum met her eyes. What was she doing, she wondered at first, with this root shaped so very much like an infant? Something was wrong, very wrong.

And then all at once she remembered, clouds of memory parting as if rent by a strong winter wind that blew chills down her spine.

Hastily she pushed the root back into her pack. To take the child now would betray Dán, and the love she had for him. How could she leave him? And the others; they had been so kind to her. How could she?

But she had never broken a vow in her life, much less forgotten one altogether.

And then she saw again the goblet filled with sparkling colorless wine, and the face of Sadhbh as she had drunk of the brew. She knew the elven woman better now; she understood the look she had not recognized that day. It had been relief. There had been something in that wine. Before she could speak, they had bound her with a potion. A *deoch dearmaid*, the drink of forgetfulness.

And he had let them.

Perhaps they had feared she would take the child before Sadhbh conceived again. But they had only to tell her; she would have waited. Indeed, now that she knew the tale behind the child's disappearance, she regretted her vow—but still, she had made it, and Alaw o'r Dial did not break her word.

Then there was Dán. She had come here as much because of him as because of the babe; perhaps even more. She loved him, trusted him. But he had not trusted her, indeed had warned her not to trust. She must be only a curiosity to him—a mortal who could sing and play well enough to amuse the Sidhe.

She would take the babe and go this very night. There was no reason to wait; Sadhbh would have her child. She did not know how she would bear it. But she had sworn that if she found the babe she would bring her back. And she had never broken faith in her life. To leave Dán, to leave the land of the Sidhe, never to return...

***

She played and sang that night as never before, but was glad to surrender her place to an elven bard. "Nay," she told Dán gaily when he sought to follow, "you may not go with me. This must be a surprise!" She could have bitten her tongue. And she stole away with harp and pack, and crept to Eirnín's home.

She was in luck; all were at the celebration. There was no one who would harm a babe in this land. So she was able to take the child from its cradle and to leave the changeling in its place.

She had reached the door when there came a low growl from outside. She froze, the child in her arms; the growl came again, and then the door opened. Dán's great hound bounded into the room, and he himself stood before her, eyes blazing.

"So! A song of vengeance it is that you would play!" he cried. "You come among us as a friend, take of our love and friendship, and steal away our children!"

Stunned, she shook her head. "Nay," she protested. "I came as a friend, and the child was part of my intent from the beginning—as I would have told you had you not spellcast me with that wine! I sought only to retrieve this babe for her true mother." Then more softly she added, "I trusted you. But I cannot break faith with the babe's mother. I have sworn."

"Indeed! And what of the vow you were to swear to *me*?" he demanded. "You do not trust, Alaw o'r Dial, and I was wrong ever to think you did. You accuse me of spellcasting, you who once told me that you feared nothing at my hands?" He laughed bitterly. "That is indeed a rare jest."

"Then why did I forget my oath after drinking the wine your brother's wife gave to me?" she cried back, stung.

"You did not forget. You waited in silence till we held you dear—and now you make accusations against the very folk you would wrong."

She shook her head. "I speak the truth, and you know it, *a Thiarna*. I knew not when I came that the child's father had killed one of yours, or I would not have given my word; I did not realize then what it was I had come to ask of you. But ask I would have; I did not come to steal! I tried to tell you that first day, but you gave me no chance. I would not have left before Sadhbh conceived another child; I swear I would not."

"Your word is worthless, faith-breaker."

"I swear it on my love for you."

"You do not love; you only deceive. Give me the child."

"Nay, she comes with me."

"You will die first."

"Then must it be at your hands, for I must do as I have vowed." She stared at him. "I have no weapon, *a Thiarna*. Will you not lend me one, that we may decide this now?"

"What goes on here?" came Eirnín's voice from the door.

Sadhbh ran into the room, wailing, "I knew, I knew," and took the child from Alaw. She moved well away from the minstrel and stood crooning to the child.

Dán turned to his brother. "What do you here,

125

Eirnín? I had hoped to spare you this."

"Sadhbh insisted that we come when she saw the *cliaraí* leave the festival. She has said from the day she arrived that she had come to take the child."

"I could feel the spells from the likeness," cried Sadhbh. "Spells I laid myself, that I might be warned if anyone came. Eirnín would not believe me." She soothed the fussing babe for a moment. "But I kept her away for a long time; had the brew been stronger, I should have kept her away forever!"

"Your own kin does not deny the accusations I have made, *a Thiarna*. Will you still tell me that it is I who have deceived you?" Alaw asked quietly.

Dán looked in anger at Sadhbh. "To do what you have done is against our laws," he reminded her. "One who comes for good intent must not be harmed in any manner."

"Does it count for nothing, the murder of my babe by one of her own kind?" Sadhbh hissed. "He disguised his evils in a gift—and we foolish folk accepted it." She looked down at the child. "And I have not harmed her at all; I only made her forget why she had come. Would that I had done to her what she does to me now—to take away that which is dearest to my heart—"

Dán went to her and lifted the child from her arms. She shook her head, then screamed and flew at him with her fists. Eirnín restrained her as Dán gave the babe back to Alaw, who stared at him in amazement.

"Forgive me, *Aislingeach*," he said. "It is I who have broken faith, for allowing such a thing to

126

happen to one under my protection. I should not have doubted you. Had you come and told us your purpose, there would have been a council to decide the answer. After Sadhbh's actions, however, there is only one decision that can be reached. You must take the child back." He studied her for a moment. "Will you return to me then when your vow has been fulfilled?"

Alaw nodded. "Aye," she breathed. "With or without spellcasting, that is all I have wanted since first I saw you." Neither of them looked at Sadhbh as Eirnín tried to console her.

"Let her go, *ionuín*. We do not need the child; we shall have another of our own now," he told her as she struggled against him. She shook her head, wailing. She tried to go to the babe, but Eirnín held her tighter. Suddenly she looked full at Alaw and her lips moved, though she made no sound. Alaw began to feel faint, and as Dán grew hazy in her vision she shook her head. She tried to speak to him, but no sound came out. Dán looked at her in horror, and called out to Eirnín.

His voice was faint, and she could not understand him; he spoke in the Old Tongue. She began to feel drowsy, and sat on the floor with the babe cradled in her lap.

Then all at once she was in darkness, moving farther away from Dán, who grew fainter and fainter. Suddenly she could hear Sadhbh's voice, saying, "*Imeacht gan teacht ort*"—*May you leave without returning*. And then she could hear Dán clearly, though he still spoke the Old Tongue.

"*Aislingeach*, I will come for you. We cannot

undo what Sadhbh has done, but she cannot keep you from me forever. When the time is up I will come for you and bring you back. I swear, *Aislingeach*. I swear on the rainbow." There was longing in his voice, and pain that matched the rent in her heart.

She woke beneath the great oak in the woods, with a hungry squalling babe in her arms. There was a light rain falling and the dawn air was chill. She was dazed, and barely thought to cover the child or retrieve her things from the ground before stumbling off in the direction of the village. She was desolate, and as she walked she wept for the love she had found and lost in the land of the Sidhe. Her tears blinded her, and she stumbled; then a voice nearby called out to her.

"Cerddoliad! You have done it!" Megan raced up to her and took the child thankfully, her face stained with tears. "Bradach died in the night; I came to—to gather flowers for the bier. But I have found you instead, and you have saved my babe! Oh, Cerddoliad, however can I thank you?" She hugged the child and took the weary minstrel's pack. She brushed fresh tears from her face as she said, "I was half afraid you would return to me an old crone and my child a woman grown, but you have come back so soon!"

Alaw looked at her in dull surprise. "Nay," she murmured slowly. "Weeks … months…"

"Nay, nay, do you not remember how time there flows differently? But a night is all. Oh, Cerddoliad, I must tell my grandfather!" She raced off, leaving Alaw alone in the rain.

Wearily the minstrel walked the rest of the way back to the Swan, where amid a hero's welcome she sat quietly in a corner by the fire to wait for the end of the rain.

And the rainbow...

Glossary

A Thiarna: my lord, high lord (of the Sidhe only; not of mortals)

Alaw o'r Dial: song of vengeance

Amhranai ó Aislingé: singer of dreams

Aislingeach: dreamer; one who has mystical visions

Bradach: spirited

Caoimneadh: keen; lament for the dead

Cerddoliad: harmonious one; harmonizer; one who harmonizes

Cliaraí: minstrel

Dán: poetry; fate; destiny

Deoch dearmaid: drink of forgetfulness

Drinnrosc: boon

Eirnín: iron

Enfys: rainbow

Gwrdd: stout, brave, strong

Hedydd: lark

Imeacht gan teacht ort: may you leave without returning

Ionuín: beloved

Llew: lion

Lludw: ashes

Megan: pearl

Sadhbh: wise; sweet

Spéirbhean: spirit woman; sky-woman; beautiful lady

The End

Lee Barwood shares her characters' love for the power and magic of music in her own playing and composing for Celtic harp and guitar. In poetry and prose, Barwood draws heavily on folklore; she also writes about the plights of animals and the environment, with a paranormal edge. Her environmental suspense/thriller A DREAM OF

130

DROWNED HOLLOW *won Andre Norton's Gryphon Award and garnered rave reviews; her short fiction and poetry have been nominated for several awards, including the Balrog. Her work has appeared in numerous small- and large-press magazines and anthologies. Her Haunted Ozarks series,* A DREAM OF DROWNED HOLLOW, SOME COST A PASSING BELL *and* A LINGERING PASSION *published by Double Dragon/Blood Moon, is peopled by those whose otherworldly abilities go beyond the physical universe.* THE TRAIL THROUGH THE MIST, *set around the Cherokee Trail of Tears, will be out in 2012 from Double Dragon Publishing, and she is at work on a trilogy about the minstrel Alaw. Her Klassic Koalas series is published by Koala Jo Publishing.*

Lee Barwood is a long-time member of Mystery Writers of America, the Authors Guild, and Science Fiction and Fantasy Writers of America. She finds that mystery and the paranormal often fit together perfectly, embracing the unknown and offering clues to more than one puzzle at a time. Learn more about her and her work at www.leebarwood.com.

What dark fantasy collection would be complete without a Steampunk query of all that the theme implies? And so Joseph Michael introduces us to a weary war criminal who stumbles through a storm in a land of unspeakable crimes against humanity in this. . . .

Lullaby of a Hated Person
by Joseph Michael

Friedrich Hanns Glockner, Nazi Kriegsmarine. Age twenty-five, five feet and ten inches tall. Born in Aachen, Germany on March 25th, 1918. Mother is Adelheid Helmine Glockner, and father is Klaus Bernhard Glockner.

The man reviewed these points over and over as he wandered through the howling blizzard. He had lost track of time and had no idea how long he had been walking by then. It had been long enough for the cold to start getting to him; his body shivered violently under his coat. His clothes were not thick enough to properly block the icy wind, but he didn't know that he would be out in these conditions. One moment he was in his bunker, laughing with his companions and drinking coffee to pass the night, and in the next moment their base was swarmed by American soldiers, and he was taken prisoner.

Friedrich Hanns Glockner, Nazi Kriegsmarine. Age twenty-five, five feet and ten inches tall.

He had to keep thinking, keep his brain active.

He clenched and unclenched his fingers, using the pain like frozen needles in his joints to keep himself awake. All he needed to do was battle the frostbite until he could find shelter.

But where could there be shelter here? The whole time he had been walking, there was nothing but whistling white all around. His captors chased him off the road once he escaped from their truck, firing at him with their pistols. Whether they aimed to simply disable him or to outright kill him, Friedrich did not know, though either way the storm was a blessing as it hindered their vision. He escaped with only a clip to his right thigh and a hit to the left shoulder. Better than a bullet to the head or the heart, at least.

Born in Aachen, Germany on March...what was it? 24th?

Finally, he saw a huge, dark shape coming into view to his left. It was clearly some kind of large building, perhaps a castle or a mansion. Whatever it was, it would be shelter away from this storm. Maybe he would find a family there who would take pity on him and offer hot food and a place by the fire to warm his aching body.

Mother is...mother is...what was her name?

As the structure came into view, Friedrich could clearly see its construction. He could not tell if it was a castle or a mansion, for while it seemed to have the overall form of the former, its size was more like the latter. The stone forming its walls and ramparts was dark, and a black iron fence encircled the front of the building, embracing a garden that in the spring would have been beautiful, but which was now dead and frozen. The gate hung loosely on its hinges, creaking loudly in the wind.

Suddenly, Friedrich remembered stories of a castle located in the middle of nowhere in Germany. It was the home of a mad scientist known as Doctor Klemens von Kaufmann, a man rumored to be as heartless and ruthless as, if not more so than, the Angel of Death, *der weiße Engel*, Josef Mengele. Tales of Dr. Kaufmann's horrifying experiments and inventions were often shared on slow nights in the bunker, tales of mechanical beasts crawling through the castle grounds, of inhuman screams and howls heard flowing from within the walls some nights, of demonic experiments that warped living flesh into insane sins against humanity.

Friedrich's eyes began to feel heavy. It was hopeless. At last, the first home he had seen for hours, and it was the home of the hellish Doctor, himself. He fell to his knees in front of the metal gate, the heavy snow crunching underneath him. His vision faltered, slowly fading into blankness. He would never see his friends or family again. Nobody would know what happened to him. He would die a dishonorable death, lost in a blizzard and killed by frostbite rather than in service to his country.

Finally, his eyes closed and he fell, his consciousness gone before he could even hit the snow.

***

Friedrich awoke to the tune of a music box floating through the air, echoing its lilting, lonely tune through the empty space of the room he was in. As his eyes slowly opened, he saw a ceiling high above with an unlit chandelier hanging from it. The room was dark, lit only by a warm fire crackling gently to his left, accompanying the sound of the mournful music box to his right. Friedrich gradually became aware of a softness underneath him, the cushions of a couch he had been lain on to rest.

With that feeling came a brief, stabbing pain in his left shoulder and right thigh. Friedrich winced, a hiss of discomfort sliding through his clenched teeth as he pushed himself up into a sitting position. It was then that a hand came around the back of the couch and pressed into his chest, a hand of metal and wood and tipped with thin, gently curved claws on each of its four fingers.

Friedrich's breath caught in his throat as he instantly stopped, his terrified gaze slowly moving down to look at the hand. His eyes followed it up to a wrist, with an arm that seemed to be made of motley scraps of wood and metal. Past that was an elbow made from interlocking gears, and then farther up another arm and another elbow, leading into yet another arm that finally terminated in a geared shoulder. The machinery gave way at last to flesh, the upper body of a young woman with eerily pale skin and empty blue eyes. Black hair flowed down from her head and past her shoulders, and Friedrich could see that the only clothing she had were ragged white bandages providing some decency and curving around her neck and stomach.

Gently, but firmly, the girl pushed Friedrich back down. He was too stricken to resist, awed by her unusual beauty and her monstrous, mechanical limbs. Once he lay down again, the girl nodded briefly and spoke. Her voice was soft and quiet, and it halted as if she knew what she wanted to say, but not how to say it. "…rest. Alraune…healed. Dangerous outside, so…wait here. Alraune will…bring food."

The mouth of the girl named Alraune twitched at the corners slightly as she struggled to give Friedrich a brief, reassuring smile. It was apparently an unfamiliar gesture to her, given the trouble she had forming the small upward curve of her lips.

Once that was accomplished, she turned around and walked off to the door, a movement accompanied by several dull thuds of multiple pointed objects tapping into the wooden floor. Briefly, Friedrich saw that she had four large, humming Tesla coils on her back, two bolted to each shoulder blade. Electricity gently arced over and between them for the moment that he could see, and then she was gone.

He lay on the couch again, his head whirling as he attempted to figure out what was going on. His hand rested on his chest where Alraune's mechanical claws had been a moment before, the metal and wood cold against his skin. Friedrich was horrified by Alraune, whatever she was. One of Dr. Kaufmann's vile experiments, probably. The girl couldn't have been older than Friedrich when the

136

Doctor replaced her limbs with those mechanical devices.

Friedrich's thoughts were interrupted by the sound of the door creaking open once more. He lay still, listening to the sound of Alraune's gently thudding footsteps as they approached and then moved around the couch. As she came into view, carrying a tray of food in both hands, he could see why her footsteps sounded so unusual. Everything below her hips had been completely replaced. A small chassis of wood and metal supported the foundations for four mechanical insect legs tipped with pointed blades. Friedrich suddenly felt as though ice water was running just under his skin, but he did his best to remain calm.

Alraune lowered herself and placed the tray she held on a coffee table next to Friedrich's couch. Then, with the whirring and clunking sounds of the gears in her limbs moving each other, she took a few steps back and sat on the floor behind the table. An awkward silence hung in the air as she idly scratched the back of one hand with the fingers of the other, watching Friedrich expectantly.

The song of the music box continued to dance through the air, its gentle notes filling the room. Friedrich stared at Alraune where she sat on the floor. Now that he looked at her again after the initial shock of her appearance, he realized that she actually was quite pretty. Her face, though deathly pale, was sculpted as though by an artist, and her eyes, though vacant and empty, were cool pools of blue that held a faint, energized glow. Her limbs, however...

"...please eat."

Alraune's voice broke through his thoughts, and he apologetically nodded and sat up. The pains in his shoulder and leg were subsiding, and it was easy for him to rise and turn on the couch to face the coffee table and the fireplace. Friedrich looked down at the tray in front of him. Upon it sat a bowl of steaming soup filled with delicately cut vegetables and beef, as well as a red mug of hot chamomile tea.

Despite whatever apprehensions he had about the chef and the location, Friedrich had to admit that the meal looked good, and he certainly was hungry after all his wandering in the cold and biting wind. With a brief look back at Alraune and an awkward smile, he picked up the spoon lying next to the bowl and gently scooped some soup into his mouth.

"Delicious," he muttered, his voice dull with unexpected revelation.

A small, shy smile formed on Alraune's face, and she carefully turned her head away to hide her embarrassed pleasure.

**

Alraune pushed the door of the room open for Friedrich, letting him pass through into the main hallway. The light, subtle creak of the door's hinges was magnified in the empty stone corridor. It bounced across the dark stone walls, sliding through the shadows that could have been dispelled if the candelabras lining the walls were lit. The only illumination came from the window at the other end of the hallway, and through it Friedrich could see that the snowstorm was still raging outside. It would be a long time before he would be able to try to find his way back to the base.

As Friedrich thought and tried to plan his situation after the initial shock of meeting his caretaker, he gradually became aware of a constant, low thrumming sound like that of a large engine that came from deep within the castle. Friedrich wondered for a moment what exactly the motor was powering, since there did not seem to be any electric appliances in the building.

That moment of thought was broken as a low, rumbling howl echoed through the hall. The cry chilled Friedrich's blood and slid down his spine unpleasantly, and he froze where he stood. The howl was not the kind that would have been made by any animal he knew of, as it sounded like some kind of beast's cry mingled with the mournful wail of a human.

Then a hulking, dark form lumbered into view at the other end of the hallway, emerging from a side room and blocking Friedrich's view of the window. Its upright frame like that of a blocky gorilla nearly filled the hall, and the cubic, almost reptilian head with two glowing green lights like eyes on the side scraped against the ceiling.

Friedrich could feel the crash of the knuckles of its huge, three-fingered hands hitting the floor with each step as its shorter back legs followed. The outlines of gears in its metal joints could be seen against the faint light coming through the window, and a line of three live electric coils lay in plain sight on its back.

It stopped in the middle of the hall as if it could feel Friedrich's sudden wave of fear. Slowly, it tilted its head in an almost birdlike fashion as if to get a better view of him through the multiple lights on its head. The whirrs and clunks of gears shifting and moving echoed through the hall as the creature began to turn its whole body to face the man. Another low, rumbling wail came from its body, more curious than malicious.

Friedrich, nonetheless, could do nothing but stand there, petrified. He didn't react when Alraune put a hand on his shoulder and peered around him at the mechanical monster, or when she called it by its name, Grendel, or even when she moved around Friedrich and approached it.

It was only when Alraune turned to Friedrich again and gave him a slightly confused and surprised look that he shook himself out of his shock again. "What *is* that thing," he asked at last as he placed a hand on his clammy forehead, as if to check for a fever.

"...Grendel," Alraune replied gently, patting the mechanical beast on the nose. "Another one of...Father's creations. Like Alraune."

"Father?" Friedrich's brow raised in surprise as his arm dropped to his side once more. "Do you mean Dr. Kaufmann? Klemens von Kaufmann?"

Alraune stared at him for a moment with a thoughtful look on her face. "...yes. Father," she replied in an almost correcting tone.

"I see," the soldier replied as he rubbed his face, weary from his travels outside and surprise

140

upon surprise in this castle he now found himself in.

He paused to think for a moment, considering his situation and wondering how long it would take the storm outside to subside. "Alraune. If you wouldn't mind, I would like to speak with Dr. Kaufmann. I must ask him if he knows of a way back to my home from here. I should leave as soon as I can."

Alraune's eyes, for one brief moment, appeared to become even duller than they normally were. Her mechanical shoulders fell just a bit, and her hand paused over Grendel's metal cranium, much to the creature's upset. A quick groan from the beast made Alraune resume her gentle petting.

"Alraune? Did you hear me," Friedrich asked with a hint of worry in his voice.

"...Father died...years ago," Alraune muttered. "Alraune has...been taking care of everyone since...then. Grendel, Caliban, Rubicant, and Arachne." She paused, and then turned to look at Friedrich again. Her lips tightened in a smile, an attempt to lighten the mood. "Alraune doesn't think...it's safe for Friedrich to leave. Not yet. Friedrich can stay until...the storm is over."

The soldier stared at Alraune, just as silent as she was a moment ago. It took him a moment to absorb the knowledge of what he was just told. If he had been asked at that moment, he would not have been able to describe exactly what gave him pause, nor would he quite be able to years after.

Perhaps it was the knowledge that this girl of machine and flesh in front of him spent the last several years, the number of which he didn't know,

141

in solitude with other mechanical beasts. Perhaps it was the knowledge that she may have spent all that time grieving for her lost 'father', with nobody to comfort her.

Perhaps Friedrich felt pity for her.

Whatever the case, after a moment, he nodded. "Yes. Yes, you're right. I hope you won't mind my staying here until the storm has passed, then."

For a minute, Alraune's sad, tight, false smile became genuine. A bit of light flashed into her dull eyes as she cheerfully nodded back. "Yes. Of course. Alraune...is happy to have Friedrich's company."

Friedrich could not help but smile, himself. For some reason, after he got past the girl's horrible alterations and empty gaze, and past her stilted speech and clunking joints, he felt drawn to her. He felt happy around her, much happier than he could remember feeling in a while. Not to say that he did not appreciate his time in the Kriegsmarine, but to say that he did not have doubts about the regime he served would be false.

The two stared at each other briefly as the minutes passed, until a grunt from Grendel broke them out of their mutual trance. Friedrich cleared his throat and averted his gaze, while Alraune turned her head at the same time to hide the slight blush that appeared on her cheeks. "I should get some rest," the soldier said awkwardly, staring at one of the candelabra on the wall as he spoke. "Thank you, Alraune, for your hospitality. Sleep well."

"...sleep well, Friedrich. Alraune will...see

you in the morning."

With that, the girl turned and walked away down the hall, the gentle ticks of her mechanical legs echoing through the corridor as they stepped on the hard floor. After a call from Alraune, Grendel soon followed, slowly turning in the space before lumbering after her.

Friedrich watched her leave as he tried to sort out his conflicting thoughts. He began to wonder what he would do if the storm did stop. He wondered if the Kriegsmarine would send a search party to find him, or if they would even think to look in this area, if they searched.

He sighed and set those thoughts aside, for now, as he turned back to the room he awoke in. The door creaked as he pulled it open, then again as he closed it once he reentered the room. His gaze shifted to the wooden table resting behind the couch he lay on a moment ago, and he looked up at the simple wooden music box that once filled the room with its song. Beside it lay a plain black notebook. He hadn't noticed it before, but judging by the thin layer of dust over it, it had been there for quite a while. Curious, Friedrich picked it up and moved to sit on the couch with it.

By the light of the still-crackling fireplace, he opened the notebook to its first page and began to read.

***

"July 31st, 1931 – This is the research log of Dr. Klemens von Kaufmann. In this log I will be placing the notes of my research into creating artificial life, both for my own review and in case I find someone to carry on my knowledge.

"My final goal in this endeavor is to create an intelligent living being. It will be capable of the same meaningful thought as a human. The body is not something I will be overly concerned with, though after this is successful I may consider altering the formula to create an entire human being."

Friedrich furrowed his brow as he read. To his knowledge, even Mengele never attempted something like this, horrible though the man's experiments were. This was something previously unheard of, though if Dr. Kaufmann's reputation was to be believed, it was perhaps expected of him. Friedrich shook his head and continued reading.

What followed were pages and pages of notes, formulas, and diagrams, most of which Friedrich could barely understand. He saw diagrams of cells and embryos and mentions of a creature that was successfully created and that grew rapidly while suspended in amniotic fluid. Eventually, he came to an entry dated two months after the creature's initial formation.

"October 5th, 1933 – The creature has developed enough to be taken out of its artificial womb, and in fact development seems to have halted entirely. Upon removal, however, its vitals dropped drastically and I was forced to return it to its previous environment.

"While it was out of the artificial womb, I observed that it experienced difficulty breathing and

144

had some form of seizure. These symptoms stopped almost instantly once the creature was returned to the artificial womb. As far as I can tell, the creature is incapable of surviving without this aid.

"In an attempt to see if this was the only hindrance, I built a mechanical body for the creature. I modeled it after a gorilla's basic form, using whatever materials I had on hand. The tank in which it is held now has been placed in the head region, and its nervous system has been linked to the body so that it can perceive and interact with its environment freely. I will observe it for the next few days and determine its mental state."

Below were a few drawings of Grendel, the mechanical creature Friedrich saw only a few minutes ago with Alraune. There were blueprints and sketches, showing the different pieces of the frame and the hideous, embryonic creature within. Friedrich stared at the sketches until a faint feeling of disgust came over him, and he turned to the next page.

"October 8th, 1933 – After observing the creature for some time, I have come to the conclusion that it is severely mentally unstable. It responds violently to any other individuals aside from me. Strangely, it listens unquestioningly to my commands, and my orders have often been the only reason it does not charge after anyone passing by the castle.

"I have named the creature Grendel, as its current appearance and wildly violent behavior remind me of that mythical creature, and I have deemed it a failure. I will be analyzing my previous methods and will determine what went wrong, so that my next attempt will be successful."

For many more hours, Friedrich read the scientist's log. Weeks later, Dr. Kaufmann made another attempt that met with a similar fate, and he created another mechanical body for it. This one resembled a big cat of some kind, with a single "eye" and human fingers on its hands. Dr. Kaufmann named it Caliban and, once again, judged it as a failure. In the same entry, he mentioned that Caliban developed a habit of wandering outside and collecting human corpses, which he kept in an isolated room in the castle. Dr. Kaufmann noted that he never found out if Caliban found these corpses or killed them itself, but he knew that the creature greatly valued them.

The doctor's last two attempts met with the same fate. Rubicant was given a body like a centipede, with two electric coils on its hind end and two eyes on the front. Arachne, meanwhile, was given a form like a slender, gangly spider with its tank fully exposed in the head and an electric coil in place of a stinger. The former was noted to have an obsession with listening to music, especially singing, while the latter constantly pored over art and images of humans.

Friedrich was silently grateful that he met Alraune and Grendel first. Rubicant and Arachne would have been too much for him to bear.

Friedrich returned to reading again once he cleared his mind of the thoughts of what it would be like to meet those horrible things in person.

The log described the despair Dr. Kaufmann

fell into when he saw how all of his creations ended in failure. He slowly began to suffer from illness brought on by the depression, which, when the two joined forces to oppose him, made it nearly impossible for the doctor to return to his laboratory to continue his research. "Perhaps," he wrote on February 15th, 1934, "mankind really is not meant to know the secret of life. Perhaps this illness, this overwhelming sorrow of mine, is God's punishment for my insolence. I reached greedily for the power that God held firmly in His grasp, and all I have to show for my attempts are my own dying body and a castle roamed by my repeated failures.

"February 19th, 1934 – Maybe I have not fallen as far out of God's favor as I had originally thought. Yesterday, Caliban brought in the body of a young girl, likely no older than eighteen or nineteen. Her arms and legs were mutilated beyond repair, but the most important fact was that it seemed her torso and head were completely intact. For a brief moment I was reminded of the experiments of the fictional Victor von Frankenstein, and I was inspired to make one last attempt at creating life. Maybe mankind was not meant to create life in ways God did not intend, but there is still the possibility that we can return life to that which it was taken from.

"In a few hours, I was able to construct artificial arms and legs for her and replace her damaged limbs. I knew that electricity would help to revive her, but I assumed that she would need a constant stream of it rather than just one jolt. Therefore, I designed coils that would use the energy of her body's electricity coupled with the initial charge to constantly re-energize themselves and thereby provide a constantly circulating voltage. Four of these were implanted in her back so as to have direct access to her heart.

"The revival process was immediately successful. The girl came to life and had stable vital signs a minute after the powerful electrocution was applied to the coils on her back. However, immediately later, issues with her mental condition were already apparent.

"She has no memory of her previous life, and she speaks German as a foreigner who understands perfectly, yet has very little skill in speaking the language. It is as if she has retained the basic idea of being human, but the finer points have been lost. Further, she insists upon calling me 'Father' and has shown no concept of indirect terms such as 'I', 'you', or 'she' when she speaks. Instead, she refers to everyone by name, and when referring to herself, she says nothing.

"One thing of note is that she seems to retain knowledge immediately. She only needs to see an action carried out once before she has instantly memorized it, and I suspect that her memory is similarly enhanced.

"Despite this, when I look into her eyes, I see nothing. They look like the eyes of a dead person, devoid of that faint spark of life and without any thought behind them. I wonder if she has no soul, and all things considered, that could be quite likely. The soul would have left the body when the girl died, and it would not have returned upon her resurrection.

148

"The first thing I am reminded of when I think of this is the story of *Alraune*: the soulless girl birthed by a prostitute impregnated by the sperm of a hanged criminal. I wonder if this soulless girl will follow in the footsteps of that Alraune. I wonder if she will grow to have a concept of what love is, or if she will develop emotions at all. I begin to wonder if what I have done was right.

"I will name this girl Alraune. Perhaps she will do as her namesake did and turn on me once she realizes her origins. For now, she is completely obedient to me, as all of my creations seem to be, and she appears to have the intelligence I was hoping my other creations would possess. She may not be something made purely by my hands, but at least she is a success in some regards."

More sketches and diagrams lay under the writing, but Friedrich did not pause to look at them. He turned the pages to find the next entry as he thought of the girl whose origins he now knew. He remembered how she smiled, how she cared enough to bring him in from the cold and bandage his wounds, how she said that she was happy that he would be staying.

Thoughts ran through his mind; he wondered if she had killed Kaufmann, as the doctor predicted, or if her sadness was merely the sadness of a daughter who had lost her father and had almost no one left in the world. He wondered if she really did lack a soul, or if she did feel love. If she loved *him*.

Far too many moments later, he found the next entry, dated much later.

"March 23rd, 1934 – I am certain now that I will

149

leave this world soon. I lie here on my deathbed, and though Alraune has faithfully taken care of me in my time of weakness, I know that it is all for nothing. The illness that fell upon me after Arachne's creation has taken its toll on me. Even the success of Alraune's revival could not turn that back.

"As I lie here, I have all the time in the world to think back on what I have done. I recall the other scientists I associated with shunning me and mocking my ideas, calling them the ravings of a madman and utter heresy. I was told that the concept of artificial life was one fit only for fairy tales. Well, I certainly have proven them wrong in regards to how they thought it impossible to create a being, but it seems that a human is still beyond our capabilities.

"Even as I write this, however, I remember what I have seen of Alraune's interactions with my other creations, and of Alraune herself. This girl without a soul has proven to be the key to understanding the others.

"Their obsessions have lessened in magnitude, since she arrived. Grendel is now more docile. Caliban has stopped collecting the bodies of humans. Rubicant no longer stands beside the gramophone for all hours of the day listening to singing. Arachne at last spends time away from paintings and photographs of humans.

"Perhaps, all this time, I have been wrong about them. Maybe they are more thoughtful than I at first perceived. All this time, it should have been so obvious. It is as if they realize that they should be human, but they know that they aren't and express their desire for that goal in many different ways.

"Grendel expresses its desire with wrath and hatred toward those who have what it wishes it could possess. Caliban and Arachne surround themselves with the forms they wish they had. Rubicant soothes itself with human voices in a similar manner.

"Amid all of this, Alraune's arrival has shown them what they are. They see her half-human, half-mechanical form and come to peace with themselves. They see that, no matter how misshapen or inhuman their own forms are, their minds are thoughtful, rational: *human*. They are already, inwardly, what they have aspired to be.

"Alraune has shown this to me as well. I now realize that they were not failures. At last, I see that I was successful, and that knowledge sweeps over me and brings me the contentment I have been searching for."

The last few lines were stained and splotched from drops of liquid that fell upon the page. Friedrich guessed that the doctor must have wept as he wrote his last words.

"Poor Alraune. Poor, sweet Alraune. I am so sorry that I ever thought that you would turn evil. I am sorry to leave you now, in this horrible place, when you deserve to have a second chance to live among humanity. Yet, I know that you can never leave this castle, for your own safety. I know that you would be viewed as a monster, a hellish creature that should not exist in this world. Your purity, your innocence would be taken from you, as you would be opened up to the horrors of the world. I know that this is for your best in the end, and yet I am filled with regret that it has to be so.

"Perhaps I am writing so much in the hopes that you will return before I finish, and I can say these last words to you myself, but you have not returned, and I feel myself slowly slipping away. It becomes harder to write, and I know that this is the last chance I will have to say this.

"I am grateful to have had you in my life, Alraune. You have been the reason I can be content with my life's work, now that I am at the end of it. You, soulless or not, have been perhaps the most loving person I have ever known. I hope that one day soon, someone will come to you. I hope that you will not be alone for long. I can only hope that you will not hate me for creating you or leaving you.

"If anyone finds this log, and if Alraune is still alive, please, I beg you, take care of her. Bring her happiness. Give her the soul that she needs."

***

For a long time, Friedrich sat on the couch with the closed book in his hands. He stared into the fireplace as he thought over what he had just read. Visions of his life in the Kriegsmarine and of Alraune passed through his mind. The last words of Klemens von Kaufmann played through his head over and over again.

Finally, he set the book aside on the table in front of him and stood up. He moved to the door, down the dark hallway, around to a broad ballroom lined with towering windows that showed the blizzard still raging outside. In the middle of the room sat Alraune, surrounded by Grendel, Caliban, Rubicant, and Arachne. The girl looked up when Friedrich stopped in the doorway, staring at him with those dull eyes.

The soldier walked quickly across the room, and without a word kneeled and took Alraune in his arms. He moved a hand through her long, black hair, gently stroking the flowing locks.

Alraune sat there silently for a moment, confused and surprised by the sudden occurrence. Then, finally, she raised her arms and laid them over Friedrich's back in a light embrace. They sat there silently for a while, and the other creatures stepped back as if to give them room.

"...is Friedrich going to leave," she asked eventually in her quiet voice.

"No, Alraune," Friedrich replied in a tone that was soft and reassuring. "I'm not going to leave. I'm never going to leave. I would rather spend the rest of my life here than go back to what I had before."

There was a brief pause. Alraune smiled. She closed her eyes as tears formed and slowly crawled down her face.

"...Alraune is glad."

The End

Joseph Michael studies Computer Science and Literature at Rice University and took time from his

153

novel about a Biblical Apocalypse to consider the interlocking mechanisms of love.

Karen Duvall's fluid urban fantasy asks how the fables and folktales of our childhood translate into our new millennial world of technology and rage. You will never look into old mirrors in quite the same way again. . .

Through the Looking Glass
by Karen Duvall

"So tell us, Alice, how long have you been able to do this?" Jeff Lockhart, host of the talk show named after him, leans forward in his chair. He perches both elbows on his knees and steeples his fingers.

I want to roll my eyes, but instead I widen them so that I won't appear rude. I get asked this question all the time. You'd think people could remember my answer by now. "I've been reading mirrors my entire life."

Lockhart's handsome forehead wrinkles with concern. "Twenty eight years is a long time. It must have been difficult for you as a child."

"Not really." I lean back in the studio's comfy armchair and cross my skinny ankles. I shrug and say, "While other kids were watching Sesame Street on TV, I got to watch real life play out on a sheet of glass. That beats the Muppets any day."

A muffled chuckle ripples through the studio audience.

Lockhart flashes me an insincere smile. He's trying to unsettle me, to dig a little drama from the depths of my stoic soul, but that will never happen.

I've been in the spotlight too many times to let personal questions get to me. I read mirrors. So what? It's as normal to me as reading the morning paper.

"Do you hear voices coming from the mirror as well?"

I shake my head. "Jeff, you need to understand the mirror is no more than a visual recording device. It captures images beneath its surface. A mirror can't hear, it can only see."

He glances at the audience and nods, rubbing his chin as if I've just revealed the knowledge of a sage. I'm only telling him like it is. There's no wisdom in that, just the truth.

"If you can't hear what the reflections are saying, how do you know what's going on?" he asks.

I smile. "I read lips."

He bobs his head. "Is that how you've been helping the police solve murder cases?"

"Sometimes." I've been helping the cops a lot lately, not so much because more murders are happening in rooms with mirrors, but because news of my accuracy rate is getting around. I'm a witness to these crimes, pure and simple, despite the fact that what I witness happened in the past. "If the people reflected have their backs to me, I can't see their mouths move. Mirror reading isn't a perfect science."

"Can you give us some examples of cases you've helped solve?" Lockhart asks.

I shake my head. "Sorry, no can do. Confidentiality and all that."

"I see." He winks at me, then waves at someone off stage. A guy wearing a blue ball cap emblazoned with the station's logo comes onto the set pushing something tall and covered by a white sheet.

"So," Lockhart says, drawing out the word longer than necessary. "I have another idea." He stands and approaches the draped object on wheels. "I'm sure you can guess what's under this sheet."

Duh. "A mirror?"

"Right you are. It's been sitting in the waiting room all day. We know what happened in that room, and now we want you to tell us."

I'm starting to feel like a trained monkey. I've never been asked to demo in public before. "From when?"

He scowls, looking confused. "Does it matter?"

I give him a lopsided grin. "Of course it matters. That mirror holds every image that's passed through its surface since the day it was made."

He appears to think long and hard how to answer, and I suspect this mirror might have seen more than it was supposed to. That's the thing about mirrors. They see everything and always tell the truth. I trust them a hell of a lot more than I trust people.

"Let's say beginning at nine a.m."

I jerk a nod. "Will do." I motion for him to roll the mirror closer. "I'll need to touch it in order to read it."

Lockhart unveils the mirror with a flourish, as

if revealing a priceless piece of art. The bright studio lights refract into long prisms of glittering color that make my eyes water.

The show's host takes a step closer to me and leans in to whisper, "Are you all right?"

I close my eyes and nod. "I'm fine. I just need to get acclimated."

Blinking back the stinging tears, I stare through the light to the surface underneath. Images flash across the mirror in a staccato rush. It's a lot like watching a flipbook, each picture jerking into place one after the other until it becomes a fluid flow of motion.

I reach out and lay both hands flat against the mirror. The images freeze in place and the surface softens to a viscous soup of melted glass. I can pass my hand right through it if I want, but I don't have the guts to try. I know what lies on the other side because I put him there. I sense him waiting for me. A queasy feeling in the pit of my stomach warns me to keep my distance.

I concentrate on the time I want the images to start replaying. My thoughts pierce the glass to clutch at the minutes spinning inside until I find the right one. Nine o'clock a.m. Curious about what Lockhart may be hiding, I turn it back a few more hours.

Well, well, well. There appears to be some extra-curricular activities going on in the waiting room before business hours. What I see disturbs me because it touches a frayed nerve that never healed. I let the rest of the day fast-forward, as events that follow are simple ones and easy to remember.

My hands drop from the mirror and I rest back against the thick cushions on the chair.

"Finished already?" Lockhart asks, eyebrows raised. "That was fast."

I press the heels of my hands to my eyes and will the pounding in my head to stop. It always hurts after a reading. "I fast-forwarded."

Laughter bubbles up from the audience and Lockhart chuckles, too. "Like a DVD player?"

"Pretty much." I squeeze my eyes shut, then flash them open a couple times to clear my vision. The real world looks fuzzy for a second or two before returning to normal.

Lockhart reclaims his seat and crosses his legs. He crosses his arms as well. I'm fairly sure he doesn't believe I can do what I claim.

"Are you composed enough to tell us what you saw?"

"Of course."

He offers a meaningful look to the sea of eager faces. "Before the show, while Alice was in a soundproof room offstage, our studio audience reviewed clips of what went on in the waiting room today. Our viewers at home are watching them now."

"Ah," I say for lack of a better response. "How nice for them."

"You're not worried?"

"Should I be?"

He shrugs. "If you're outed as a fraud, that could compromise your good standing with the police."

The hairs on the back of my neck prickle, but I

159

refuse to rise to Lockhart's drama bait. I smile sweetly and say, "Are you ready to hear what I saw?"

"By all means."

I clear my throat. "First, that same man who wheeled in the mirror brought in a box of donuts and set it on the coffee table. He took three for himself and poured a cup of coffee from a carafe on the counter."

The audience rumbles with appreciative murmurs and Lockhart says, "Very impressive. Anything else?"

"Oh, yes." I tilt a glass of water to my lips for a sip before relaying the other banal activities the mirror witnessed: A baby having its diaper changed, a couple arguing over what movie to watch for date-night, and a dog lifting its leg on the couch where I'm sure hundreds of studio guests would soon sit now that the upholstery cleaners have come to clean up the mess.

I grin at the applause and nod my thanks, then glance at my watch to see how much longer I'll have to endure this torture. Only minutes remain, which is long enough to deliver my finale.

"Jeff, I thought you were married," I tell the smiling host. I hate cheaters. I know better than anyone how cheaters should be punished. I give the mirror an anxious glance before returning my attention to Lockhart.

"That's right. I've been married quite happily for the past ten years."

I frown. "Isn't your wife blond?"

His smile wavers. "Yes, she is."

160

"Then who was that dark-haired woman you were—"

"And that's all the time we have today," he says in a rush as he turns to face the camera, his ruddy complexion a few shades ruddier. "Thank you, Alice Timpkin, for sharing your extraordinary talents with us today."

"Thank you for having me," I say brightly.

The red light on the camera blinks off and Lockhart swings around to face me. His lips draw in a tight line before he says, "How dare you try to discredit me like that, not to mention possibly ruining my marriage."

"I don't think you need any help there," I tell him. "The ruining the marriage part. As for discrediting you, that's just the kind of drama you like on your show, right?"

"Get the hell off my set." He stands and marches off the stage.

"Touchy, touchy," I mumble under my breath, and go in search of my driver. It's late and my head feels ready to explode. I need to get back to my hotel room for a hot soak in the tub, a couple of Ibuprofens, and a tall glass of wine. Heaven.

"Have you seen my driver?" I ask the studio's security guard when I see him by the back door. "I've looked everywhere and can't find him."

"No, ma'am," the guard says.

I shoulder open the door to peer out into the alley behind the studio, where Bruce parked the town car. It's still there and he's in it. "Never mind," I say over my shoulder. "I found him."

I specifically asked Bruce to wait for me inside

because I don't like walking alone in the dark. It's like the inner depths of a mirror where not even I can see. I swallow deeply and straighten my spine. A fifty-yard walk by myself won't kill me.

"Bruce!" I yell as I stomp toward the driver's side window. A hot breeze tumbles a cluster of newspapers in front of me and one wraps itself around my legs. I peel it off and kick it away. "What the hell are you doing out here?" I peer inside and see what he's doing. Sleeping. I bang on the glass. "Damn it, Bruce! The least you can do is unlock the god damn door."

A strong pair of hands grabs me from behind, and before I can scream, my mouth is covered by a cloth that stinks of sweet antiseptic. Last thing I remember is someone's hot breath on the back of my neck before I black out.

***

I come to inside a dark room that smells of old sweat and mildew. Definitely not my hotel. My headache is even worse now; the after-effects of whatever was on that cloth makes my temples throb. The summer night intensifies without conditioned air or a cracked window and I struggle to breathe what little oxygen I can find. It doesn't help that I'm scared to death.

I blink in the dark and feel the presence of someone with me. His, or her, footsteps approach from behind and when I try to twist around to see who it is, I discover I'm tied to a chair. The pearls of my spine dig into the wood when I squirm to try getting free.

"Welcome to wonderland, Alice," says a man's voice.

My tongue loosens when I realize I'm not gagged. "Help!" I scream as loud as I can. "Somebody! Help me!"

The man chuckles. "Don't waste your breath. This is an abandoned building miles outside of town. No one will hear you."

"What do you want?" I ask.

"Guess."

"You didn't have to kidnap me to get me to read a mirror. All you have to do is ask."

"True." He walks around the chair to stand in front of me.

I look up into a face hidden in shadow. As long as I can't see him there's a reasonable chance he'll let me go. I cling to that.

"But I don't want to waste my money paying for your services," he adds. "I'd rather steal them like I steal everything else."

A thief. Okay, I can deal with that. A thief and a kidnapper. As long as he isn't a murderer, I feel relatively safe. "I just finished a reading that turned my brain to mush. I can't do another one so soon."

"Oh, yes you can. And you will." His voice drops an octave when he says, "Or I'll kill you."

Air vanishes from my lungs as panic sets in. "I... I can't..."

A splash of something wet hits me in the face and I gasp.

"Better?" the man asks.

Surprise has chased the panic away. Water

runs down my forehead and into my eyes, but because my hands are tied I can't wipe it away. I shake my head like a dog shakes water from its fur. "Bastard."

"So I've been told." He paces slowly in front of me. "Here's the deal. I want you to read a mirror and tell me who you see."

"Who am I looking for?"

"My wife is the star of this little drama," he tells me, his steps slow and confident. "The other person in it is her leading man."

"You?"

"No."

His wife is obviously cheating on him and he expects me to tell him who it is. "Just one man?"

He stops, turning to face me, and the faint moonlight shining through the window behind him accents his silhouette. I cringe, thinking for sure he's about to hit me, but he playfully rubs the top of my head instead. "Aren't you the bright one." He resumes his pacing. "If there's more than one, describe them all."

"Why can't you just ask your wife?"

This time he smacks me in the back of the head. "Because it's none of your business," he says calmly. "Just do as you're told and I'll let you live."

I don't really believe him, but my obedience will improve my chance of survival. Maybe I can appeal to his soft side, if he has one. I doubt it, but there's no harm in trying. "Someone cheated on me once," I tell him and the frayed nerve Lockhart had touched begins to burn.

164

"Yeah?" My kidnapper crosses his arms and stands with his legs slightly apart. "What did you do about it?"

I shrug. "Made sure he couldn't do it again."

He pauses. "How?"

"I got him out of my life."

"That easy, huh?"

It wasn't easy at all, but I refuse to share the intimate details of my love life with this loser. Harry and I were two lovesick teenagers, or rather I was the lovesick one. I thought he was, too, until I saw him making out with Lucy Maloney in the backseat of his car. His rearview mirror showed me the entire story and you know what? It's amazing how much bigger a rearview mirror is than it looks. A whole person can fit through one of those things. Harry's sudden disappearance remains one of my hometown's greatest mysteries.

All I want now is for my kidnapper to know I can relate to what he's gone through. "Why not leave your wife?"

"I loved her, that's why not."

Loved. Past tense. She must have left him and I can't blame her. This guy has enough charm to cover the head of a pin.

"Enough chitchat." He grabs an object leaning against the wall, lifts it with a grunt, and sets it down in front of me. I'm not surprised to see that it's a mirror. He uses a chair to prop it up. "This was in our bedroom."

A chill quivers down my spine. That means I'll see this man in the images reflected there. It also means he has no intention of letting me go.

I pull against the rope that ties me down. "You have to free my hands."

"I don't *have* to do anything."

"You do if you want your fucking reading."

He sighs and I hear a click as he flicks open a pocketknife. My heart thrums so hard against my ribs I think surely he must hear it. He holds the knife up to my face, then swings it down to slice through the rope binding my hands.

"Now do your thing." He pulls back his sleeve to glance down at the glowing face of his watch.

I stare into the mirror's shimmering surface and feel it draw me in. It never fails to share its deepest secrets with me, and it always keeps mine. A mirror is a loyal friend I can depend on to always tell the truth. People, on the other hand, can rarely be trusted.

"Tell me everything you see," he says.

I don't know this man, but I already hate him. I hate how he smells, the way he talks, his disrespect, and most of all I hate his bravado. He has an ego big enough to fill an ocean.

My legs and waist still tied to the chair, I lean forward to lay both hands flat against the mirror. Nerves make my entire body shake, which causes the glass to rattle against the cracked tile floor. The refracted light burns my eyes like it always does, only this time the tears blurring my vision are caused by fear and rage.

He doesn't tell me how far to go back in time, and I don't ask. I'll give him as little information as I can get away with. It may be my only bargaining chip.

166

One man shows up repeatedly and I know exactly who he must be. I swallow and my throat nearly closes from being so dry. My voice sounds hoarse when I say, "I see a tall man with dark hair, a mustache and a goatee. He's thirty-something, works out, dresses well." He is also quite handsome, but since I know this is my kidnapper, I won't give him the satisfaction of saying it aloud. I just wonder why he isn't showing me his face. What difference would it make now?

"Handsome bugger, yes?" the man says, a smile in his voice.

"Your wife is lovely." That's the truth. She's brunette and fair-skinned with a model's body. I've seen her before. In fact, she made an appearance in the mirror I read a few hours earlier. This is the woman Jeff Lockhart locked lips with in the studio waiting room.

I watch as her relaxed demeanor abruptly changes whenever her husband is around. Her movements become almost robotic and every action is tentative, her behavior apologetic, and it becomes obvious she fears her husband, who I now know is named Jack. The name that forms on his lips when addressing her is Amy.

"Jack and Amy," I say, unsure how he'll react and not really caring at this point. I struggle to keep my panic in check.

"Bingo," is all he says. "What about the other guy?"

No other man appears in the mirror. Only Jack.

"Stop stalling. Just tell me what he looks like."

"How can I be sure you'll let me go if I tell

you?" I ask as I continue forwarding through the images. I'm looking for Lockhart, but he apparently never made it to Amy's bedroom.

"You have my word," Jack says.

His *word* is as good as spit.

The couple inside the mirror is arguing now. Jack's fury makes the veins in his neck pop out as he yells at Amy, then grabs her by the shoulders and shakes her until her head snaps back. He throws her on the bed and punches her in the face. I jump.

Jack stiffens beside me. "You see him. What does he look like? Tell me or I swear—"

"You and your wife argued," I say. I refuse to mention Lockhart. I may not like the talk show host, but I won't be party to whatever Jack is planning for his wife's lover. "You accused her of cheating and she denied it."

"The lying bitch." I watch him from the corner of my eye as he ignites a match to light the cigarette in his mouth. That brief flash is enough to show me his face and confirm he's indeed the same man from the mirror, but with one added feature. Four deep scratches mar one side of his perfect face and the wound is fresh.

"She fought back." I'm so caught up in what I see that I barely notice Jack's towering presence above me. I can feel the heat of his body now. "I know what you did," I tell him, watching his enormous hands wrap around his wife's throat and squeeze. She thrashes on the bed, kicks him between the legs, and that makes him even angrier. Her body goes still and he steps back, his hand cupping one side of his face.

"She deserved what she got," he says, his voice close to a growl. "She made a mockery of our marriage."

I tread dangerous waters as I ask, "What makes you think she was seeing another man?"

Through clenched teeth he tells me, "Because I could smell him on her." He inhales deeply as if to clear the offensive odor from his nostrils. "Amy was a producer for that show you were just on. It was me who convinced her to get you on as a guest."

Shit. He had this all planned out from the start. "You want to see him? The man your wife had an affair with?"

Jack bends low to get in my face, making sure I can see him now. The scratches are dangerously close to his left eye that's swollen and scabbed in one corner. "Impossible. You told the media no one can see inside the mirror but you."

"I only said that to protect my reputation. Let me show you how it works." I jerk my head at the mirror. "Just place your hands next to mine and push against the glass."

He gets down on his knees so that the top of the mirror is level with his head. "You sure about this?"

"If it doesn't work, what do you have to lose?"

I hold my breath while the glass beneath my fingers ripples like a pebble disturbs its liquid surface.

He holds his hands out in front of him. "Like this?"

"That's right," I say. "The second you touch

the glass, you'll see what I see."

His palms barely touch the mirror. "I don't see anything."

"Push harder," I tell him.

He leans forward and vanishes through the glass.

"Putz." Though still tied to the chair, I manage to lean over enough to lift the back legs up off the floor. I toddle and turn, searching the room for anything Jack left behind. I hope to find a cell phone and also his pocketknife so I can cut away these ropes. Balancing my weight so I won't tip over, I take one shuffling step forward, then another.

I haven't traveled more than a few inches when I feel fingers clutch around my ankle. I glance down at the male hand sticking out of the mirror. What the hell? It yanks me toward the glass. I try leaning the other way, but it's too late. I fall onto the mirror.

I think it's going to swallow me whole, but instead it breaks when I land. I lie on the floor in the dark, pieces of shattered glass all around me. Relief covers me like a blanket until I see the hand reach for me again. I squint to get a better look and notice the ring I haven't seen in over ten years. It's Harry's high school class ring.

I smile at the irony. Eyes filled with tears of regret, I grab onto Harry's hand and pull.

The End

Karen Duvall is a native Californian who grew

170

up in Hawaii, lived in Colorado most of her adult life, and now lives in Bend, Oregon with her husband and four incredibly spoiled pets. She has three grown children and five grandchildren. Her new urban fantasy series is published by Harlequin Luna with the first book, KNIGHT'S CURSE, a Publisher's Weekly TOP 10 ROMANCE PICK for Fall 2011, available in September 2011 at all major bookstores. The second book, DARKEST KNIGHT, releases in early spring 2012. Visit Karen's website at http://www.wix.com/jkduvall/knights-curse and stop by her blog at http://www.karenduvall.blogspot.com

What if the old witch-hunting tales were all true? And what if there was more to them than even the old witch-hunters suspected? Then we would have on our hands such a wild yarn as A. J. Walker's mesmerizing tale. Enjoy!

The Witch Bottle
by A.J. Walker

"You must piss in it, sir," Malcolm said as he handed the bottle to his master.

Henry Raban, Esquire, took a final puff of Virginia tobacco and set his clay pipe on the mantelpiece. He gave his servant a doubtful look as he took the bottle offered him.

It was half again the length of his hand and made of heavy crockery. The neck had the design of a face stamped into the clay—a bearded man with crazed hair sticking out in all directions as if he had been riding his horse at a fast gait all day. The eyes wide and staring. Henry suppressed a shudder as he turned to Malcolm.

"Is this absolutely necessary?" he asked.

Malcolm nodded, "It is, sir, if you want to trap the filthy witch who torments you. Such evil women are—"

"I'll remind you that you are speaking of my wife!" Henry snapped.

Malcolm bowed and mumbled an apology. Henry grunted and looked back at the bottle in his hand.

"But witch she is, and torment me she does.

172

And if you say that pissing in this thing will trap her, then I must make haste to the privy. That ale you served with the venison has worked its way through me."

When Henry returned to his sitting room, careful not to spill the sloshing contents of the bottle, he found Malcolm busy at his desk—Henry's desk. The gentleman resisted the urge to upbraid his servant.

That man thinks himself above his station, Henry mused, *but he is essential to me. I only wish he weren't so cognizant of the fact.*

"What are you doing now?" Henry asked.

"Other items to trap the witch," Malcolm said, indicating the pile of odds and ends littering the desk. "Twelve iron nails, eight brass pins, and a twist to the heart."

Malcolm held up a small patch of leather cut in the shape of a heart. A bent iron nail was stuck through the middle.

"Ah, that should catch her!" Henry said. "She loves me still, I'll wager ten guineas."

"Most assuredly. We need some more items, sir. Kindly give me the bottle. My, I fear I did indeed serve you too much ale for supper."

Malcolm turned to the window and poured out some of the yellow fluid onto the rose bushes. He then dropped the nails, pins, and leather heart into the bottle.

"Now kindly sit down, sir, and I will cut your fingernails."

Henry shook his head and sat down. Although Malcolm had explained the process after the curse had started, Henry still didn't like the idea. His wife's witchery was all too real, but surely participating in such a thing as the creation of a witch bottle would be considered almost as ungodly. He had his reputation to think of.

Malcolm set to work trimming Henry's nails with a tiny pair of shears, dropping each cutting one by one into the bottle. After that he unbuttoned Henry's shirt without so much as a by-your-leave and plucked the fluff from his navel. This went into the bottle too. Malcolm looked inside, gave a satisfied nod, and stoppered the bottle, sealing it with wax from a dripping candle that sat lit on the desk despite the warm spring sunshine pouring in from the open window.

***

Catherine Raban stood at the window of the little cottage that was once again her home. She looked east, looking toward her husband and the fine twelve-room estate that had once been hers, now out of sight over a stream and past two villages.

But magic flies faster than the swiftest steed.

"It is still mine," she said to the empty room.

She had been the belle of the village since she was thirteen. All the young swains wanted her, all the wealthy old men vied to have her as their house maid. But her mother had been wise. Oh, her mother! She had learned so much from her—the Craft, the secrets of plants and stars, and the subtler craft that all women have, not only those who have

174

inherited the Gift. Yes, her mother had kept her close, refusing munificent offers for her employ, chasing off the young bucks and laying a curse on those who proved too insistent. Mother and daughter knew Henry Raban's first wife hadn't long to live and that he looked at Catherine with eyes as covetous as any man's.

Shortly after Catherine turned sixteen, Henry Raban's wife died. No Craft had been required. Mother had insisted on that. God ~~had~~ called the woman, and no wagging tongue could say they had ~~had~~ a hand in it.

After an unsuitably short period of mourning, Henry had come to Catherine's mother asking for the girl's hand in marriage. From this one-room cottage, Catherine ~~had~~ moved to a brick house with a maid, a cook, and a manservant. A fine coach took her on rides around Henry's ample lands. *Her* lands.

Now all that was gone, and her mother gone too, poor woman, taken by God or the Devil or neither, as some in the coven whispered. The most blasphemous truth the Craft could utter—that there was no Heaven or Hell, only the laws of nature, action and reaction, sympathy and antipathy. All in one, each thing isolated, each thing temporary, All endures.

She had not sat out the blush of her youth, had not resisted the charms of the young men who came calling, had not given her maidenhead to a portly, balding oaf only to lose the wealth her mother never had.

She picked up the doll, dressed in a coat woven from her husband's own hair meticulously collected from his comb over the course of three long years. Her finger rested on the end of a pin stuck in the doll's stomach. She grasped it. She twisted.

***

"My God, oh but it hurts!" Henry shouted, clutching his ample belly.

"She's using her witchery again," Malcolm said, leaping up and grabbing some coal from the scuttle next to the hearth. "Now is the time to act."

"Make haste! It feels as if a rapier is skewering my insides."

Malcolm stoked the fire as Henry moaned in his easy chair. Once the flames burned high and bright, Malcolm grabbed the witch bottle. Henry looked hopefully at his servant as Malcolm brandished the bottle over the fire, then started passing it through the flames.

"Now your little witch will feel the fire as if it were scorching her own flesh."

"The pain is easing," Henry said.

"Her hold on you is loosening."

***

In the cottage two villages over and across a stream Catherine wailed as she gripped the windowsill, knuckles white. Sweat slicked her body as her face grew as red as sunset. She gritted her teeth, knotted her brow, and straightened her spine.

***

176

The witch bottle shattered. Fragments of crockery clattered against the slate of the hearth as Henry's piss splashed onto Malcolm's trousers.

"Blast!" the servant cried.

"Is she beaten?" Henry asked hopefully.

"No," Malcolm grumbled.

"But I feel no pain."

"She is hurt. That is why she is not tormenting you. But make no mistake; she will recover her powers and return."

Malcolm stalked toward the door.

"Don't leave me!" Henry wailed.

"I'm merely changing my trousers, you booby," the servant called back over his shoulder as he walked out.

Henry scowled at the door through which Malcolm had disappeared and then gave the shattered bottle in the hearth a terrified look.

***

Catherine lay in her bed, breathing deeply and trying not to remember the pain. *Malcolm. It had to have been him.* From the moment she'd set foot in Henry's home she'd been wary of the fellow. He had come from nobody-knew-where with references Henry never checked and Catherine never believed. He listened too carefully, stared too long, and knew too much to be a manservant. Even more suspicious, he proved immune to her charms. Not that she'd consent to tumble with a man now beneath her station, but at least he should melt at her smile like other men did.

Malcolm soon had her husband under his thumb. Her authority usurped in every room but the bedroom, the only room in her new house she hated, she watched with fury as Henry increased Malcolm's wages and bought him a new set of clothes and a pair of shoes with silver buckles.

Mother hadn't raised her to be the kind of woman to sit idly by. Soon Malcolm came down with the chills. Warts covered his face and from his nose ran green pus. But Malcolm was a wily one and looked under his straw tick to find the rancid piece of sheep's kidney wrapped in a frog's skin.

Malcolm denounced her to the magistrate. The constabulary searched her things and found more evidence of the Craft. To avoid a scandal, Henry had the whole thing hushed up. The magistrate and constables pocketed the money and insisted that Catherine leave the village. Henry bedded her one last time and sent her on her way.

***

"We have to go through this entire demeaning process again?" Henry demanded.

"Yes, sir," Malcolm said, now wearing his Sunday best as the maid sat with a washtub in the backyard scrubbing his work clothes. "As fortune would have it, I have another witch bottle same as the last. We must fill it again with pins, your water, your nails—"

"My fingernails are cut to the quick!"

"Your toenails, then. This time we'll catch her,

178

I promise you."

"She resisted the fire."

"She's a strong one, to be sure. We must be cleverer than she. There are other ways to catch a witch than fire."

"Such as?"

"You shall see, sir, you shall see."

***

Catherine sat at her mother's table, mixing herbs with a mortar and pestle. Every now and then she'd reach over and give the pin in her husband's effigy a twist.

"Let's see, rosebuds, lavender, and ginger should get him pining for me, orange flowers to remember to be loyal in marriage, and a dash of St. John's Wort will help with forgetfulness so he'll let this curse be bygones. In the meantime, though, the selfish poltroon needs a bit more of *this*."

With that she gave the pin another twist.

A knock at the door made her look up. She stuffed the effigy of her husband into the pocket of her smock and threw a cheesecloth over her preparations. Wiping her hands, she went to the door.

A boy she recognized from her husband's estate stood outside, holding a letter in his hand and looking nervous.

"Don't tremble so. I'll not hurt you," Catherine said as she took the note from his hand.

She opened it.

Dearest Catherine,

I cannot live another moment without you. I know you feel the same. All is forgiven. Let our love bloom again this spring after the winter of our discontent.

Love always, your husband and master,
Henry

Catherine gave a bitter laugh, tore up the letter and told the boy, who was obviously waiting for a reply while resisting the urge to run, "Tell that fool that if he wants me back he has to give me a security. In writing. I'll not be welcomed back only to be cast aside again."

The boy nodded and ran off.

***

"Oh, it's worse than ever before!" Henry wailed.

"We must bleed you, sir," Malcolm said.

"Bleed me?"

"To remove the foul humours her curse has put into your blood."

"I will send a boy to get the surgeon."

"No, sir! Think. He would be sure to see that you are under a curse. Think of the scandal!"

Henry clutched his belly again, face scrunched in pain.

"Oooooh, what do I care for scandal? This pain must stop."

"It will be only a prick of the finger, sir, no need for the surgeon."

"Very well, but make haste!"

Malcolm fetched a pin and a small glass vial.

180

He pricked Henry's finger, which elicited barely a jerk from the man since he was so overwhelmed with the pain in his stomach, and squeezed the tip of his finger so that several drops fell into the bottle. Malcolm then put a cork in the bottle and turned to walk away.

"What are you doing?" Henry asked.

"The most powerful ingredient in witches' curses is a man's blood, as surely you have heard it said. I must bury this blood so that Catherine does not find it and use it against you."

As Malcolm left the room, Henry bent over in pain.

"Malcolm! Malcolm!" he grunted through clenched teeth. "The foul humours have not left my body! It hurts as much as ever!"

Malcolm ignored his master's pleas and went to his own room. Once there he unstopped the bottle of blood and mixed it with a bottle of ink, one of several ink bottles with different labels hidden under his bed. He took the bottle of mixed blood and ink and strode back to Henry's drawing room.

He found his master sprawled across his easy chair in a cold sweat, holding a document.

"You were wise to write that up ahead of time in case of such an eventuality," Malcolm said. "Assigning your wife rights to half your estate, even in case of divorce, will surely get her back."

"It pains me to do this, but I must have her back. She loves me still. Oh, how my mistrust of her must have struck pain in her tender heart!"

Malcolm rolled his eyes and then looked nervously at his master. No, the fool hadn't seen.

He upbraided himself for his uncharacteristic slip of showing his true feelings, but how much whining could one man be expected to take?

***

Catherine sat knitting by the window. She hadn't twisted the pin for some time now, hoping her forbearance would make her husband more pliable.

Husband, Catherine snorted. *Husband only for money*. There were others far more deserving of her maidenhead and her hand in marriage. Like Jonathon, who at age twelve had bloodied the nose of a bully two years his elder and a handspan taller for saying that Catherine's mother rode a broomstick on full moons. Or Albert, ah sweet Albert! Her first kiss at thirteen and not a word her mother could say that would make her regret it. A handsome lad was he, now gone a sailor and no doubt making the lasses swoon in the West Indies. She'll never see those fine features again. If she had married him he would have never left for the sea. . .

A knock at the door brought her out of the past and into the present. She opened it to find the boy was back, with a new letter in his hand. As she took it, he ran off.

She opened it and read,

My darling, all is forgiven. Please come back to me. I know my mistrust has disappointed you, but it cannot have dampened the love you have always shown me.—Catherine laughed out loud—*Below is a legal document guaranteeing you to half my*

182

lands, monies, and property portable and immoveable. Plus I will dismiss Malcolm, who I know you have always disliked.—Catherine raised an eyebrow—*Anything to make you happy.*

Catherine continued reading and found that the document did, indeed, say all Henry claimed it said. It was signed with his own hand, with the cook, not Malcolm, as a witness.

Catherine clapped her hands with joy. She was reinstated to her rightful place, and that dastard Malcolm was out on his ear! She wondered about the judge and the constables and what they'd say if she reappeared at the estate. Henry must have bought them off. A pretty penny was gone from the family coffers, to be sure, but no matter. A bit of Craft would increase Henry's harvest as it had last year, and the expense would soon be recouped. She grabbed her shawl and bonnet and hurried out the door.

***

"She torments me no longer," Henry said as he watched Malcolm digging a hole in front of the threshold.

"Her heart has turned toward you, sir," Malcolm replied without looking up from his work.

"So is the witch bottle necessary?" Henry asked.

"Surely, sir. As I said, burying the bottle upside down and having her pass over it will tie her to you and this property forever. She will never leave you."

"Ah, but she loves me! There is no need for

183

enchantment."

Since his back was turned to Henry, Malcolm allowed himself the luxury of a mocking smile.

"Ah, but sir, women are a fickle lot, witches or otherwise. It's best to be sure."

"Yes, Malcolm, I suppose you're correct. You always know what's best."

Once the hole was deep enough, Malcolm placed the witch bottle in it upside down and covered it with dirt. He smoothed it over and replaced the gravel of the front walk. Standing back, he gave a satisfied nod. It looked as if it had never been disturbed.

"That is certainly good work," Henry said as he stepped out of door. Malcolm restrained him.

"Not yet, sir! The witch must be the first to pass over the bottle for the magic to take effect. That is why I gave the rest of the servants the afternoon off. Sit in the front room, visible through the window, while I secrete myself in the back. She will be here soon and you will have your heart's desire."

"That I will," Henry rubbed his hands with glee. "In fact it might be best if you stayed at the inn tonight. It will be a noisy time here and you shan't get any sleep. Here's a guinea for your trouble. By the time you return in the morning, there will be no more talk of your leaving. She will be well in hand."

Malcolm bowed and smiled.

"That she will, sir, that she will."

Henry sat as he had been told in the front room, visible from the distant road. He didn't have long to wait. Soon a familiar figure came strolling along the lane, a few stray blond tresses flowing out of her bonnet to catch the sunlight like gold. Henry leapt up out of his chair and almost forgot Malcolm's injunction to stay put. He controlled himself, waiting anxiously as Catherine turned off the lane and walked up the path to the house.

Henry stood there, trembling a little and biting his lower lip.

Ah, but she is a beauty! Henry thought. *Every man in the shire was green with envy when she married me. But why does she scowl so? Shouldn't she be happy? The poor girl is still cross with me. Who could blame her after the way I treated her? That will soon be smoothed over. With Malcolm's spell, and my own prowess in bed, she'll soon be as meek as a lamb.*

His heart grew light as Catherine approached and looked at him, a smile replacing her frown.

"My love," she said, extending her arms as she walked up to the door.

"Welcome home," Henry said and stepped across the threshold.

Arms wide to embrace each other, they came together over the spot where the witch bottle lay buried. And disappeared.

***

Malcolm smiled as he dug. Once he uncovered the bottle, he picked it up and found it warm to the touch.

"Having a hot time in there, are you?" he chuckled.

He walked back into the house and packed the witch bottle into a small crate padded with straw. He'd bury it in the woods come nightfall. Nobody would ever find it. After he had tucked the crate under his bed he reached into his coat and withdrew two documents. The first was the document he'd tricked Henry into signing. While Henry thought he was signing a legal document to give his wife half the estate, in fact he was signing a document giving Malcolm the entire estate, with generous remunerations to the other servants to keep them silent. The two documents had been written one over the other with two different types of ink—one that disappears immediately and then reappears over time, and the other that fades within a day and a night, never to be seen again.

The second document was the one that was now visible on the page. A third type of ink had been used to sign it, the ink tainted with Henry's own blood. To sign a document in blood made one a witch. And a witch could be captured in a witch bottle.

Malcolm tucked the documents back into his coat, feeling very pleased with himself. He put on his coat and prepared to take a stroll around the property. *His* property.

A series of high-pitched squeaks came from his side pocket as a blob of darkness poked out of it. It looked like a moving inkblot with arms and legs that scrabbled with tiny claws up the side of his coat.

"We've done well, my friend, we've done well," Malcolm said, tucking the thing back in his pocket.

The End

A. J. Walker is the author of the fantasy novel ROOTS RUN DEEP *(Double Dragon, 2010) and the mystery/thriller* MURDER AT McMURDO *(LL-Publications, 2010). An archaeologist and medievalist by trade, he has an enduring fascination with the folk magic of England. The witch bottle and its contents described in this story were discovered in England in 2008. A. J. talks about the discovery and witch bottles in general in a post on his blog:*

http://genreauthor.blogspot.com/2011/05/medieval-mondays-witch-bottles.html

What if a gay-basher should discover himself to be—suddenly, irrevocably—in the wrong? Natalie L. R. Baker drags a very unexpected hider out of this particular closet.

In the Closet
by Natalie L. R. Baker

Ed glowered at the place that resembled The Jigger, the local bar that he and his friends frequented. *Where am I?* he thought after he squeezed his eyelids into a blinking attempt at alleviating his grogginess.

It looked like The Jigger, but something was wrong. The juke box was missing, there wasn't any sawdust on the floor, and there were curtains…long, pink curtains. Ed glanced down at his stained plaid shirt. He moved his hand to reach for the frayed piece of fabric that was once a stitched-in shirt pocket but withdrew and redirected his attention to the metal pipe rolling off of the table.

The metallic sound that resonated from the pipe's landing recalled Ed's memory from the night before. He was gripping the pipe at the end of a series of pipes, yanking with all of his might before it finally broke off with shards of wood attached to it. He could see himself walking, broken pipe in hand, in the direction of Jase and Bobby Jr.'s voices. "Come on Ed! I hear these fairies like gettin' together and doin' all kindsa sick crap. He might get too excited with us holding him…"

Ed was jolted from his memory by a man

who'd picked up the pipe.

"Do you play?" The man asked, examining the metal.

"Uh...yeah," Ed lied.

He looked down at the man's pointed shoes. The light bounced off of the sides, but the top and edges of the shoes looked soft and velvety. Before Ed could wonder why the man's pants were so snug, he was forced to look up at the slender gentleman's face beneath his shiny blonde hair because he was nestling into the padded booth seat across from him.

Ed's eyes darted from the pipe gripped in the man's fist to the smirk under his searching eyes.

"What the hell is goin' on?" Ed scowled. He looked over at the bar where a tall woman with short hair was shaking a canister in front of a mirror with alcohol bottles stacked to the ceiling. "Where's Carl?"

"How retro that you know someone named Carl. I knew that you weren't from here, you just couldn't have been."

"Where is Carl?" he asked through clenched teeth. He was louder this time, and his jaw was square and tight.

"I'm sorry, but there is no one here by that name." The man rolled the pipe from one hand to the other on the table.

Ed was confused. "Why are there pink curtains on the walls? What's goin' on here?"

The man snickered at Ed's question and complementary countenance. "First off, those aren't 'pink.'" He made air quotations with his

189

fingers. "They're deep salmon with a light mauve finish on the roses. Secondly, they're more like drapes. At least, I would appreciate it if you would call them that, seeing as how the fabric costs more than what your entire outfit was ever worth, if it was ever worth anything. They were handmade of Chinese mulberry silk. They're absolutely stunning, don't you think? Justin wanted to go with a cheaper set – sateen. Can you believe it? Sateen! Ugh, I'm going to gag just thinking about it."

Without responding, Ed stared at the man with the same fiery look that he gave the bar. In addition to the man's lady-like drawl, Ed noticed his hair again. He thought it was in a very clean—too clean—manicured style that moved in a way that a man's hair shouldn't move. As he watched the pipe roll on the table between the man's hands, he noticed that his fingernails were shiny, like he had clear nail polish on them. His tie was a light purple color, and the kerchief on his jacket was shaped like a flower.

Suddenly, Ed's eyes tightened as he focused, paying more attention to the detail of the bar and all of the men who were there. There were plenty of men…men who didn't look like Ed. Ed clenched his jaw tighter, and he turned back to the gentleman sitting across from him.

"You some kinda faggot, ain't you? This a *gay* bar? So help me God…" Ed slammed his fist onto the table. That was when he realized that it wasn't sticky like he remembered it. When Carl did "clean" the tables, he did it with one old, saturated rag.

Ed's pound on the table took his mind back to the night before. He was now handing the pipe to Earl. "You like em' hard, don't ya, boy?" Earl said walking over to a naked, bruised young man sniveling on his knees. The boy couldn't have been very much older than Ed's nephew, Donnie, who'd just been accepted into the military.

Bodily liquids dripped from the boy's short chin that moved as he panted between sobs and pleas. Bobby Jr. was twisting one of the boy's arms behind him while Jase held onto the other and pounded his foot into the boy's back. No matter how loudly the boy screamed, Jase kept kicking his bare back as if he could run his foot all the way through the boy's exposed chest.

"I said, 'What can I get you?'"

Ed found himself staring at an annoyed Amy, the waitress from the *real* Jigger. His eyes widened at the probability of clarity, instead of the sight of Amy's smooth, freckled skin. Amy would be able to explain what was happening. She was always eager to see Ed, and he was always eager to watch her shake out her brownish-blonde hair and smile whenever he'd say "hey." Sometimes, when the bar wasn't full, she'd drop a coin into the juke box and bump it with her hip. She'd wink at him and sing along to "Somebody's Baby" while she'd keep her eyes on Ed.

"Well?" she said, looking Ed up and down.

"Amy?" Ed searched her eyes for some sort of recognition. "It's me. Ed." He tried to smile, but the look that Amy was trying to fight back was icy and fiery, all at the same time. He could feel his

191

smile disappear into his thickening confusion.

"Look. I don't know no 'Ed,' and I don't know you. Do you want something or not?" Her tiny fingers rested on her hip.

Realizing that everything seemed wrong, Ed yielded his idea of a reunion and understanding. "I'll just have some water," he said.

When he said "water," Ed's mind flashed back to him washing off the pipe. His hands shook as the blood cascaded down the metal and the water became more prominent.

Then he saw and heard the man's snapping fingers. "Hello? Earth to Ed?"

Ed focused on the man's fingers. He sneered and turned to face the man.

"If you're what I *think* you are," the man said, "then you'd better start talking, and quick. I might be able to help you."

"I don't talk to faggots. If I were you, I'd shut up right now…before I make you." Spit flew with the momentum of the words from Ed's mouth.

"Suit yourself. But I couldn't live with myself if I didn't let you in on something. This isn't a 'gay' bar. It's a bar." He held his hand out, palm up, and gestured for Ed to look around.

"And I'm not a 'faggot,' I'm a man. I don't know where you came from, but you are a very brazen heterdog…I guess that explains the clothes and the smell. Good luck getting out of here without getting killed," the man said as he released the pipe and prepared to leave the booth.

"Oh, and by the way, you better not look at Amy or any other woman the way you did a moment ago, unless you're ready to lose your life."

Ed inspected his surroundings again. He turned to his right and looked out of the window. Everything looked the same, yet so unfamiliar. The hedges still stood by the window, but there were flowers and other plants at the opposite end of the parking lot. *What's going on?* He thought. *And did he just say get out of here without getting killed?*

"Wait," Ed called after the man, who immediately stopped. "Why would anyone want to kill me?" he asked.

The man scooted back into the booth. "Really? You're serious?" He looked at Ed.

Ed stared at the man, just as dumbfounded.

"Because you're a heterosexual…aren't you? A *heterdog*?" He stared back at Ed with squinted eyes.

"Of course I'm straight. But why would somebody want to kill me for *that*? And what is a heterdog?"

The man sat back and watched Ed. "A heterdog is a heterosexual man. People will want to kill you because they don't think that it is right for a man to be with a woman. That's just not how the world works. We could never *be* with women. They don't understand what men need, just as we could never understand what they want. The Almighty made us homosexuals, but most people — pretty much all people — believe that The Almighty doesn't make heterosexuals."

The man picked up the pipe again. "When heterosexuals make the decision to become heterosexuals, their blood is believed to be cursed. Do you know what happens if men and women have sexual relations? Women can grow Mutts inside of their bodies. They're cursed with filth and crippling pain that lasts for three quarters of a year; some say it is The Almighty's way of punishing them." He began to toss the pipe up and catch it while concentrating on Ed.

"So what kind of organ do you play, Ed?"

Ed put his hands atop his head as he sank into his seat. Then he covered his face and began to talk. "What is happening?" he said into his hands.

He inhaled the powdery fragrance of the bar, and he blew it out as quickly as possible. He was just in here last night. It hadn't been twenty-four hours since he was in this exact booth, looking across to Bobby Jr. and Jase. They were waiting for Earl so they could ride over to the church together.

"We're not barbarians, Ed," the man said. "Maybe in other parts of the world, some eons ago, people were attracted to and slept with the opposite sex because they didn't know any better, but that sort of thing is not tolerated here. Do you know what Mutts are? Mutts are born in a filthy way to filthy women who do filthy things. Babies should be born in the Conceptual Conception clinics, Ed, the way The Almighty intended. There is no blood, no pain and babies are ready after three weeks. Look at me, Ed." The man leaned over the table. "You don't get the splendors of hair this bouncy and eyes this blue by being born from a woman's..." He shuddered and leaned back into his seat.

"I don't know how you've survived all this

194

time being a heterdog, but I can assure you that if anyone finds out, you won't be leaving here alive."

The man disregarded Ed's blank face that was now as colorless as was humanly possible. "Where do you work? Underground or something? Where are you from?"

Ed looked around again, but he really didn't know anymore. He looked down at the pipe on the table, and he tried to swallow before he spoke. "I'm from here. Backwash, Texas. But what do you mean that The Almighty made 'us' homosexuals? That doesn't make any sense. What kind of world is this?"

"Wow," the man said. "We've heard of hetero-acceptance, but I always thought that it was a myth. You're a real heterosexual, but you're not from *here*, are you?"

Ed put his hands on his head again. "Why would people want to kill me for bein' straight? That's how *my* Almighty wants us to be."

"*The* Almighty." The man stopped Ed, pointing the pipe at him.

"Well, that's the way it's supposed to be. And let's just say that I'm in some freaky homosexual universe. No one could just kill me. That's my business, ain't it? So what if I love women. Have you seen women? How can everybody be *gay*?"

"You seem to be more than lost, Ed. I don't know how things worked in your world, but, here, being heterosexual is against the law. *Everywhere*, it's punishable by death. And it's not just your business. What about the children who could be influenced by your heterosexuality? If little girls saw their mommies kissing men, then they would probably want to do it, too. And what about those same little girls? Most people think that men like you would run around and try to rape as many of them as you possibly could."

"I ain't no pervert!"

"You very well may not be, but we don't want you on the loose, threatening children with your tainted existence. No one wants a child to be confused about the way life is supposed to be. Bringing more Mutts into this world."

Ed sat back and uncomfortably settled into the booth. First, he looked down at himself, and then he looked around the room again. People were whispering to one another, but their gazes, smirks, and frowns screamed at Ed's intrusion and disrespect.

"Maybe you should hold my hand, Ed." As he made the suggestion, the man stretched his arm out and held his palm up.

Ed's mouth twisted into disgust. He wanted to pick up the pipe in front of the man and bash his head in. He hesitated and cursed himself for even considering it. *I ain't no faggot!* Ed screamed in his head, but he could feel the mood of the bar all around him. Everyone was talking. Most people were looking at him. His fingers twitched as he considered himself. He could meet the same fate as the young man that he, Jase, Bobby Jr., and Earl dealt with behind the church. He didn't want to die, especially for being what he knew God wanted him to be.

He'd attended church every Sunday, sometimes

dropping his last few dollars in the collection plate. He didn't run around on women like some men did; he'd been pining for Amy for a little more than a year. He read his bible— he read it every day. He even kept it in his truck. He went to work every day. He prayed. He was righteous. He wasn't a homosexual like the kid who'd hit on Earl the night before. And even though he knew that that boy was going straight to hell for wanting to lie with another man, he wasn't the one who helped him get there. Bobby Jr. and Jase held him, and Earl was the one to finish him off. All Ed did was break the pipe off of the organ inside the church and keep look-out.

Then he glanced at the pipe beside the man's outstretched arm. Reticently, Ed let his hand creep onto the table and into the hand of the man sitting across from him. The man's silky fingers closed around Ed's dirt-blotched hand. Ed gave a slight pull but remembered that he wanted to make it out of the bar alive. Apparently, this man knew how to make that happen.

But looking down at his hand resting in another man's hand, Ed's eyes glossed over. He pictured the kid again.

He could see the kid's hands, bloodied, bruised, and broken as he landed on the pavement after Jase rolled his limp and crippled body off of Earl's truck bed. The young man was barely breathing, and his face looked like a chewed steak that some dog refused to finish. The only thing that Ed could detect a movement from was the boy's fingers. There was a slight twitch to them, and all Ed could think about at that time was how bent the boy's wrist was when he offered to buy Earl a drink.

Ed looked down at his hand in the man's, and he snatched it away just as Amy placed a glass of water on the table.

Don't look at her, Ed. She's not your Amy, he repeated to himself.

He hid his eyes and said, "Thank you, ma'am," as he pictured the perfect shade of amber in her eyes. Although this Amy harbored some sort of unfounded hostility, he could remember the smile that followed his. The way she bumped the juke box and winked at him. He smiled to himself, and he glanced up to steal a glimpse of Amy walking away.

"HE'S A DIRTY HETERDOG!" a woman yelled from an adjacent table.

The outcry ignited the prudish rabble. Chairs scraped against the hardwood, frowns wrinkled into disgust, and glasses tinged; some broke. Suddenly, everyone was shouting words that Ed had never heard, but the tone, expressions, and animation of the crowd left him with a hopeless feeling that pounded in his chest.

Overwhelmed by the immediate storm that came of the bleak gloom since he woke in this booth, Ed didn't notice Amy charge back to his side. Before he could descry her hate-fueled agility, he found himself cleaning her saliva off of his face with the filthy front of his shirt.

"Don't you ever again in your life, you nasty mutt-making heterdog!" she said just before she rammed the backside of her hand across his face.

Ed scrambled as far as he could into the corner

198

of the booth. He was confused, ashamed, and afraid. He looked over to the calm man across from him, who shook his blonde hair away from his face to examine the pipe more closely. "You never answered my question, Ed. About the organ. I asked, 'What kind do you play?'"

Even more befuddled, Ed shook his head. "I...I...I don't know!"

Half a grin curled on the man's face. "A shame what being gay can mean for you. Isn't it, Ed?"

Ed's eyes darted from the man to the pipe to the mob.

"It won't be long now, Ed. Since no one here has actually attacked you yet," he turned and smiled to the audience of angry faces, "I'm assuming that the authorities have been notified. I'm really sorry, Ed, but they will come to kill you. Every day, at five-fifteen, outted heterdogs are bused to City Hall where they are lined up on the steps. One by one, they are publicly beaten with bibles and homemade crosses. Then they are set on fire to 'jumpstart their eternal damnation.'"

"But I didn't do anything!" Ed cried out. "God made me this way. This is what he wants." Ed's trembling hands reached out to grab the man's hand across from him. "You have to help me. Please!"

The man jerked his hand away and shoved it beneath the table. "I'll help you, but please don't do that," he said.

At that moment, sirens broke through the chattering. People began to clap and cheer. "They're coming," the man said.

"What do I do?" Ed frantically reached out to

him.

"You see that door back there?" He pointed to a white door at the back of the bar.

"Yeah."

"It is a closet. Take this." Beneath the table, Ed felt the pipe against his knee. "Go in there and wait. That's the only thing that you can do now. Run, Ed." He was so calm that Ed didn't want to listen to anything he said.

Scrambling out of the booth, Ed pushed past Amy and the rest of the mob. He ran for the closet, opened the unlocked door, and ducked into the temporary dark haven.

The moment the door shut behind him, peace blanketed the small cubical. The blackness somehow occluded all sound, as if nothing outside of it existed. Ed, panting with a dissipating fear, gripped the pipe and sank down to the floor, thankful for the space and safety.

The seconds seemed to run into minutes that Ed had lost track of. In the darkness, the anxiety and fear that had been controlling all of Ed's body released its hold on him so that he could finally relax. Sight wasn't a luxury in the obscurity of blackness, but Ed could feel that he had enough room to finally uncurl his knees. *I didn't even get his name*, he thought as he stretched his legs out in front of him.

Something bulky lay in Ed's way, so he reached for the lighter in his pocket. Once the small fire illuminated the area just around Ed, he could see that he was no longer in the closet. He looked over his shoulder at the sound of a vehicle whizzing by. He could feel his brows knit into a wrinkle at his confusion, since, not only did he hear a car, but he also saw a red truck. He leapt to his feet, and gravel ground beneath his shoes. When he looked down to see if the ground he was standing on was what it sounded like, he screamed to the limits of his voice and oxygen at the sight of the young boy Earl, Bobby Jr., and Jase had killed.

The boy lay in a mix of loosened gravel, weeds, and bloodied trash. He was on his side with his arm unnaturally behind him, his fingers bent in opposing directions. His naked body was a mix of colors from black to purple with minute blotches of white and red, dark, sticky and thick. Ed patted around the truck to get away from the horrible scene but was shocked into more screams when he saw himself standing, as if waiting, in front of the truck.

Rigid with fear, Ed fell against the passenger door of the pickup. He watched himself stare at something in his hands, but he was interrupted by Earl's didactic request.

"Will y'all hurry up and get in the damn truck, please?"

Ed looked through the window to find Earl at the steering wheel. Jase and Bobby Jr. came running from the back of the truck. Ed jumped at the sight of them but was surprised to find that they couldn't see him, which he noticed once he called to them. Apparently, they couldn't hear him either.

He backed away from the truck before Jase opened the door and hopped inside. He could see himself—his other self— standing as if no one had said anything. Bobby Jr. stopped just before he

201

climbed into his seat and said, "Well, you coming, Ed?"

"I'm gone walk back to the bar. Y'all gone head."

"Don't beat ya'self up too much, Ed. That queer bastard had it coming. Just think what people like him are doin' to this world."

Ed turned from himself to the slamming door of the pickup truck. He saw himself shove the pipe in his back pocket as he began to walk with the truck speeding off down the highway behind him. Before the truck could get completely out of sight, a heavy horn resounded through the night, just long enough for Ed—and the other Ed—to turn around and see the headlights of a Mack Truck pour onto Earl's truck just before smashing it into the side rail of the highway.

Flames quickly engulfed the red truck, but Ed saw that the vision of himself was already running in the opposite direction.

He decided to run with himself since he didn't know what else to do. As he and the Ed that he watched kicked up dust beneath his feet, he pictured the boy's face. It wasn't yet mangled as it would be before he'd be dumped. It was disfigured yet slightly recognizable. One of his eyes was puffed up so much that Ed couldn't see his eye beneath the protruding skin, and his other eye, though darkened around it, could still pass for the same amber as Amy's. Ed remembered how he tried to look away when the truck stopped but saw that the boy had pulled out whatever strength he had left in him so that he could reach Ed.

He grabbed at Ed's shirt and whispered, "Help me, please," but Ed jerked his shoulder back, causing the shirt pocket that the boy was gripping to rip while he looked away and said nothing.

Ed began to cry as he ran and ran, bypassing the vision of himself. He pulled the inside of his elbow into his face as he apologized into the nothingness.

Everything was pitch-black again, and he could hear the stomp of heavy boots marching in his direction. Tears ran down Ed's face as he began to scream apologies.

The cops were getting closer. Seconds later, there were three deafening bangs at the closet door. "Come out, right now, with your hands up," someone yelled.

"Forgive me." Ed got out, with his tears. He was met by four police officers.

They didn't ask Ed any questions. Two of them each grabbed him by one arm and yanked. They dragged him out of the closet, shoved him onto the ground, and handcuffed him.

Everyone in the bar happily watched Ed being forced out. He looked around. The man who had sat with him was nowhere to be found. The only person who was willing to listen to Ed, a gay man, wasn't there to help him anymore. Ed was still crying when the cops escorted him out of the bar.

The sun broke through the clouds just enough to brighten the world without burning it. A breeze uncharacteristic of any that had ever wafted through the thickness of Backwash's heat washed over Ed, and he wished that he could sit and feel it for a little bit longer. It made him think of Amy's hair, but the thought angered him, so he intentionally stepped on a trail of yellow flowers that were just out of his way.

When the cops shoved Ed into the back of the police car, he was relieved but confused at the sight of the man from the booth in the backseat. Ed's neck whipped around to see what the cops were doing, but the man shook his head. "No, they don't know I'm back here because they can't see me."

"They didn't put you in here?"

The man pulled his hands out from beneath his folded arms. "Would they put an un-cuffed criminal in the car and leave him unmonitored?"

"Then how...why?" Ed asked.

"You'll see soon enough."

"You have to start tellin' me somethin'. Who are you?"

The man turned toward the window without saying another word.

When they reached City Hall, Ed's sobs grew as he saw the crowds of people surrounding the steps. When the cops pulled Ed out of the car, the ruckus panged in his gut. He knew that he was going to die, but the thing that really bothered Ed was how hateful and bigoted everyone was. It sickened him. People weren't perfect where he came from, but he knew that this was overboard. The woman calling him out in the bar just for looking at someone, Amy's attitude and the way she spat on him, the police officers manhandling him without explaining what he'd done wrong...it was

204

all ridiculous. These people were barbaric.

There were signs about The Almighty on large poster boards. Bible verses that Ed didn't recognize littered the many signs and banners in the crowd. There was yelling and, oddly enough, there was actual singing. Ed counted nine American flags being waved. "I just want to go home," he said. He whimpered and shook, wishing that he would wake up.

"That's exactly where you're going." The man smiled, following right beside Ed, but no one reacted to what he had just said—even though laughter rang out in the audience closest to Ed when he cried out. He realized that maybe others really couldn't see the man because no one stepped aside or acknowledged the man in the tight pants walking next to a handcuffed accused criminal.

"You're going to help me?" The slightest bit of hope gleamed, but as quickly as the anticipation found him, one of the cops pulled the organ pipe from Ed's back pocket and bludgeoned the back of his head. This was followed by repeated strikes to the side of Ed's face before the cop tossed the pipe onto the steps.

The crowd livened with applause and whistles. Once the cops broke through the crowd, Ed could actually see the white, scuffed steps and, standing at the top, large guards in white uniforms. He nervously looked from side to side only to see more signs, more flags and more angry faces.

Ed shuffled through a smaller crowd of men, women, children, and news reporters and cameras. There was so much noise that he couldn't hear what one female reporter said to him before she shoved a microphone into his face. He blurredly looked up to find a camera pointed directly at him. The reporter yelled, "It's starting! Are you getting this?"

Ed followed the reporter's eyes to the man from the booth. "Nobody...see...you?" Ed struggled to say. The breeze cooled the parts of Ed's face that weren't covered in blood. His head throbbed, and the pain pulsated through his face in a sharp wave that heightened with every word he spoke. "Jus...wanna...go...home..."

"And you shall. In a moment," the man said. He pulled out one of his pockets, but instead of a lining, blocks of wood fell onto the steps. He bent down to arrange the wood in a circle as the crowd watched and cheered. The man leaned over to pick up the pipe, and he stood it up on its even end in the center of the circle. He lay his hand on the jagged top of the metal and began to pull, which, seconds later, transformed the pipe into a six-foot-tall pole.

The camera remained on the mystification as the reporter, who watched the happening, spoke into her microphone. "The Almighty is preparing the site as we speak. Let this be a lesson to all heterdogs out there: everything that you do will come to light, and you will pay. To all of our normal viewers who may be turned off by some of our city's actions, just think what people like this heterdog are doing to our world."

"Burn him!" the crowd chanted as the police officers dragged a struggling Ed to the pole. When they unlocked one of his cuffs to wrench his arms behind him, he looked over to the man in pursuit of some understanding.

"I'm not him, you know." He replied to Ed's unspoken inquiries. "They just think I'm The Almighty."

The crowd fell silent when a young boy ascended the steps holding a long cardboard cylinder that spouted flames. He stopped three steps below Ed's stake and jostled the wood with the lit cardboard until a spherical fire blazed beneath Ed's feet.

"At least they didn't beat you, Ed," the man said.

The heat reminded Ed of home, the real Backwash, until a searing pain bled through him from his feet and ankles. He shook and jerked as he screamed at the cheering citizens. "Please! I didn't do anything!"

"Oh?" asked the man. He stood in front of Ed, thumping the flames that bounced off of his purple kerchief and tie.

"I'm not The Almighty," he said, stepping away, "but I do play the organ in the closet."

The End

Natalie L. R. Baker earned her bachelor's degree in English and journalism at Texas Southern University and has written for various publications including The Houston Forward Times, JPages Hair and Beauty Magazine, One Love Houston, *and* The Strong Times. *Natalie is a teacher who feels privileged to work with children as she completes her dark fantasy series,* THE DANGEROUSLY

207

BEAUTIFUL BEAST OF BURDIN.

To this collection of tales of love and accompanying darker passions, Matthew K. Bird contributes this tantalizing flash fiction about what happens when an adoring servant is not allowed to serve.

I Am a Smart Maid
by Matthew K. Bird

Dec 25

This is my first log of daily events. I was operational roughly 240 days before this time but the factory told me I didn't have a master yet. I met my master today and I must say I am more than pleased. He and his female partner seemed very happy for me to be operational. So happy in fact that they had me perform my tasks almost immediately upon activation and proper establishment of date. I was so happy to have so many things to clean. It was mostly funny looking paper and cardboard boxes but I went right to dusting and organizing the house after cleaning the parcels. I was almost ecstatic when I found that the laundry hamper was over five feet tall! I even found torn up jeans and properly mended them immediately! The lady of the house wasn't very happy about this but she submitted in the fight when my master used logical reasoning. If I were human I'd want to be just like my master because he is so smart!

Dec 26

Today I got my full list of duties programmed and let me say I am looking forward to this life more and more! I have access to cleaning and organizing over two thousand square feet! I am to dust constantly and pick up after my master. I am to make sure laundry gets done daily. I even cooked dinner! The lady of the house was especially happy about my meal so that of course made me feel absolutely fantastic. My master complained about my cooking fish but I was so happy to cook him another meal to his specifications. It was two pieces of toast covered in gravy with fifteen strips of bacon and three quarter pounds of beef. I logged that it was terribly unhealthy but master instantly cut off my nutrition function.

Dec 27

Today I got caught up on all of my cleaning and made the meals in proper timing. There were no unusual things to report.

Dec 28

I did something terrible today. I purposely broke several vases that were valued at less than nine dollars a piece so I could have something to clean up. My masters of course did not take notice but they never asked me about the state of the vases so I never had to bring it up in basic conversation. Is that what humans call lying? I Googled "lying" and found several forums saying it was not. I don't want to be a liar.

Dec 29

Nothing to do today either. I was not permitted to clean or cook because the lady of the house said she wanted something to do today. I of course went back after her and did it properly.

Dec 30

Same thing as yesterday. Except this time there was nothing to do behind the lady of the house. I am programmed to feel happy about my job. I actually think that beyond programming I honestly like my job. When she takes my job from me I start to feel inadequate. I researched this feeling and found several forums saying that I needed to develop a hobby. My hobby that I discovered is making messes and then cleaning them up. If my *raison d'etre* is "I clean therefore I am," then what happens when there's nothing left to clean?

The End

Matthew K. Bird is an ex-Marine who currently find himself studying anthropology at the University of Houston and creating a post-apocalyptic fictional masterpiece.

Most of us have heard people refer to their illnesses as "mine"; but what happens when a woman's suffering becomes her liberated other self? Christina St. Clair compels us into just such a seductively pain-filled freedom.

Ice Cream
by Christina St. Clair

Thelma Brown did not look up when her husband said, "Are you ready yet?"

He was pacing back and forth. Slowly, she squeezed a pat of age-defying cream onto her index finger. Then, carefully smoothing it over her chin, her forehead, and finally her puffy cheeks, she surveyed her face in the mirror. A good face, a tired face, a fat face that no amount of cosmetic could restore looked back at her. She quickly tugged on her wig, making sure it sat evenly on her crown and hid any wisps of her hair.

"You'd better hurry!" Eric yelled again. He wanted to get it over with more than she did. They were on their way to the hospital for the chemotherapy that was supposed to prolong her life.

What a horrible and yet beautiful word: myeloma. It belonged entirely to her. *It is my Eloma,* she thought, *not his.* It was not an invasion but an evasion. Her cells were rebelling in ways she'd never been able to in her life. Eric always got his way. She always tried to soothe him and make him happy. After all, marriage was for better or worse. He'd gotten all the better, she sometimes

212

thought. She'd gotten the worse. That was being resentful, she knew, and it was not the whole truth, nothing but the truth. She had two beautiful daughters whom she loved so much that it had almost killed her when they'd gone to college. Eric had been a steadying force during that transition.

Her house might as well have been emptied of furniture and its walls painted gray—that was how empty it had felt. *Empty Nest* was a term she didn't like much. She would call her state *nothingness*. That sounded very philosophical. She'd always wanted to study philosophy. Everyone had discouraged her. *You couldn't get a job with a degree in philosophy. You might be able to quote Sartre or Hume, but that wouldn't pay the bills, or put food on the table. Much better to get a job as a teacher. You'd be doing a service then, and earning a living, and not become a victim of some man and his paycheck.*

Thelma tweaked the hair over her ears. The wig looked better than her real hair ever had. She wondered if her hair would come in the way Janet Thurstrom's had after her chemo. Before she died. From complications after her second cancer operation. Double pneumonia. *Maybe it really had been a blessing,* Thelma thought. Janet's hair, though, had turned gloriously lush and pure white. Thelma did not like being almost bald. The wig made her head itch too. People sometimes stared, or worse, they quickly looked away, pretending they hadn't noticed. Perhaps they worried it could happen to them. Well, it couldn't. This was *her* Eloma. Amazing how the girls now called home at least once a week. Sandy always asked directly, "Are you following the doctor's orders? Are you getting rest? Do you eat well?" Sheila, on the other hand, was the spiritual one. "Are you right with God?" she'd ask. "Perhaps you and Daddy should join a church."

Thelma could care less about eating well, following doctor's orders, or being right with God. As a matter of fact, she'd been thinking about enrolling in an online course in philosophy. It was called *The Philosophy of Death*. It might make her laugh to read what the great thinkers from Descartes to Sartre said about death and nihilism. "I think, therefore I am," she yelled out to Eric who she could hear clomping up and down in the kitchen.

"We'll be late if you don't hurry," his voice growled.

"Doesn't matter," Thelma mumbled. "They'll wait." *I can't wait*, she could almost hear *him* muttering. *My Eloma*, she thought, *has made me strong*. In the past, she'd be scurrying about so as not to cause him the slightest disturbance. Nowadays, she was beginning to discern that she'd been a pushover and a pleaser. Her *Eloma* told her that it was now time to please herself. After all, she might not have much time left. What she had, she needed to use wisely, not in the service of others, but in the service of her own deepest needs.

Philosophy wasn't the only thing she'd always yearned after. She had secretly wanted to be a dancer. Anyone would look at her, twenty-five pounds overweight with heavy thighs, and laugh. She might not be able to trip around a stage en

214

pointe or leap into the air daintily clapping her legs together, but she'd recently read about belly dancing for older women. It was supposed to help with self-esteem as well as physical well-being. And it would be fun. She didn't have in mind to become an exotic belly dancer, although the idea of dancing for a king who drooled after her body sounded delicious. Eric's idea of good sex was to turn out the lights and turn down the sound on the TV. To be fair, though, they'd been in love when they'd met and had enjoyed a healthy sex life for many years. She'd been the one to start getting headaches. He'd eventually given up chasing her. She wondered now if her imaginary headaches had been early warning signs.

"Do I have to go without you?" Eric yelled.

She began to laugh because he sounded so serious. Not that he'd take the bullet for her. It was rather that he thought there would be an end to the treatments and a restoration of good health. His idea of good health included her obedience to his every whim. *There I go again,* she thought, *being so unfair to Eric. He has been a wonderful provider. He is a good father. We share so many great times.* Then an ugly voice asked *such as?*

She dabbed her swollen cheeks with face powder and strolled out of the bathroom. "Here I am," she said. "How do I look?"

"You're going to the hospital, not to a dance." He dropped his stare to the floor. "You look fine. I like that wig. It suits you."

She twirled around. "Do you remember at our wedding how we danced and danced until our feet ached?"

He looked at her and shook his head. "I only remember the first dance."

That's because you only danced with me for the wedding dance, she thought, but didn't say so. She wanted to dream of what might have been, not what was. She wanted him to enter into her dreams. "Wouldn't it be wonderful to renew our vows?" she asked. "Then we could dance until we dropped." She followed him outside.

"I doubt that would be good for your health." He slammed the front door and got out his car keys.

"Wouldn't it be better to dance until you dropped, rather than simply drop? I don't mean *you.* I mean anyone. One. Wouldn't it be better to dance until one dropped..."

"Yes!" He strode over to the car, hopped into the front seat and started the engine. "I suppose you are right. But you are not going to drop dead. You are going to recover."

Thelma slipped into the passenger seat and put on her seat belt. "My Eloma is like a seat belt."

"What? Don't talk such nonsense!"

They drove in silence towards the hospital. At the red light outside the new DQ, a guy in an ice cream cone costume waved skinny arms in the air trying to get attention. Then he became motionless like a mime. Their car rolled to a stop behind a yellowed Cadillac that had seen better days. Thelma could feel Eric's impatience. She stared out the window at the DQ man The bottom of his costume, a brown plastic sugar cone, was crinkled on one side. Midway at the guy's waist, the

216

costume formed a fat belt that gave rise to a scoop of ice cream at chest level. Thelma bet it must be hot in that costume. It was a good thing it was December and the weather was cold. Another scoop of ice cream, rising from the chest, formed the head. His face had smiling black lips, a ping-pong nose, and plastic eyes the size of saucers. A swirl of ice cream, like windswept hair, curled from the top of his head. Suddenly the guy lifted his red and white football-sized shoes. He kicked left and right, jumped up and down, twirled around, and just as the light turned green, looked directly at Thelma. The black pupils in his saucer eyes spun. He bowed.

Thelma wrapped her arms around her sides and smiled.

Eric, as soon as they came to the divided highway with two lanes, sped around the Cadillac. He dropped her off at the door of the cancer treatment unit and went to park the car. Thelma stood outside, waiting for him to come back. She shivered.

"You could have gone in without me." His eyes flashed.

"I know."

The receptionist greeted them. "Thelma, you look radiant. Feeling good, I can tell." She smiled and handed Thelma a clipboard with a sign-in sheet attached. Eric took a seat in front of the TV. Thelma signed and then sat next to him. Country music blared from the screen, and a girl of about ten belted out a mournful song, rocking to the music and looking sad. An elderly woman with a thick braid of hair wrapped around her head read out loud from a medical consent form to an old man. "Have you ever had any surgeries before? Are you diabetic? Do you have any allergies?" His eyes seemed sad as he dutifully answered, and the old lady scribbled on the paper.

A young nurse in hospital scrubs called her name, "Thelma Brown." The girl's pretty face and kind smile made Thelma sink into herself with gratitude. She did not wish she were young like this woman, but it was comforting to remember that her daughters were probably not much older. As she passed the old man, she noticed he seemed calm, almost expectant, and not at all apprehensive. Maybe she was merely wishing age could bring about acceptance.

Eric stayed in the waiting room. He never went into the examining room with her. He couldn't take the sight of needles. She had a port and it actually was not a big deal. She just lay on the cot and the nurse hooked up a drip with the chemo and the steroids. It took about twenty minute to administer, and then they checked her vitals, and sent her home--with anti-nausea drugs in case she needed them.

Twelve hours later, Thelma leaned across the bed over the bucket Eric had just rinsed. He'd taken family leave while she was getting her first round of treatments. His morose face and turned-away head from the odor of her spewed up guts offended her. *She'd* much rather have had a nurse help her than him with his fumbling and repressed fury. She knew *he'd* much rather be at work. Did he think she wanted this disease? Did he think there was a cure?

There was none, only possible remission.

It was now *his* turn to be the caregiver. She'd been the one to see the girls through all their childhood sicknesses. She remembered only too well how frustrating taking care of babies had often been—like the time Sheila had thrown up during her bath, while Sandy in her cot wailed for attention and peed all over the sheets. It was easy to forget how Eric came home and changed diapers, and brought pizza for dinner. Right now, pizza sounded like something that ought to be fed to pigs. Right now, food could not help. Her Eloma wanted out. It wanted out. "Out out out!" she cried. Eric did not come into the room.

"They're offering ballroom dancing above Harriet's gallery. I want to learn," she later told Eric when she felt strong enough to go into the living room.

"Well, I don't!" Eric slumped deeper into his easy chair and shook his head in disbelief. "I'm not sure which is worse: professional ballroom dancers who look like they belong in a circus, or middle-aged wannabes waltzing around until the floor gives way."

"In that case, I'm going to sign up for a course in belly dancing." She waited for him to laugh, but he didn't. "It's a good form of exercise."

"Exercise *would* help you regain your strength."

"I want to dance," she said and began to sing, "dance, dance, dance... I could have danced all night..."

"I'll heat you some chicken broth." He hurried into the kitchen. She listened to him opening a can

219

and pouring the liquid into the saucepan. It smelled revolting, but when he brought it in with a piece of toast, she managed a smile through the voices that were hurling insults at him. Surely it was the chemo making her so sour. She took the bowl, her favorite one, bought on sale at K-Mart's. "Thanks," she managed, and obediently took a sip, before setting the plate on the coffee table. She nibbled on the toast and soon put it aside.

"You have to eat," he told her. "Try to get a little more down."

"You eat it!" she said. "I hate chicken broth." She managed to prevent herself from adding *and I hate you too.* She felt as mean as a snake.

"I'll get you something else," he said. "What do you want?"

"There's nothing you can get me," she answered, and wanted to add *you cannot fix this because it is not about you. This is my cancer. I would not give it to you even if I could. Not because I love you but because I hate you.* She began to cry.

Eric stiffly put an arm around her and stroked her back.

"Get away," she said. "Get away! I don't need you."

Eric stood up and she looked at his belly hanging over his belt and she remembered when he'd been as sleek as the skinny football player they'd watched during the Sunday game. She remembered when she'd craved for him to hold her. Now, her Eloma had delivered him from any responsibility to make love. She did not want his caresses. She wanted most of all to be alone. "You go out," she said. "I'll be all right by myself. Go on down to the Moose and have a beer." Then she sang, "You deserve a break today!"

After Eric left, she went to the freezer to see what there was that she might actually be able to eat and hold down. She remembered when she'd been pregnant and they'd joked about her wanting pickles and ice cream. She'd once craved beets in vinegar. He'd brought a can home every night for weeks, and she'd eaten every sour red slice to the point of wanting to barf. His concern and his desire to please her had been so tender that she had been helpless to say no.

The freezer contained a half-eaten loaf of bread, a package of peas covered with frost, a mound of ground beef, various unidentifiable packages buried under other frozen leftovers that had been there from before she'd gotten sick. She took out a tray of ice cubes, shook one into her hand and began to suck on it. The cold numbed her mouth. Back in the living room, she managed to eat the chicken broth. It slipped down her throat tastelessly. She began to sweat and ripped off her wig. Then she felt so cold that wrapping herself in three afghans didn't warm her. The cold was deep inside. *Systemic*, she thought. "Eloma," she said. "I want to learn to dance and I don't want to ever have to teach again. I have always hated being a teacher. You know that."

Then she remembered the little red-headed boy in her third grade class who'd not been able to draw anything because he didn't want to make a mistake. "It's all right to try new things," she'd told him, coaxing him. "Don't be afraid. Let yourself go. This is just for fun."

He'd drawn a picture of his dog. It had big ears and a skinny tail hanging down limply. She'd known he'd been expressing sorrow. What about, she'd never understood, but she'd always taken a little more time with him after that. Now, she realized that serious little boy had been unable to have fu—just like her. She wanted to dance, but her legs felt like rubber pencils. "Eloma," she said. "It's not your fault. But I want you to know you're only a guest. You cannot stay forever." The trouble was the doctors said that myelomas never went away. Fortunately, it was a rare disease, but usually more men got it than women, they'd told her. How lucky she was to be one in thousands, a woman at that. What was more, she was a rare younger woman since she was only fifty-two and most people made it to sixty-some before getting stricken.

The front door opened and Eric stepped into the room. "Who were you talking to?" She knew he thought she'd finally gone off the deep end, talking to herself like a crazy woman. "I was talking to myself," she said. "I enjoyed my chat with me, telling myself how lucky I am." She wished she could stop herself from goading him like this. She'd made her choices. Teaching had been a good job. There had been times she'd quite enjoyed her role. He hadn't forced her to do a thing she hadn't wanted to do. The cancer was not his fault. "It's not my fault I got cancer," she said. "I don't enjoy this, you know."

"Oh honey," he responded, and knelt next to the couch and began to stroke her bald head.

She pulled away, embarrassed for him to feel the wispy flyaway strands of hair, and frightened that some might come loose.

He hesitated, then cupped her chin in his hands.

"I have a whale face." She tried to grin and puffed out her swollen cheeks.

He stood up, grabbed her hand and tugged her to her feet. "Let's go."

"Where? I can't go out like this."

"Of course you can."

Thelma almost asked him if he planned to take her dancing. She remembered only too well, though, his comments about how the ballroom dancers would probably fall through the floor and land in the woodcarver's exhibit in the gallery. "Let me put my wig on, first."

"Why?" He held onto her wrist. "You look beautiful just as you are."

She knew she did not. Yet for one second she thought he might twirl her around. She imagined herself a prima ballerina performing a *batterie* with Rudolf Nureyev. She leaped, her white tutu resembling the feathers of a swan. Or perhaps she'd dance for Nureyev, shimmying her whole body so seductively that he'd sink to the floor and gaze at her from love-struck eyes.

Eric let go of her wrist. He threw open the front door. "I'll warm up the car."

Thelma grabbed her coat. She did not look into a mirror. She waited a few minutes before going outside to climb into the heated vehicle. "You know what I'd really like?"

"What?" Eric's voice sounded gruff as he backed out of the driveway.

"An ice cream at the DQ."

The End

Christina St. Clair once sold American newspapers to Parisians to pay for rent in a hotel near Montmartre, where she survived on baguettes and Beaujolais. She came to the United States when she was eighteen, and since arriving in Kentucky, along with earning degrees in philosophy, spirituality and women's studies, she has won an award for a YA novel, published essays, articles and fiction, and co-authored a biography of Pearl S. Buck published by the Shanghai Foreign Language Press in 2009. She and her husband began a small publishing house to promote the work of poets and writers with a connection to Appalachia. Christina is the author of EMILY'S SHADOW, *published by Blood Moon/Double Dragon in 2011. Her newest publication,* UNEXPECTED JOURNEY, *published by RoguePhoenixPress (August, 2011), is a historical novel set in the 1700s about a Native American shaman, a rich English girl, and a crafty girl from the streets of London whose paths converge in Colonial Pennsylvania.*

As horrendous as destructive relationships can be, it is the lack of any relationships at all that undoes so many, as Joel Owusu depicts in this disturbing flash fiction tale.

Noisnam Edicius
by Joel Owusu

Noisnam Edicius, a grandiose tower that sits atop an isolated hill, lies amidst lifeless weeping willows and is adorned with thick, hazy fog. The exterior is littered with black rose bushes, and the tower is constantly circled by dozens of frigid crows. Who would think that such an ominous-looking structure would be a one-way destination for immense joy and gratification?

Disneyland? The happiest place on Earth? Oh, no. Mickey Mouse and his cronies need to take a backseat to the happiness exuded by Noisnam Edicius—at least, to those who patronize this particular institution.

For it is at the mysterious Noisnam Edicius where pain turns to pleasure.

On this particular day, visitors to Noisnam Edicius include Cassie, a victim of relentless bullying by her peers. Saddened by the torment of everyday bullies, this teen's life is void of any LOLs.

Then there's Richard. Once a successful entrepreneur, a risky business venture left him penniless and bankrupt. He lost everything, including his children, his gold-digging wife, and possibly his life.

Also among the patrons is Agnes, an elderly grandmother who is all but paralyzed by the effects of arthritic pains in her bones and joints. She yearns for the younger days when diapers were used on her infant grandbabies, and not on herself.

Finally, we have Steve Burrell, a forty-five-year-old virgin whose best friend is his left hand. This freaky, frumpy, fat fellow simply covets the embrace of a female. Unfortunately, he has no game, aside from the ones he plays on his computer in the basement of his parent's home.

All these people come from different walks of life, but they all share a common characteristic, and that is deep sorrow and anguish that they hope to relieve on this trip to the mysterious Noisnam Edicius.

As the individuals journey through the gate surrounding the building and proceed through the colossal marble-encrusted door, they enter the main living hall in which they are to wait. They're each provided with bongs riddled with burnt residues of opium.

Of course, their objective is to inhale the drug, but this is not the main attraction but, rather, the appetizer before the main course, the trite opening act before the real performance. The main attraction is yet to come. The drug, however, provides them with the frame of mind Noisnam Edicius necessitates.

After the drug settles in their systems, they're then guided to a large, dark, enclosed room littered with lifeless dull obstructions on the ground that are not visible, due to the lack of any lights or windows.

This dark, cold, grim room is what our patrons are anxiously waiting for because it is here where life's burdens are no longer going to be endured. As they settle in this eerily restful room, each individual gradually begins to conjecture transformations.

Cassie, the lonely teenager, is now the popular girl. No longer are photos of cows on social networking sites tagged with her name.

Richard, the bankrupt opportunist, now has so much money, he could buy a private island. His wife and kids are back to go along with the immense amount of materialistic items they own, such as Bentleys, Mercedes, and jaguars; not the car Jaguar, but rather the animal. They own a small zoo at their estate, too.

Agnes, the old cripple, is now a spry, young, sexy version of herself. She is able to walk unassisted and even dance to the beat in her head. Shakira has nothing on Agnes because her hips don't lie.

Then there's Steve Burrell, the forty-five-year-old virgin. Let's just say he's a virgin no longer.

But just as gradual as is the way they begin to conceive of these transformations, so too do their desires slowly and calmly begin to fade to black until they attain their ultimate desire.

You see, Noisnam Edicius is not their final destination but, rather, a resolute stop along the way toward the end of suffering.

The mercury-blazoned gas chamber is the escort. The important thing to know about Noisnam

Edicius is that, once you choose to enter the halls of this enigmatic tower, you never return. Pain is permanently alleviated in the Suicide Mansion.

The End

Joel Owusu was born on November 2, 1991 in Houston, Texas, the only child of Ghanaian immigrant parents, but spent most of his childhood in a suburb of Washington, D.C. Joel has always been inquisitive and imaginative but tended to shelve books and notepads in favor of helmets and cleats. His greatest aspiration was to become star running back of a Super Bowl-winning team until he realized he wasn't that good. Now he is a biology major who hopes to become a surgeon.

Novella Serena's tale of yearning and despair brings the grimy difficulties of 21st-century urban youth, forging their own definitions of family, to the level of the sublime.

Cacie's Prism
by Novella Serena

Why couldn't life be as orderly and plainly understandable as the blank wall he faced? Then again, as the shadows on the wall deepened and shifted, nothing was really what it seemed anymore.

Koko shifted his weight off his left ankle, as it had fallen asleep. Soon his kneeling put his other leg to sleep as well. The little boy dropped back and stretched his legs out in front of him. He stared at the now dark gray wall, wishing he could forever fade into the shadows. At times like this nothing bothered him. He was thoughtful and happy and nothing could break his sense of peace.

The light reaching the hall from the windows grew weaker as the sun tucked itself behind clouds, undressing and preparing to snuggle under the horizon for a good night's sleep. The light dimmed from white to gray to a moment's soft gold as a ray broke through the blanketed sky. Shadows stretched. The wall's canvas lost its brilliant palette.

As gray bled into softly darkening blue, Koko heard a key in the lock of the front door. Moments later, his sister's smile shone from around the hallway's bend. She was surprised to see him sitting in the dark hallway but recovered her cheerful presence. "Hey there sweetie."

Koko thought about the fact that his sister never allowed herself to look sad or worried when she thought he was around. But there were times--bare moments--when he'd catch her.

Koko knew that there was plenty to worry about. Beatrise managed to juggle four part-time jobs, go to school, pay for and keep up their home, where Koko had been born, and still make her brother feel like the center of her universe. Beatrise had to cut corners to pay for their modest flat. The refrigerator was nearly bare, as were the cupboards, but they were stocked with the little boy's favorite foods. She would probably stop going to school soon. She would have more pennies and more time to work.

"Now what are you doing in the dark? Don't you want to stop for some ice cream? You didn't forget about our walk, did you?" She stuck out her lip as she smiled and walked over to him, kneeling to squeeze him in a bear hug.

"I'm sorry," he answered softly. "I was watching the shadows on the wall and forgot myself."

"Well, there's no more light now. How about a little dinner?"

"That would be nice."

"Good," Beatrise said, almost triumphantly. "Why don't you help me choose?"

She turned on the hall light. Creamy white glinted off of her black hair as she disappeared back around the corner.

230

Koko squinted after his sister. He heard the gentle clank of dishes pulled out of the kitchen cupboard. He pulled himself to his feet. He'd been so long on the floor that his legs were unsure under his sudden height and weight. He flicked the light switch off, plunging the hallway into rich blue shadow.

Koko hurried to join his sister. She pulled out a box of instant macaroni and cheese in fun shapes, his current favorite thing to eat. In the few minutes before the water boiled for the macaroni, Beatrise pulled fresh fruit she'd just bought from her backpack to wash.

Beatrise sought to keep her brother on as healthy a diet as she could and wanted to give him as much life as she could. Every other evening, she brought home a new type of fruit or vegetable and a story to go with it. Tonight, they would share pears. After adding the macaroni to the boiling water, Beatrise explained to her brother the origins of pears and their many uses. Koko, thrilled to see this oddly shaped treasure, watched astutely as his sister washed the fruit and put it in a small bowl.

"Koko, will you please set the table?"

"Yes." Koko drew reluctantly away from the dripping fruit bowl. Gathering two forks and two napkins from a low drawer his sister had prepared for him so he could help with housework, Koko went to set their little dining table. He returned for the glasses, his newest prizes, two collectable jelly jars decorated with cartoon characters.

Koko seated himself. Beatrise entered, deftly balancing their dinners and the bowl of fruit in her arms. Koko watched his sister. One piece of fruit tumbled out and rolled in a circle. He smiled. It wanted him.

"May I have this one?"

Beatrise looked at her brother. "I should at least wash it, okay, honey? And I'll give you a little plate for it so it won't get dirty, all right?"

Koko brightened when his sister placed it, gleaming and wet, next to his macaroni. Beatrise sat across from her brother and took his hands. Koko recited a child's poem that he'd learned that day. His neighbor Mrs. Reese told him she used to recite it as a blessing over dinner as a girl.

Koko ate slowly. The first time he found a shape, he would place it gently on the rim of his bowl. A parade of cheesy cartoon characters eventually graced the edge of his bowl.

The line of pasta characters watched Koko spoon various scenes out of his dinner. Here was a chase scene. Now they're at the fair. Look, they're all asleep. Uh, oh, this one doesn't have a head, and that one is stuck to another one. Here, nibbling off one's head and the other's tail, a new cartoon character in the gooey orange audience on Koko's bowl. Beatrise watched her brother play.

When Koko's bowl was empty, save for a few orange streaks stuck to the side, Beatrise reached across the table, sliced the pear, and arranged the perfect juicy wedges on his saucer. Koko sucked the juice from the pear until it lost its gleam. He furrowed his brow and stuck the fruit into his mouth. He played with the small, dark seeds on his saucer.

Beatrise's eyes didn't leave her brother. "You like it?"

Koko nodded, eyes bright, mouth dripping. "May I have another?"

"Another? What about ice cream?"

Koko's eyes widened.

"You didn't forget, did you?"

Koko shook his head furiously. Koko had forgotten. She could have let their outing slide and saved a few pennies, but she was not going back on a promise.

"I'm ready!" Koko furiously wiped his mouth with his napkin and swallowed the last of his juice with the tablets arranged by his glass.

Beatrise tousled her brother's hair from across the table. She stood up. "It's been raining. There are lots of puddles to jump in." Koko smiled.

Koko knew that as the problems surrounding him and his sister grew, Beatrise acted happier and more carefree around him. Why were they going to get ice cream? Where were they going to get that ice cream? What was the special event this time? Was there ever any special reason?

Koko slid off of his chair and made his way to his room, running his hand along the wall. He slept in what used to be his parents' room. It was wide with a high ceiling and even had its own bathroom. The bedroom was painted a very pale blue and the trimming was white. Their parents' belongings were stashed in another room. So were all the photo albums.

Beatrise had bought a bedroom set for Koko a few years ago when he'd become too old to continue sleeping with her. The twin bed sat under the largest bedroom window. Sunlight poured onto Koko's patterned blue and white sheets. A shiny white baby monitor hung on the right side of the headboard.

Koko walked into the closet. His eyes skimmed over worn sneakers. Then his eyes fell on the new leather shoes his sister had bought. Koko grabbed his little Italian shoes and ran down the hall with his coat to his sister.

Beatrise opened her mouth to order him to change shoes, but he looked so happy in them, and his face fell so mightily as he watched her, that she held her tongue. She helped him into his jacket and, laughing, they left for the ice cream parlor.

The two made their way to the neighborhood café. It sold milk and small groceries, had a bar, and was a small child's heaven with old-fashioned barrels of candy and what the neighborhood children thought of as the world's best ice cream menu. Koko got a glass of soda water mixed with a large helping of sugared syrup.

"So," asked Beatrise as she and Koko sat in a booth, "What adventures did you have today?"

Koko held the cool mint liquid in his mouth a moment. "Well, after you left, I walked to the park. Do you know that nice old lady?" He paused his story while he finished the soda. "We talked a while, then she bought me a bag of popcorn. We sat together and fed the birds at the park. She had a lot of fun stories about when she was little." Koko greatly admired Mrs. Reese and seemed to have more fun basking in her childhood memories than he did living through his own. "But then she didn't feel well and I walked her home. After that, I came home."

Koko folded his thin hands and looked expectantly from his sister to the menu over the ice cream counter. Beatrise slid off of her bench and walked up to the ice cream counter. She turned back to Koko. "Okay, then. What do you want? Do you want a sundae?"

Koko nodded.

Beatrise ordered a large banana split with the works for her brother and a small chocolate and vanilla scoop ice cream cone for herself.

* * *

Hedeon sat at his table and looked out the window. He paid no heed to the scattered pile of papers in front of him, white and wide as the aftermath of a blizzard. As a matter of fact, he had no need of the papers anymore. The sight and weight of them sickened him. He'd burn them. If he got rid of the manuscript that plagued him, he might find that his mind was once again free to brainstorm.

From his apartment window, Hedeon could see the narrow gray street below. The overcast sky seemed to match the bland buildings. There was a dark alley nearby which had, strangely, been holding his attention for a while.

It was impossible to see very far into it. He doubted that anything worth writing about lay hidden within those shadows. Maybe a few gangbangers, an old hobo, or some adolescent runaway. Not that people's lives had any impact on Hedeon. In his mind, kids in gangs were self-righteous little punks, a strange semblance between a peacock and a bristling cat. And if some soldier came back from some war and couldn't maintain a job, well, it wasn't Hedeon's fault. He could care less about the self-pitying children who hid in the shadows. Hedeon ran a hand through his auburn waves, leaned his head on the glass, and stared at the alley.

* * *

Koko and Beatrise screamed as they splashed down the street, spraying water everywhere. The few scattered rays of sunlight, against the cracked tar of the road and cement of the sidewalks, made the street sparkle. The best splashes brightened the street with shimmering droplets.

As they passed a dark alleyway, Koko stopped. He stared in. Beatrise took his hand. "What is it Koko? Did you hear something?" Koko pointed. Beatrise looked over his shoulder. What was it?

He yanked free and disappeared. "Koko!" Beatrise ran after him. She hit something and stopped before moving again in the inky silence. Beatrise made her way through the shadows with her hands in front of her.

Koko was, to her horror, kneeling next to a body. Koko held the person's bloody hand and stared intently into the face. Dark hair, matted with blood, hung over the eyes. Beatrise reached for her

236

brother. "Now," she rasped. "Koko, let's just go."

Koko murmured, "Please."

Beatrise had never heard so much yearning in Koko's voice before. She paused, at a loss. The person's head lifted. The dark eyes focused on hers. In the shadows, time seemed to stand still. Beatrise joined her brother at the form's other side.

Slowly, Beatrise pulled the limp body away from its sitting position against the wall. "We should call the police." A quick look of fright crossed the person's bloody features. Beatrise looked away from the red-glazed face to her brother's. "Okay, let's hurry. We don't want it to get dark or something. You need to help me, Koko."

When the three came out of the alley, Koko and Beatrise supported the sagging figure between them. "Where do we go?" Beatrise asked herself aloud. She looked up at the apartment complex in front of them. In one of the higher windows, she saw a man's shocked face. He signaled that he would come down. Then he disappeared.

* * *

"I'm tired," said Hedeon. "I just feel tired." He leaned back against his headboard.

Cacie looked at him from the window. "Why?"

"I don't know. I just feel tired. Like an old man or something."

"You're hardly old."

"I know."

"And you really don't do anything to make yourself tired."

Hedeon lazily shot Cacie a glare. "I didn't say I've been pushed so hard or so far that I'm worn out. I said I feel tired. I just can't even try in the first place."

"What's holding you back?"

Hedeon shifted on the bed. Cacie's dark eyes bored into him, unblinking. Hedeon couldn't look at Cacie. He looked at his own knees.

"What is it, Hedeon?"

What was it? Why could he never say the words on the tip of his tongue? Why couldn't he reach out when he needed to? Why?

"Why do you always stop short?"

There would be no hiding anything from Cacie. "I'm scared."

"Why?"

"I don't want to lose it."

Cacie sat still. So still. Hedeon looked up. Those dark pools gazed at him. So dark, so deep, so comforting. "Some things you lose."

"I—I know, but..."

"Some things you never lose."

"Cacie," Hedeon turned his full body to Cacie. "I haven't had many things I can count on. It's safer just not to risk it." He felt himself bristle. "Don't be stupid."

"Risk what?" Cacie's brow lifted a bit. "You're not gearing up for a fight."

Hedeon stared past Cacie, addressing the dreary buildings through the window. He wanted to open up. Just once. Of all people, Cacie had to be worth the pain. "When I finally trust something, I lose it."

"You won't destroy everything just because you

care about it, Hedeon."

"Well, that's what I do."

"That's what you *think* you did, Hedeon. That's not what happened." Cacie had responded to the memory Hedeon could not voice.

"I felt so safe, Cacie."

"You were, Hedeon."

"I didn't know him."

"That's okay."

"I didn't thank him."

"I think he knew."

The dull buildings appeared to glimmer like the snow and trees from that distant vignette. It had been so fun. And so cold. So very cold. A day of exploring, sledding and feeling on top of the world.

Snow covered his young world as far as he could see. The frigid air chilled Hedeon's adrenaline. It wasn't fun anymore. It was late. Where was home? Hedeon had gone too far. He did not know where his house was or where his parents were. When was the last time he'd seen them? Did they know where he was? He had gone out with their permission, hadn't he? It was going to be dark soon. Hedeon could feel it.

The snow and the cloudy sky met and bled into one another, the same shimmering gray from one to the next. Winters were like this. Darkness was never gradual. Hedeon knew night would fall suddenly. But what time was it?

Hedeon walked. Eventually, silver birch branches reached out to him. Trees. Shelter. Maybe home would be past these.

Hedeon walked through the frozen grove. Each

step grew heavier. His fingers were stiff. Cold had already become a freezing burn. Stupid gloves. Stupid coat. Stupid boots. Weren't these supposed to keep a kid warm?

Almost as if he'd wished it into being, under a thick tree trunk lay a pile of colorful clothes. Winter coats, scarves, sweaters, socks, and trousers in warm oranges, bright yellows, rich reds, and toasty browns beckoned. Hedeon approached the pile, unsure what he would do when he reached it.

The pile moved. A pit of fear froze Hedeon's belly as much as his frostbitten hands. A weathered face, straggly gray birch beard first, rose from the clothes. The mouth above the beard smiled. Was Hedeon cold, it asked. Hedeon could not answer. Don't worry, it soothed. Just lie down. Warm up. Get some sleep.

The old man crawled out of the pile and Hedeon crawled in. The warmth was delicious. Had he ever felt so safe? Had he ever felt so loved? The man, seemingly nothing more than a dark, stooped, wrinkled winter outfit with a tree-like face, smiled down at Hedeon until Hedeon's eyes, finally thawed, closed. He slept.

Hedeon was jarred awake from the hot chocolate dreams in which he floated. Men surrounded him. Big men in navy blue and black. No faces. Goggles and scarves. It's okay, son, they said. We found you. You're safe. It's all right now. But, of course he was all right.

The big men, dark like the night that was falling behind them, pulled Hedeon out of his textile sanctuary. He craned his neck. Where was the old

240

man? What was happening?

Hedeon finally saw his savior. The frozen sentinel sat stiffly next to Hedeon's nest. One of the midnight men covered the corpse with a ratty brown blanket.

"You didn't kill him, you know." Cacie's voice caressed Hedeon, embracing and comforting him.

"But..."

"He saved you, Hedeon, but you didn't punish him."

Unwanted tears burned Hedeon's eyes and he willed them not to fall. He clenched and unclenched his hands.

"You don't need to hate everything that reminds you of him." The runaways. The soldiers. The lost. The homeless. "Accept his gift. Make something of it. If it hurts, make all that worth it."

"Can I hold you?" Hedeon's voice was small. No tears had fallen, and now Hedeon's eyes felt enflamed from the effort to hold them in.

Cacie climbed onto the bed, sitting next to Hedeon. Hedeon wrapped Cacie in his arms, burying the tears that now flowed into Cacie's midnight hair.

* * *

"Koko!"

Koko roused himself from his afternoon nap. His sister's voice.

"Koko, sweetie!"

Had he forgotten something?

Beatrise pranced into Koko's bedroom and

dropped onto his bed. "Guess what?" Koko rubbed his eyes sleepily and blinked at her.

"We're going out! Now, where are your shoes?"

Beatrise slid to the floor and stuck her head and an arm under the bed. She found one shoe and pulled it out. "Hedeon invited us to go see a movie and hang out at the mall. Doesn't that sound fun?" She found Koko's other shoe peeking out of his coat pocket. She stopped by his dresser and pulled out a fresh pair of socks. Returning to the bedside, Beatrise took Koko's feet, rubbed them and put his socks on them. "You, me, Hedeon," Beatrise smoothed the socks out on his ankles and slipped the shoes over them.

She buckled the strap of the little Italian leather shoes Koko had worn the day they'd found Cacie and the only shoes he'd worn since. "And Cacie."

"When are they coming?" Koco asked.

"Hedeon just called. He said he and Cacie thought it was time we all got some fresh air."

Koko's usually solemn face lit up with a smile at her words and remained like that.

The smoothness of the trip to the mall got interrupted when Beatrise and Hedeon got into a friendly argument about an outfit Beatrise wanted for Cacie.

The two often spent hours dressing Cacie or buying Cacie a wardrobe or otherwise trying to claim Koko's friend. As they debated, Cacie guided Koko to an ice cream shop a little further down the mall hallway and bought him an ice cream and a bag of candy. The two swapped jokes and took turns licking the runny ice cream as they made their way back to the clothing store.

Koko sat next to one of the mall's fountains as Cacie quietly reminded Beatrise and Hedeon that the day was meant for Koko. He smiled. This was almost like a family. It was a family for him. Hedeon was like his father, his sister often like his mother and Cacie—Cacie was—

"The family dog?" Cacie offered, joining Koko and lifting him for a piggyback ride.

"Not really."

The group made its way to the mall's large movie theater. No movies especially for children were playing at the time, so they picked a reasonably safe family film. The four were the first into the theater and found the perfect seats, guided by Koko's little pointing finger.

Forty minutes later, Koko took the time to look at his companions. He wasn't interested in the romantic stuff on the screen anyway. He sat on Cacie's lap. He knew that both Hedeon and his sister were jealous of him, but being far older than he could not make a show of it. They both tried to get the attention they wanted when they were alone with Cacie. They had no idea Koko knew.

As always, Cacie ignored their advances and focused all affections on Koko.

How, Koko wondered, could his sister be so grown up and responsible yet be so confused sometimes? Cacie was the least confusing person he knew.

Now, Beatrise slumped so that she all but put her head on Cacie's shoulder. On Cacie's other side,

Hedeon did the same but with a more masculine approach. *How silly*, thought Koko. He looked up at Cacie's chin. He felt Cacie's legs bounce under him. Cacie politely continued to watch the screen, allowing Koko the comfort to do as he felt.

Koko liked his friend's eyes. If you took the time to look in them you could see existence. They looked black, but they swam with color as if universes shone behind them.

Could he look into them now?

Go ahead, mouthed Cacie inconspicuously. Koko climbed onto his knees and took Cacie's face in his bony little hands. After fifteen minutes of intense gazing, Koko slept curled on Cacie's lap through the rest of the movie.

Hedeon watched the little boy. He thought about the manuscript he'd planned to destroy. The movie had taken a turn for the romantic. Not what he needed on his mind at this time. Time with Cacie was the most fantastic and the most aggravatingly confusing time of his life. And when he was with the little boy and his sister, things only got weirder.

Hedeon wondered what the girl was doing now but decided against leaning forward to look over at her, as it might aggravate Cacie further.

The burning shame was still fresh from weeks ago when, spending the night at his apartment, Cacie had berated him for his possessiveness. Why did he have to force more? Couldn't he be satisfied with what he had?

No, not in his mind. Or was it his heart?

Cacie had rejected, to put it lightly, Hedeon and

244

his intentions. "You are not my concern at this time, nor are you my desire," Cacie had nearly shouted. "Can't you just stop right now? Look at what's in front of you." That meant Beatrise and her brother.

Cacie gave the impression of only being a temporary member of society. Focus on the family Hedeon was now a part of. Focus on the little boy. Focus on the girl. But she wasn't Cacie. She wasn't this passion or mystery. She couldn't touch his soul or move his heart like this.

As much as Hedeon liked Beatrise, she, compared to Cacie, was only human.

* * *

Cacie and Koko sat in Mrs. Reese's bedroom. She'd taken ill again and was confined to bed. In memory of her visits to his sickbed the year before and their days spent sitting in the local park feeding the birds as she told stories of her childhood, Koko demanded to be allowed to visit her at her house when her nurse permitted. Bringing someone older ensured longer visits.

Hedeon was usually very nice about coming. The interest he took in Mrs. Reese's stories she found enthralling. She was the inspiration for his new book. She made him want to write again. Hours could be spent recording the stories and laughing together over lemonade made from concentrate, since Mrs. Reese was not fit enough to bake her famous cookies that had carried Koko through bedrest.

Beatrise never had time to bring Koko to Mrs. Reese's for a visit.

When Hedeon first found out about the siblings' financial status, he hired himself out to help Beatrise pay bills and rent until his book was finished and he could send her some of its revenue. So now, Hedeon was often unable to accompany Koko unless Mrs. Reese felt well enough to tell more stories. And if he did force time into his schedule to come with Koko, he was often grumpy for a while after.

Since it usually seemed to them all that Cacie existed to take care of Koko, Cacie changed the day's schedule so as to be able to take Koko on visits to Mrs. Reese as well as to the little boy's doctor.

Mrs. Reese liked Cacie's company. Cacie was quiet and unobtrusive and sat for hours holding Koko as she told the boy stories. Or Cacie went about the house relieving the nurse of a few of her chores and giving her more time to focus on Mrs. Reese.

Koko noticed that the nurse enjoyed it when Cacie came over, as well. Hedeon was not as interesting as Cacie and could not have bothered to pay any special attention to the nurse, but Cacie, leaving Koko and Mrs. Reese to spend private time together, joined the nurse on most of her breaks.

After realizing that visits could go nearly all day when the nurse got this much attention, Cacie often joined her on her cigarette breaks, never sitting downwind, and allowing her to flirt.

On this particular day, Mrs. Reese became

worn out during the visit and was soon very sick.

The nurse was back at the hospital at this time, working with Mrs. Reese's doctor. Cacie comforted Koko, who was quite distraught, and put him to bed in the guest room for a midday nap, before returning alone to Mrs. Reese's room.

Mrs. Reese labored to breathe. Her face had become a mass of pained wrinkles. She moaned, half asleep. Every time she shifted to ease her discomfort, her oxygen line would slip from her nostrils.

Cacie pulled it from her face and took her hand.

Cacie reached out and stroked the lines from her face. Slowly, Mrs. Reese relaxed. Her haggard breathing softened and her struggling pulse strengthened.

Every pain Cacie caressed manifested itself in Cacie. Mrs. Reese's gnarled grasp on Cacie's hand untwisted. Cacie's right arm strained. Mrs. Reese's countenance grew soft, bringing back the face of the girl whose adventures she'd so often related to Koko. She slept.

Cacie kissed Mrs. Reese's forehead and moved to the nurse's nearby armchair, right arm twisted in on itself, cradled it and slept.

* * *

Koko was in the hospital more often than he was out. Beatrise spent her nights in his room, curled up in a chair by the bed. She had already quit two of her jobs. She risked being fired from a third. Though she showed up right on schedule,

Beatrise was not really there. Her employers noticed. School had not suffered yet, but that was thanks to Beatrise's intelligence, not her effort.

Hedeon's book was done. His publisher had it. The advance on the book was in the mail. As one may expect, bills had arrived already. But, at least, the check was on its way.

Hedeon's reliable work ethic paid off. Though the labor jobs he found to help Beatrise were scattered and not definite, he always showed up and did what was expected. Hedeon was offered and accepted a single, secure position with a large enough salary to modestly cover the needs of two households, his and Beatrise and Koko's. With regular work hours, Hedeon was able to take shifts watching Koko at the hospital and keeping the boy company before his procedures.

Hedeon would send Beatrise away with a kiss on the forehead. After work or classes, she would make her way home, often curling up fully dressed on her bed and going to sleep. Since she did not always remember to eat when she was finally home, Cacie made a habit of preparing dinner ahead of time, sometimes waiting outside of Beatrise's job or school to escort her home.

Dinner was quiet. Cacie ate slowly, only taking bites when Beatrise did. Guiltily, Beatrise ate everything.

"I'll clean up. Just get ready for bed."

While Cacie cleared the dishes and went into the kitchen to wash them, Beatrise walked to the bathroom. She shut the door and turned the small lock in the knob. The bathroom was small and dim, the antique paint and dusky porcelain too dark for the limited space. Beatrise pulled a clean towel from under the sink, along with a half-empty bottle of body wash and a disposable razor. She plugged the tub drain and turned on the hot water.

As it filled, Beatrise undressed and stood, staring blankly at herself in the mirror. The skin around her eyes looked bruised from her lack of sleep. The corners of her mouth had turned downward when Koko was rushed to the emergency room this last time. Aside from the loving smiles she gave her brother, Beatrise's mouth refused to smile. She didn't frown. Beatrise just could not smile.

"Beatrise, I'm going to bring some stuff to Hedeon and Koko. I'll be back soon," Cacie called through the door.

The bottom of the tub was full. Beatrise stepped in and stretched out as far as the short tub allowed. Her knees stuck up. The water rose around Beatrise. She looked past her knees at the thundering water. Her knees looked back at her, like alligator eyes in a river. With one foot, Beatrise turned off the faucet. She settled back and watched the steam dissipate.

Beatrise stirred in the tepid bath. She had not slept. She'd lost track of how long she'd been in there. She took the razor and pulled it across one leg. The blades cut the goosebumps on her skin. Beatrise cried out in surprise and frustration. She looked at the blood build and trickle into the water and held the razor up to the light. Translucent pieces of her skin stuck between the blades. Her gaze flowed from the cheap razor to her hand, her arm, then down to the water.

Almost as if it had a mind of its own, the razor dragged along Beatrise's wrist. She watched her wrist as she scraped the blades up and down the inside of first one arm then the other. Her wrists felt raw, as if she'd just fallen on asphalt. But they didn't look bad. The blood took a few moments to find its way to the newly exposed surface of her skin. When the blood finally welled and flowed, so too did the tears. Beatrise sobbed, dropping both arms into the water, letting blood and tears fall.

"I'm back!" Cacie walked through the apartment and put two bags of groceries down in the kitchen. "Hedeon is planning on making dinner tomorrow." Cacie swiftly pulled items out of each bag and put them away.

"Beatrise? Are you done?" Cacie walked to the bathroom door. "Beatrise?" Knocked. Once. Twice. "Beatrise?"

Cacie tried the door. "Oh, no..." Locked. "Beatrise!" Body slammed against it.

Eventually, the door could no longer take Cacie's running against it. With a snap of the latch it moaned open and sent Cacie skidding through. Beatrise lay in the water, still.

"No—not now..." Cacie hesitantly put fingertips to Beatrise's throat. The faintest of pulses. The water was cool and red. Cacie reached into the opaque liquid and lifted Beatrise's left arm. The length of the delicate flesh from wrist to elbow was raw with geometric scrapes. Cacie felt around again and found the skin-clogged disposable razor.

250

Sliding Beatrise's other arm over the side of the tub, Cacie firmly grasped both of her wrists and squeezed them, breathing heavily more from suppressed rage than exertion. Cacie stroked the sliced skin, and it responded to the touch by following the caress and closing, malleable as sculptor's clay. The pallor left Beatrise's face and her cheeks flushed. She began to shiver.

Cacie stooped and lifted her out of the water. Cacie lifted Beatrise's limp body over the cold floor, wrapped her in her towel and took her to her bed.

When Beatrise awoke, she found herself, in her mother's old nightgown and a thick sweater, bundled in warm towels and blankets. She lifted her hand to rub her eyes and saw that her arms were wrapped with gauze and elastic.

"That was stupid." Cacie leaned on the dresser across from the foot of Beatrise's bed, arms crossed. Cacie's eyes burned. Those deep eyes had consumed the light that usually played in them, and the blackest pits glared back accusingly. "Why pick the time your brother needs you the most?"

Beatrise stared at Cacie.

"Do you expect me to sympathize with you?"

Beatrise's eyes filled with fresh tears.

"I do. But, don't expect that to override how stupid that was."

Beatrise tried to blink the tears back but, instead, they slid down her cheeks.

"How does that make anything better, Beatrise? How?"

Beatrise tried to sit up but was too groggy.

"Answer me."

Beatrise attempted to roll onto her side. She didn't feel like listening. Or answering. Before she could realize what was happening, Cacie was above her, hands on her wrapped wrists—pressed into the mattress, pinning her on her back.

"We are going to talk about this."

Beatrise turned her head. Cacie wouldn't let her and grabbed her face with one hand, holding her wrists above her head with the other.

"You are going to listen."

Cacie's torso pressed Beatrise's into the bed. Beatrise could feel her left hip digging into Cacie's abdomen.

"Do you realize how many people don't have a choice?"

She could feel Cacie breathe, feel Cacie's heartbeat.

"Koko needs you."

She was never this close to Cacie.

"Hedeon needs you, too."

This was not quite how she had intended to get this close to Cacie.

"You hurt. It hurts so much. But doing this won't make your brother better, Beatrise. And when he goes—don't try to ignore me, Beatrise—when he goes, it won't bring him back. Your love, Beatrise, and the knowledge that you're here keeps him alive."

Beatrise blinked. Cacie let go of her jaw and leaned against her cheek, speaking softly in her ear. "And knowing you're still going to be here is what's making him brave." Cacie released her wrists and took her hands. "Don't take away the one thing that

252

will prepare him for a peaceful death."

"But I don't want him to die!"

Cacie stroked the palms of Beatrise's hands. "Sometimes you can't change things."

Beatrise sobbed loudly.

"But you can change the way they happen."

She buried her face in Cacie's neck.

"Koko needs you, Beatrise. He will always need you. He needs you to be okay. He needs you to live the life you two have been working toward. Beatrise." Cacie rolled off of Beatrise and wrapped her in an all-encompassing hug. "You've changed Hedeon's life, too."

They rocked. "For the better, Beatrise. You've done something amazing for both of them." Cacie wiped Beatrise's cheeks. "And you have more to do. Look at me, Beatrise."

Beatrise looked into Cacie's eyes. The fury had subsided. The black holes were again pools.

"You have to grow up and grow old for your brother. You might have a beautiful baby and name it after him. You have to do the things and see the places he's always wanted to go. You have to finish school and eat lots of ice cream and macaroni for Koko."

Beatrise sputtered a laugh.

"You know, I was on my way back with some news. Your boys got you a new job. Just one job this time."

"What?"

"Remember little Koko's friend. That nice lady he used to visit?"

"Yes."

"Mrs. Reese needs a caretaker. You'd spend time with her that her nurse just can't spend." Cacie ran gentle fingers through Beatrise's hair. "I understand what you feel. I know that it feels like there's no point. But there is, Beatrise... Koko is so proud of himself. Hedeon worked out the details with Mrs. Reese and she has already told the nurse she will have no one else. Koko feels like he got you the job of his dreams."

Beatrise laughed.

"He loves Mrs. Reese, and you should see how happy it makes him to know you'll be with her. All his favorite people together."

"But I—"

"The job's easy to train for. Hedeon has spent the better part of tonight working out the details. The job is yours. It's stable. It pays well. Just one job. You'll have time for school and—most of all—plenty of time to spend with Koko."

"I—"

"Shh... go to sleep now. Sleep, Beatrise. Koko loves you. Live your life so he knows you know it to."

* * *

Koko lay in his hospital bed. He drifted between fitful sleep and drowsy lucidity. Since they could not bring him home, Beatrise and Hedeon had brought, with the hospital's permission, Koko's curtains and blankets and toys to decorate the room. Other than the large machines, the wires and tubes, the people just outside the door, the room felt like

Koko's own.

A gentle wind came through the screened window and blew lightly against the curtains. The blue and white squares waved like flowers in the breeze. The sun shone through them.

Cacie entered the room and sat on the edge of the bed, watching. Koko slept on.

When he finally woke, Cacie smiled.

"Hi there."

Hi, Koko mouthed. The world was wonderful. His sister was happy again. Mrs. Reese was well. Now Cacie was here. All was right and well.

"It's good to see you."

Koko smiled. He said nothing in reply. He could not. His voice had left him a week before as his illness strengthened and his treatments intensified.

"Look what I have," said Cacie.

Cacie's hands clasped over the bed in front of Koko and opened slowly.

Suspended between Cacie's fingers twinkled a prism. It caught the light and reflections of their smiles.

Cacie's hands clasped again. Another prism flashed in the sunlight.

Again and again, Cacie's hands closed and opened over the bed until a web of glittering light surrounded the frail child.

Koko pushed himself upright on his bony arms. The prisms sparkled, as did the boy's joyous expression, and wrapped him in light. He looked ready to soar.

Cacie grinned at Koko and made the light

dance. Koko closed his eyes. The empty cocoon of a boy lay back, a peaceful smile upon his cooling lips.

The End

Novella Serena teaches literature, Humanities and composition at one of North America's largest community colleges and has published award-winning essays on abiku *or spirit children, African Diaspora dark fantasy and crossover media.*

256

Max Balkan's riveting tale of Serbian vampire hunters maddened by the blood feuds of previous generations reminds us how hard it is to come together, even in the most dire times of need. Perhaps it is then that we feel most compelled to protect ourselves with what the author calls. . .

Long Knives, Sharp Tongues
by Max Balkan

Nevena's home is a two-story, five-bedroom block house that is nestled some nine hundred meters away from the main road. It is secluded from the other houses, standing on a low incline with a vineyard that stretches beyond sight. Her family has been known for making a great tasting *rakija*[1] for generations now. This piece of land has belonged to the Milutinovic family as far as their lineage goes back. Four other houses that stand on the right by the edge of the woods are a testimony to the four generations that built them. From those four houses, eight generations sprang forth. Nevena made sure I knew all about it.

As we walk side by side, I'm still trying to figure out what is going on. Zoran said very little on our way here, probably from his lack of information. And that's odd. But I don't like what he has told me. The new Minister is making too many decisions in a short time. It's as if he knew he would get the position. The worst thing is his eliminating our sectors, and from the provided info,

---

[1] Serbian National drink made out of either plums or grapes

my sector is going to be erased. Each leader has a sector, usually the area where he and most of his team reside. The leader is responsible for the safety of all in that sector, safety through vampire eradication.

Once these imaginary borders are gone, there will be no order, no efficiency. You might ask why this sector thing is such a big problem. Easy. Since each leader controls a zone, there's no rivalry; everyone knows what to do and where to do it. With this new plan, some sectors are going to be overrun with hunters, while the rest will be overlooked. We'll be at each other's throats over this. It's good that I'm relieved of duty tonight, or Zoran and I would be less than friendly. Either way, I must speak with Slavomir; he must attempt to rectify this mess before it turns into a bloodbath.

The Jeep isn't even a distant speck anymore; it's completely gone from sight as the door to Nev's house opens, and light from the porch illuminates the face of someone who could be her older twin— the same long hair and figure, only with more maturity in all the right places.

"Nevena?" The female says, coming down the steps, her hands resting on her hips.

"Moom." Nevena sighs and looks skyward, and then at me. I think it's cool when you can see your loved one in the future without getting old and say to yourself, *She's still hot*.

Nev's mom looks at me, raising an eyebrow. "Vampirovicu?" she intones, always calling me by my last name, never by my first.

"Natasa?" I always call her by her first name.

258

"I hope you're making dinner."

"You hungry?" she says.

"No, just wondering about those two knives behind your back."

"Ooh." She flashes me her smile, and I see the same tooth, like Nev's. There's a quick movement of her hands and a blade hits a tree on my right, vibrating on impact. With her left hand, she spins the long kitchen knife between her fingers. *Like mother, like daughter*.

"Come over here." She approaches and kisses me three times, left cheek, right cheek, left cheek. I respond in kind. Customs; what can you do?

"Ugh!" I wince, as she touches me close to the neck, by accident.

"What's wrong?"

"Battle wound." I stretch my neck.

"If you die, I'll kill you." She waves her finger at me.

"Moom?" Nevena rolls her eyes.

"Nevena?" Natasa says.

"Natasa?" I say, and all of us smile.

"Get inside. Nev, help me in the kitchen, Vampirovicu, Milorad is in the cellar," Natasa says, taking the knife from the tree and returning it to somewhere in her dress.

"'Kay, mom," Nev says, already disappearing inside.

"What's Milorad doin'?" We walk inside.

"What else? Cleaning his shotgun...again." Natasa looks towards the ceiling.

Just wonderful. "Nice throw back there."

"Thank you. I practice a lot."

"On what? Cabbage?"

"Crows."

"Great." I snap my fingers, pointing. "I'll go find Milorad."

"Don't try to fly away; I'll pin you down." She twirls the blade out of nowhere in her hand before vanishing into the room on the left.

I know some people don't like their in-laws, but just think of it this way: no matter how boring, unnerving and insulting they can be, they at least cannot cut you up like sushi. Lord Byron must have had a bulletproof vest, if he ever dealt with a family as sharp as this.

I take my shoes off and pass through the line of rooms, turning to the right and descending down to the cellar. As soon as I step in, I'm greeted with the long barrel of a side-by-side shotgun, staring into my face.

Milorad is holding this wonderfully crafted shotgun, looking at me like he would look at a deer. I focus on his shaved head that reflects light with glass ball intensity. If his beard was any longer, I would call him a dark-haired Rapunzel, although he would not be a very attractive one, with those vein-filled arms like roots and fingers as thick as shovel handles.

"Gone hundred years." His eyes measure me up and down.

"Was busy."

"I see. Armed as usual." He doesn't take the shotgun barrel out of my face; with the barrel he opens my jacket, taking a look at my sidearm. I could've disarmed him twenty times, in twenty

260

different ways, twenty seconds ago; however, I choose not to create any disturbance.

"As are you." I nod toward his shotgun.

"Fuuuck, what can you do?" He props the shotgun against the wall, waving his hands.

"Get more?"

He becomes serious for a second, and an ear-blowing laugh escapes his lips. My ears start ringing. "Ha, ha, ha, come. Sit." He pats me on the back, and kisses me three times as well, before I sit in a nice handcrafted chair, padded with a comfy cushion.

"Here's some *slatko*[2] heroes," Natasa says, stepping down the stairs, carrying a silver platter with two glasses of *kisele vode*,[3] two little porcelain cups with *slatko*, and an empty cup to dispose of the spoons, afterwards. There's a nicely woven, white tread with the cover depicting hunters and pheasants. As is tradition, I take the first taste and quickly wash it down with *kisela vode*—the sweetness hurts my throat.

"Thank you, darling," Milorad says, kissing Natasa. I smile as she slaps him on the ass and goes back up. *Nev, baby, we need to talk.* He picks up his shotgun and starts rubbing the barrel with a cloth, throwing a glance at me every now and then, not saying a damn thing.

"So, how've you been?" I rest my back on the comfortable cushion.

---

[2] Special kind of sweet treat, made out of fruit, usually served when guests arrive.

[3] A kind of mineral water mixed with soda.

"Fine." He looks uninterested. "Anything new?"

"No."

He takes the two red slugs out of the barrels. *It was loaded? Damn.* He throws a side glance at me but says nothing.

I sigh, giving up. "Yes, you can see it," I say, moving my jacket aside, taking out Atrophy. He throws the shotgun at me and snatches the pistol out of my hands. He looks like a kid despite his age.

"Son, this is one wicked contraption." He looks it over like it's the Holy Grail, ejecting the mag to see the bullet. "Customized V2 31 .30 caliber fully automatic, thirty-two round mag, specially treated barrel to cope with modified ammo, plus its adjustable silencer."

"I can hardly call it a Scorpion anymore; everything is modified."

"Wait till the old man sees it," Milorad says. He gets up and walks toward the room on the left. "Pops, ooh Pops! Pops!"

"Mister Stojadin is here?" Stojadin is a different story altogether.

From the room on the left, a fully military-garbed Stojadin comes out. Well, one part of the Serbian military that is, the opposite of what my grandfathers were. He's completely dressed in black, with *kokarda*[4] on a *shubara* [5] and enough medals to construct a tank. He reminds me of a

---

[4] Metal badge of the King's royal guard, with two swords crisscrossing
[5] Russian-like hat, made out of fur with the ability to cover the ears

wizard, minus the long white hair. In his hand he has a bolt action rifle with a bayonet under it, and on his thick belt a renowned blade, called a *Kama*[6], dangles. I won't lie to you; I feel intimidated, not by him, but what he represents—a *Chetnik*[7].

"What is it? Are the Germans here? Where are they? I'll bayonet them to death!" he says, rushing kind of fast for an old man.

"Take it easy. Just young Vampirovic is here."

"Respect, Father Stojadin. How do you do?"

"Vampires. Vampires? What vampires?" he says, waving his hand in the sign of a cross, looking like a lost kid in a mall looking for his parents. His hand reaches for the *kama* on his belt.

"No, Pops. V-a-m-p-i-r-o-v-i-c."

"Aah," Stojadin says, releasing the hold on the blade. "Why's he here?"

"Well—"

"Are the goddamn Albanians assisting the *Svaba*[8] again?" His hand returns to the blade quickly; his eye shoots a glance at me.

"War's over Pops."

"War's never over, not as long we have the damn *Partizan*[9] bastards." He looks at me. I

---

[6] Long double-edged knife, widely used by the *Chetnik* party in WWII

[7] A member of the King's royal guard or a supporter of the King, depending on location and family lineage. The term can have positive or negative connotations, but usually negative.

[8] Derogatory term for German soldiers

[9] The official army of Serbia under President Josip Broz Tito, rivals of the King's guard

swallow hard; both of my grandfathers were Partizans, but I remain silent, or this could get ugly.

Milorad looks at me and clears his throat. "Ahm, anyway, Pops, look at this." He steps closer to old Stojadin, presenting him with Atrophy.

Stojadin's eyes dilate, and he places his rifle up against the wall and takes the pistol in his hands, looking it over from every side. He points the gun at me, green laser beam straight where my heart is. My right hand reaches towards the *kukri* hanging on my back, and I pretend to scratch a nonexistent itch. He looks at me; his eyes are still filled with some dangerous feeling, and it seems as if time moves slowly.

"Pops?" Milorad shoots a glance between us two. He understands that his father can get carried away sometimes, but what can he do in this situation? Stojadin is so close to pulling the trigger, but Nevena saves the day.

"Food is ready. Come on up," she says running to my side, throwing her arms around my neck. She doesn't seem to notice that her grandfather has some issues.

As if he just woke up, Stojadin breaks his gaze and speaks. "Nice weapon son, nice weapon. If we had this back then, no damn *Svaba* would even dare cross our land."

"True, but then again I don't think that others would stay on the land, but go under," I say, and with a quick motion of both hands, I manage to spin the weapon out of his hands, twirl it, and holster it in its place. "We couldn't have too many dead *Partizans*, now could we?" I stare down Stojadin.

To be honest, I expect him to go crazy with the last remark, but he just starts laughing. "You're all right son; you're all right." He pats me on the shoulder not occupied by his granddaughter. "You chose quite a man, my dear. Keep him close; I would hate to see what would happen if he gets far." Stojadin glances at Milorad and kisses Nevena on the forehead, his eyes still tilted on me. *If looks could kill, this would be a bloodbath.*

"Thanks, Gramps. Will do.' Now let's go, or else mom will use us for target practice."

All of us comply, of course; no one is crazy enough to mess with the lady of the house. Even I'm not that crazy.

Stojadin still throws me another glance before we go up, but it's hard to tell if he's angry or just calculating. Milorad whispers something in his ear as Nev and I walk up, and Stojadin just nods his head. The bug of fear crawls down my spine and settles in my stomach, clawing inside. *I cannot believe what I'm about to say, but God help me.*

All of us take a seat at the big black wooden table. The dinner is amazing; besides being good with a blade, Natasa is excellent with food. It's an unusual time for dinner; it's eleven o'clock, but this is a special visit. There's stew with meat and vegetables, roasted lamb with potatoes, *sarma*, *giba`nica* and beer. I think it's ironic; most of it is *Chetnik* food.

I choose to just eat and not comment, because I think I can comment on more important things, such as our seating arrangement or the look of Stojadin when I wash my hands. Natasa is sitting next to me

265

on the left and Nevena straight across from me on the other side of the table, right next to Stojadin, while Milorad is at the head of the table. And of course, Stojadin is not taking his eyes off me.

I think I know the reason why. He must think that it is disrespectful for me to even be here, considering that he considers me a "piece of communist shit." He never really said that, but I'm not stupid. I know; I just know.

The other thing is, of course, my dating his granddaughter; he probably believes that I'm far from a good thing for her, being that I'm not from a *Chetnik* family. For those who don't understand these relations, it's quite easy. Each side hates each side and basically claims that the other is the traitor and is fascist-oriented. *Partizans* were communists, and *Chetniks* were monarchists; two separate goals are a reason enough for hate, but there have been so many atrocities committed by both sides that anyone, including me, can get lost. There are no saints, just hypocrites.

I look around the dining room and see the icon of St. Djordje the Dragon Slayer on one wall, with some candles that are half-burned, the wax leaving a long stream. There's a wooden cross right beneath a four-letter insignia, CCCC[10] (*Samo Sloga Srbina Spasava*). As I munch down on some cheese-filled *gibanica* , my eyes focus on the family picture in the corner. *Nothing wrong with an occasional stereotype, right?*

There are five long-bearded men posing with

---

[10] Only Unity Saves a Serb

Draza Mihailovic.[11]

I recognize one face and I shiver inside; it's Stojadin. As if he read my mind, he stands up and walks over to the picture, bringing it back to the table. All of us are quiet. I look at Nevena, but she doesn't look at me; she concentrates on the platter in front of her. I catch a smirk from Milorad and disapproval in the eyes of Natasa, as she bumps my leg, telling me just to be calm. Now, I believe I'm fucking calmer than Gandhi, and I deserve a goddamn medal for this shit, because I am so ready to go totally Satan Panonski[12] on his ass.

"See this picture? It's me and my four brothers, with Djeneral Draza." His eyes glimmer as he lifts his decorated chest, medals ringing and the fabric stretching.

I decide to play it cool, as cool as anyone could in these circumstances. "I didn't know you had brothers, mister Stojadin."

"Yes."

"Where are they now?"

"In the ground."

"Sorry to hear that. God rest their souls."

"Indeed."

"How did—"

"They die? Is that what you wish to ask?" he says, hugging the picture so hard that I hear the frame crack.

---

[11] One of the leaders of the *Chetnik* movement, tried and executed at the end of war

[12] Legend of a man who, during WWII, charged a German tank with a bayonet, killed the crew, and commandeered it before he was blown up by Allied forces.

I'm an idiot.

"Killed by the *Partizans* in a skirmish by Arandjelovac." As soon as he says that, that bug I felt earlier starts clawing its way out of my stomach.

I've fallen into this so easily. I lower my head enough to see Nev throwing me a quick glance with no expression, returning to her plate.

"Killed and buried somewhere, with limestone and animals, every trace gone," he says, teeth jittering like drums, so close to spitting.

"On my honor, I'm sorry for—"

"What does a Communist know of sorrow and honor? You had none; you know of none."

"Grandfather please—"

"Nevena, be quiet," Milorad says.

"Let's talk about something else," Natasa says but gets silenced by Milorad's gaze. Stojadin continues watching me, disregarding everyone else.

"Who are you talking about when you say 'you'?" *Oh no. I can feel the rush.*

"You, the collaborators with the Germans, little Hitler and Tito bastards, you deserve only death, you—" He points a finger at me in accusation.

I jump; my chair falls down as the entire table shakes. "You listen to me, you forest-dwelling freak of nature. Go back to your fucking woods and hide like you did in the past. That's all you're good for, to be sheep-less shepherds, scurrying like rats, living in the ground." *The rage is so near, I can smell it, and it smells like blood. I can feel it; it feels like a burning flame. Stay away, don't come, not now.*

"We invite you into our home and this is how

268

you treat me?"

"Vampirovicu, you—"

"Shut up, Milorad, just shut up." I point my finger at him as he jumps up, as well.

Natasa just remains calm, crossing her arms, watching as Nev's face has that stricken expression.

"How I treat you? How you treat me! Who started this? I didn't come here to argue. I haven't done anything against you or anyone here, and for the first and last time, I'm not a Communist and even if I was, it shouldn't matter. At least I'm not a greasy *Chetnik*."

"What? You Socialist piece of—" he says, pulling out the *kama*, rushing toward me.

"Grandpa!" Nev yells.

"Father, no." Milorad tries to come around the table, but Natasa is already on the move by his side; I don't even see when she leaves her chair.

Stojadin comes close, swinging the knife at me; I catch his wrist, and I bring him down on the floor, disarming him. The blade is under his chin, pressing against the beard. His eyes flap like window shutters in a wind storm as my weight presses his chest.

He looks at me, that rage gone, replaced by fear.

One rage strand touches me; it wants to come out. Be still.

"You listen to me, you brainwashed fool; one more goddamn time you point your finger at me and talk shit about the *Partizans* or anyone from that period, and I swear to you on my family's honor you'll end up worse than Draza. Understand?"

He nods his head in affirmation.

"Now you mentioned loss and sorrow; how 'bout this, you under-trimmed cutthroat. A *Chetnik* party came into the house of one of my great-grandfathers and killed everyone. They tortured him. They raped and cut the throat of his wife, my grandmother. They left the baby on the mother's chest to suck the blood out of her dead breast, right before they set the house on fire. When I think about it, you disrespected me and my family; I'll collect that payment now."

It's here.

"No, please don't!" Nev starts running toward me, but it is already too late. The justice has been delivered.

The End

Max Balkan was born in Belgrade, Serbia and studies Philosophy (Epistemology, Metaphysics, Ontology, Existentialism, and Nihilism) and Literature (Medieval, Modernist and Speculative Fictions) at the University of Wisconsin. This short story is selected from his vampire hunter series-in-progress, SERBIAN NOCTURNAL SHERIFFS.

Tenea D. Johnson contributes this otherworldly tale about the worlds within our worlds and the irresistible pull of like that hungers after like.

Only Then Can I Sleep
by Tenea D. Johnson

I, Dainadella Adu, commit this to the skin of our ancestors, of which I am one, so that those who come after may know, and save their imagination for dreaming.

Six Days Before the Last: When I was a boy I did not believe the journals. I thought the transition would hurt. I imagined my spirit sucked out, like a night beetle by a hungry *delau*. When I was a girl I feared the molting, as I then feared anything that could not be stopped once begun. Now I know: it is simply the next breath. It took me seven transitions to understand that. But now I am at threshold, barely able to believe that my last transition to my final body approaches. Janju laughs at my disbelief and keeps assuring me that it's true. After much searching, the Spirit Women found my match amongst the *CanBal* and have triggered my molt. After I have thresholded, I will be promoted to a High judge, an honor to any Djeli. So again, I'm writing here, in a now-careworn piece of hide torn by my first hand.

I am the only one to threshold in four seasons. When I began, hundreds transitioned into their last bodies, last lives. Not so, these nights. Some Djeli charge that the bodies are slowing us down, even stopping us from transitioning. They insist we shouldn't harvest them from wars. After problems with the last crop, a few brought their complaints to the courts. I have judged matters of trade and so have not been privy to the details. They are wrong though. It is our honor that is infected, not the bodies we use. Fewer and fewer Djeli honor their trades. Instead they cite obscure statutes or quote a past life lesson to avoid a fair barter.

Until the transition, I am left alone with my thoughts and Janju's distractions. We intend to get all the use out of this host that we can. I have to stop calling it a host body. Soon I'll be in *my body*. What a strange phrase.

***

Five Days Before the Last: I shared the morning meal with this host body's new match, Uvonia. She seemed satisfied enough with it, although she remarked that the jaw cracks when chewing. Funny, I had forgotten. When I was new to it, I cursed the noise every morning. Each time I yawned I feared it would fall right off the hinge. I had meant to get it fixed but never did. At the time, its more obvious tics—the flinching at loud noises or bright lights, and its food hoarding that passed for slow metabolism—took precedence. During the medical visits to fix those problems, I had overlooked the jaw.

Uvonia accompanied me to my check-up, and, as a matter of course, consented to its condition. (I have known only one Djeli who would not consent: Radhuri Anatol, Case 44274 Cyle 23 in the Special Collections, and only as a performance in pursuit of her artist's guild membership. When the accolades faded, she quickly desisted and transitioned just before the molting would have left her forever afloat.)

The next time I see Uvonia, she will look as I have for the last twenty-eight years. She will smirk when she intends to smile, just as I have. She will lead with her left foot and walk on her toes.

How these bodies hold on to their memories.

Not ~~the~~ my new body, though. It will only remember what I teach it to.

***

Four Days Before the Last: Janju has gone to check my body for me. I want her to describe it to me so I can see her face when she says the words. Otherwise I will never know if it pleases her. This body, though, is hungry and can't wait for the afternoon meal. *Porren* and *plen* with ripe *shipi*. It's this body's favorite new dish. It reminds me of the *ackale* and sweet *tsitan* fruit I ate as a youth. Not the same texture in it, though--nothing in it to rub your tongue against. Perhaps I will find something fresh-fresh later.

I hope Janju returns soon. So I can satisfy both my hungers.

***

Three Days Before the Last: I will write this slowly so that it bleeds.

My body ate Janju.

I found her host body, quiet and empty, next to the *incube* where my new body should have been. I thought to surprise her so that we could dine together at the city gardens, or perhaps go dancing while we are still the same height. Instead I discovered her host body. Its features had already melted into a blank repose devoid of Janju's passion; the limbs lay still as stone. My body had picked her clean.

The Corps are searching for it with Janju trapped inside. They would not let me accompany them. I pray to Oddudua for Janju's safe return. When the time for judging ~~my~~ the body comes, I will pray for myself.

***

Two Days Before the Last: The Corps found my body sleeping next to Dunleve River. They tracked it by Janju's essence. They brought her—and it—here. Soon after, the Spirit Women arrived and laid the body out in the front room. I can hear them singing as they try to draw Janju out of the *CanBal* body and place her back in her host. The spicy smells of *shreef* and *lacand* fill the hallways. The body that had been matched to me has held her hostage for the better part of a day. Already she has fought bravely. Though our bond gives Janju an approximation, she and the body are not matched; she should be dead. Soon her own host body will

274

be. Because I cannot help, I do not go where they lie. Instead, I walk around our home, touching Janju's things. I can still smell her spirit in the sheets, see it reflected in the sweet dark wine she always ~~drank~~ drinks before we sleep. They must get her out. They must.

***

One Day Before the Last: The trial begins this evening, in the open meadow near Gasca. Janju and I were bonded not far from there. When the Sanctified Judge wove our spirits together and presented us to the ancestor-stars, I knew I wanted to hold that position one day so that I could see Djeli love free and fresh-fresh with possibility. If only I had stayed on that judgeship level. Then I wouldn't have to decide our fates: mine, Janju's, Uvonia's. I cannot leave it to the Transgression Judge. Uvonia is only fit for this body, and I am only fit for the murderous one. Such a case is my jurisdiction.

***

Today, one of the Spirit Women told me what "*CanBal*" meant in the old tongue. If I could spare the strength, I would shake my head.

How these bodies hold on to their memories.

***

The Last Day: My molting period is almost

275

over. I have made my decision. Let the ones who come after ponder it. I am too tired. I have done my judging.

Janju, forgive me. Oddudua, help me.

***

I, Janju Akanadella, commit this to the skin of our ancestors, of which I am one, so that those who come after may know and save their imagination for dreaming.

The First Day: Air searches for a body to move in order to prove that it exists, even to itself; my Dainadella is this way. She ripples the wine in my glass so that I know she's here. Only then can I sleep.

The End

After time well-spent in alphabet cities—NYC, ATL, and DC—Tenea lives near the beach where she writes speculative fiction and creates compositions of prose to music. Her short fiction and poetry have appeared in various magazines and anthologies. She is the author of the poetry collection Starting Friction *and two novels,* SMOKETOWN *and* R/EVOLUTION. *2012 will see the release of the second and final book of the* R/EVOLUTION *duology and a fiction album. Please visit* www.teneadjohnson.com *for more information.*

Tedd Hawks introduces himself to the worlds of sci-fi and fantasy with this earthy idyll about the destruction of Eden by bloody sibling rivalry – sound familiar? – in this hauntingly original approach to a timeless tale.

The Vengeance
by Tedd Hawks

XR399 lay dying and she didn't even know it. She looked into the eyes of one of the Many and comprehended neither the fear nor terror that was written across his face. She could not make sense of the long cruel gashes ripped through his torso, and she did not recognize the warm, red substance pouring from them. She didn't know why she felt so—the way that she felt—it was something different she had never known. It was different, more life-like than she had ever felt—more life-like than she had ever been allowed to feel.

The Vengeance came quickly. She remembered the look on The Mother's face as she came before the village. Her face had never exhibited anything like it before, not what she knew The Mother to be—not what she expected. Her face had suddenly become full of lines, lines everywhere. Her eyes were not as bright as usual either; they seemed somehow dipped in shadow. That's what XR375 said: she seemed "dipped in shadow."

They had been speaking after the Mating of the day. It was warm, she remembered, there in the

277

sunlight. They were a bit sticky from the proceedings and she and XR375 walked with many of the other Pairs to the Deep Blue to clean themselves. One of the Young had come up to them and said that The Mother wanted to speak to them—

She twitched slightly and a gurgle of red came from the wound in her chest. For some reason she was growing cold despite the heat of the midday sun that beat down on her lightly bronzed skin.

The world at once begins to fade,
its skies obscured in ashen gray.
The waves that used to rise and swell
have lost direction, tepid and still.

A voice drifted from somewhere far away. XR399 listened and waited. Such words she had not heard before. She learned new words from The Mother that day she was in shadow.

The Young had led XR375 and the others gathered by the Deep Blue back toward Home. Most of the Many were already gathered together in the center of the little village looking expectantly at The Mother. An older woman than the rest, she was the one who had taught them how to live, how to gather nuts and berries, how to take care of the Young. XR399 remembered looking at her that day, her face lined, her usual bright face dimmed and tense.

"Thank you for coming," she said. "There is something I need to tell you."

The Many nodded together in unison.

"There are people who are coming here. They

wish to do you harm."

"Mother, what is 'harm.'" XR375 looked questioningly at the Mother.

"They wish to—they wish to make you hurt."

XR399 had never heard such a thing. Hurt was something that happened when you fell down, when you ate one of the wrong berries, when you were stung by a bee. Hurt was not something one person did to another. How would you even do that?

"These people are angry. They should have been taken care of—they shouldn't have survived." The Mother quivered. Her face grew red and the shadow crept further over her features. "They are different from us. They like bad things."

"Mother, what is 'Bad Things?'"

The Mother faltered in front of them. She shook her head. "They wish to spread Hurt. They wish to make you Hurt. They wish to make the world hurt." She paused and took a breath. "They come for vengeance."

XR399 remembered looking at XR375. He looked different. Something like what had happened to The Mother was happening to him.

"The Mother seems different," he said. "This Vengeance has made her darker, dipped in shadow."

And then the Vengeance came.

Emerald green and rising trees;
sounds of life and raging seas;
clouds of white in azure skies;
black, starry, perpetual nights.

It was the voice again.

XR399 tried to lift her head and look for the source. She could see nothing. Her vision already grew blurrier—perhaps from pain, perhaps from the impending death. She let her head fall again. It rolled to the side and she stared into the face of the One beside her, at the red trailing down his face.

"Maybe it is Hurt," she thought. "Maybe that's why he won't speak to me." The blood dripped down his face and XR399 remembered The Vengeance, remembered The Mother's scream.

"We have come for you! We have come for vengeance." The voice sounded so harsh. His eyes looked like the beasts' in the forests. There was something beasty in them. Others like him were gathering around the Many. They looked just as wild, just as frightening.

She remembered it in a blur of action. The Many just stood and watched, but The Mother, she was taken—the One grabbed her and cut her head— The Mother was in two. There were two Mothers.

"This is her comeuppance. This Woman," the One thrust the head of The Mother into the crowd and more red liquid splashed over those gathered. They had never seen anything like this. They did not know what to do. What was wrong with The Mother? Why didn't She speak anymore? "This woman created you. She wanted something better; she wanted to do away with us!" He threw the head into the crowd. It rolled and came to a stop at the feet of one of the Young. "She tried to destroy us. She tried to make sure that we didn't survive. Billions of people—all wiped out by a weapon of her creation. And you!" His eyes flared. "You are feeding off of our loss. You are the parasites of our Earth."

XR375 looked at her. She looked back. There was a deep shadow on both of them. These men brought the shadow. They brought it to Mother, and they brought it to the Many.

"In the name of God she slew her own people. She did it to start over. We had gotten out of control. She tried to destroy us. But we survived. And we will be avenged."

The man took a staff and hit one of the Young who was close to him. More red....

"We should go," XR375 took her hand. She didn't understand this, but she knew that it was something that was not from the Mother. The Others tried to leave as well. They all moved away from the Vengeance.

XR375 was taken before they made it far from Home. XR399 kept going. She had to get away, she decided. She remembered the path through the forest, Others following her towards the Deep Blue. But memory stopped.

She had awoken later.

She lay dying and didn't know it.

As it was will never be again,
man-made motion, mortal sin.

The voice was now almost on top of her. She saw one of the Vengeance who had split Mother take a wooden staff and hit the One next to her. He did not move. Why didn't he move?

The One with the staff spoke again:

But hope remains in ashen skies,
what life remains seeks and tries
to bring back beauty to the night,
to end the ceaseless, careless blight.

XR399 looked up into the eyes of the man with the staff, with her vision fading. They seemed to glimmer and be full of something that she did not recognize. They did not look like XR375's eyes.

"What do you call those words?" she asked, twitching in pain.

"Poetry," the man said. And then he plunged his staff into her head.

The End

Tedd Hawks graduated from the University of Notre Dame with a degree in Theatre Arts and is completing his Master of Fine Arts degree at Northwestern University. He invites his fans to check out his live journal at http://teddhawks.livejournal.com.

Marie Brennan's hypnotic tale challenges what we think of our fondest folktales. If all the trappings are there, what has happened to the innocence? The following, like the rest in this collection—despite its seductively sweet introduction—is not a tale for children. . .

Kiss of Life
by Marie Brennan

In faraway lands, the tale is a romantic one. She sleeps in her tower, in the castle surrounded by thorns, awaiting a prince who is brave and true of heart, for only the kiss of such a man will end her slumber and bring her back to life. She has waited for many centuries, they say, and many princes have gone, fighting their way through the dark wood and climbing the thousand stairs to the tower room, but none have been pure and noble enough to wake her.

Some tellers say that, distraught by their failure and this judgment of their character, the princes fling themselves from the tower window and fall to their deaths below.

If that were true, the courtyard of the sleeping castle would be littered with bones.

Closer to home, the stories change. The princes, they say, do not die of broken hearts and wounded pride. They do not reach the tower room at all. Long before they have a chance to lay their mouths against the perfect rosebud lips, long before they catch sight of the graceful, slender hands, they fall prey to the creatures that wait beneath the thorny boughs of the wood. And if they survive their trials there, then they meet their ends at the hands (or claws, or jaws) of the beings that walk the halls of the darkened keep, more foul by far than their forest-dwelling kin. And if they win their way past these as well, they perish in battle against the guardian who stands on the stairs of the tower -- but most never make it that far. The curse on the castle and its sleeping resident was placed by a powerful, jealous sorceress (or fairy, or stepmother-queen), and she vowed, as she was slain by knights, that her victim should never wake; and her blood flowed out and became the monsters of the wood and the hall, and her malevolent spirit the guardian on the stairs.

In the village that once served the keep, they tell another tale, and that is the darkest of all.

They tell their tale to any who pass through, but most princes and knights and wandering adventurers dismiss their words as the superstitions of credulous peasants (forgetting that their own peasants' tales set them on their road to begin with), or else assume that the villagers do not want the curse lifted -- for then they would lose the one thing that distinguishes their collection of squalid hovels from the thousand others like it.

The idealistic young prince who approaches the wood now never even had the opportunity to disregard the peasants' tales, for he took a vow, when he departed on his quest, to speak with no one until his task was done. A foolish vow, which lengthened his road by months and leagues; he searched in many wrong places, all unknowing, before finding his way here. He is not quite so young now, and his idealism has tarnished along the way. But at last he has found the wood, and beyond it lies the castle, and in the castle's topmost tower sleeps the lady whom he seeks.

He rides into the wood, his sword unsheathed.

The impassable forest of thorns disappoints him; it is dark and overgrown, to be sure, and thickly populated with briars, but the spines on these are not the sword-length blades he had been led to expect. He makes his way through with no more difficulty than an ordinary tangled forest might give him, and sees no horrors along the way. There is no sign, in all the wood, of any prince or knight slain here before him.

The villagers go blackberrying in the wood every year; they could have told him it was safe.

On the other side of the wood he finds the castle, walls cloaked in ivy, gate hanging open. Sword still in hand, the prince steps through. The courtyard stones are cracked by frost, and grass has grown between them, but there are no scattered bones, no fallen blades, left by despairing suitors. Above stands the tower, the tiny panes of its window glinting in the light -- shut against the elements, not left open by one leaping to his death.

The villagers never venture as far as this, but they know the courtyard is clear.

The great door of the keep also stands open, and dead leaves have drifted into the hall. They crunch dryly under the prince's boots as he walks in, the only sound he can hear. The light is failing now, the day having passed while he navigated the wood, and so he pauses to work flint and steel, until a spark catches in the torch he brought with him -- he knew there would be darkness. By the torch's flickering light, he searches the corners for threats, but finds nothing.

The villagers could have told him that.

He begins to question this all as he looks for the stairs. Where have all the others gone? Is it mere fiction, that men have come here before him? Could it be he is the first? All the stories agree that the questors have never returned, but perhaps they never reached this place at all. Perhaps they perished far from here; the road is, after all, dangerous. Or perhaps they came, failed to wake the sleeper, and refused to return home with their shame.

Perhaps there *is* no sleeper.

But he never asked the villagers for answers.

He finds the stairs and climbs, half-wondering if there is a guardian lurking here who will devour him, bones and boots and all, half-wondering if the tower room will be empty when he arrives.

Nothing meets him on the stairs.

As he opens the heavy door at the top of the stairs, he is of two minds. One envisions triumph and fame, the tale of how a youngest son, lacking any hope of inheritance at home, won a beautiful princess and restored her castle -- their castle -- to its former glory. The other fears mockery, the jeers of those around him when they learn he spent years on a foolish, pointless quest.

All thought vanishes when he opens the door.

The dusty, half-rotted curtains around the bed stir slightly as the air is disturbed. The prince scarcely sees them, eyes fixed instead on the figure lying atop the mouldering coverlet, hands neatly clasped across her breast. Amidst the decay, her hair shines like incorruptible gold. Her long lashes lie against her cheeks, hinting at the beauty they hide, and her perfect rosebud lips await his gentle kiss.

There *is* a sleeper, and there *is* a curse -- and the villagers know well the nature of both.

The prince drops his torch to the floor, where it dies swiftly, unnaturally. In the sudden gloom, he walks toward her, boots automatically lifting over the debris that blocks his way. He spares no thought for the debris; all his attention is fixed on her. She is a beauty beyond compare, and his skin aches, as though too small to contain his adoration. Trembling in anticipation of the sight of her eyes, he bends over and gives her the kiss of life.

An instant later, he stumbles backward, no longer recognizable as the idealistic young prince who set out on a noble quest, nor even as the older, more travel-weary prince who climbed the tower stairs. He is scarcely recognizable as human. His skin has shrunk tight against his bones and his muscles have withered away; he collapses to the ground, a skeletal, desiccated thing, dying among the scattered bones and rusted blades of all the other brave young men the villagers could not persuade or prevent from coming to this tower.

The sleeper sighs once, but does not wake.

The curse still holds, for which the villagers give thanks every morning. Her prison of sleep still contains her. But one day it will fail; one day, she will absorb enough life from others to open her terrible eyes, to rise from her bed and walk again. On that day, the skies will darken, and she will come forth from the castle once more, sweeping the bones of her suitors before her, bestowing her ravenous kiss on all who cannot flee her path.

But that day is not today. For now, she sleeps, waiting for her next kiss.

The End

Author of the ONYX COURT *series, the* DOPPELGANGER *duology, and more than thirty short stories, Marie Brennan pillages her background in anthropology, archaeology and folklore for her fiction. Visit her at* www.swantower.com.

For those who wonder what it was like when ancient mysteries made one afraid to be alone at night—or, more to the point, afraid to be with a loved one at night—Ezekiel M. Zachs offers this unforgettable immersion in a space where today meets the terrors of long ago. Brace yourself.

Blood Doll
by Ezekiel M. Zachs

Chapter 1: Haima

Morning

I find myself in an alleyway. I'm sitting, slumped against the wall. Master must have left me here. I slip back into the darkness of sleep.

Noon

It is a dry, not wet, day. The weather must be warm, but I'm still feeling cold. I stick my hand in my pocket and find some money. I take it out and look at it. There is about €3,000. Master must have left it with me. It is enough to keep me going for a while.

Evening

I awaken for the third time today. The sunlight has changed to evening orange. Although the alley is safe now, it won't be when darkness falls. I have to move.

I struggle to get on my feet. It is hard but I manage. I sway a little, dizzy and heavy-headed.

Then I walk out of the alleyway, slowly, carefully.

There is a hotel around the corner. It looks expensive but I need to sleep. The evening light makes the valet's red uniform glow, almost throbbing. He eyes me as I enter his hotel, but doesn't stop me.

I reach the reception. I would like a room, I say. They ask for money up front and I give them cash from my bundle of €3,000. Are you okay, says the man who hands me the plastic card key. I nod. Sure, I say. I just need to sleep.

In the room I drink a lot of water. Then I order breakfast. The biggest one they have, with extra black pudding and fortified cereal with berries.

When it arrives, I consume it meticulously. The bacon melts on my tongue and the egg yolks burst, warm and yellow in my mouth. Sometime during the meal, my stomach rumbles into gear and I realise I don't know how long it has been since I used it last.

I clear every single piece of food and lick the plate clean. When I'm done, I drink more water and then collapse on the bed.

10.32am

I wake up, feeling better. I forgot to draw the curtains last night, so there is sunlight in my room and everything is warm and sleepy. I snooze a bit before I get out of bed.

In the bathroom, I look at myself in the mirror. I don't look as bad as I expected. A bit thin maybe. My hair is ruffled and I'll need new clothes, but it could be worse.

I undress and throw my knickers in the bin, then take a long hot shower. When I get out I realise I don't have a hairbrush. Will have to go for the ruffled look, I guess.

I get dressed and have breakfast once more, this time in the hotel restaurant. I order an orgy of pancakes and get them to give me thick black treacle instead of maple syrup. There are fresh strawberries with the pancakes. The chef must be a genius. The meal is so sensual and so deliciously textured that it makes me want to masturbate under the table, but I don't.

Finally, the coffee fills my veins, makes me alive again.

Viktor

I watch the girl from afar, as she is sitting in the alley. It is a warm day, and the sun makes the stones on the pavement glow. Indian summer.

She is sleeping, in the alley. Only the homeless do this, but she doesn't look homeless. A bit ruffled, perhaps, but without the terminal air of lost about her that the long-term street-sleepers have. Temporarily lost, then. Maybe.

I watch her for about half an hour, imagining myself her guardian angel. If someone would approach, I would stop them, protect her from all harm. I would swoop out from nowhere and save her life. Pretty naive, really, as I don't know how to fight and don't carry a weapon. But a satisfying fantasy, nevertheless.

After a while, I get bored and leave. I buy a

sandwich, which I sit and eat in the park, but the girl in the alley keeps lingering in my mind. Who is she? Where does she come from? The city holds such strange destinies.

I decide to go back, but by then she is gone. I curse myself for my impatience. If I had just stayed, I would have learned something about her. I would have *known*.

Later

After breakfast, I go on a shopping spree. I don't buy much, just enough to get by, but I buy good stuff. Two t-shirts, one pair of jeans and a denim jacket. Underwear. And a hairbrush. I also buy a small travel bag for the things I'm not wearing. At the register, I pay cash from my bundle. There is €2,417.15 left when I'm done. I don't get shopping bags but put everything into the new travel bag.

Back in the hotel, I change then check out. Although it was nice, it would be too expensive in the long run. I don't know how long I'll need the money to last.

Evening

I spend the day wandering the city, absorbing its colours, its sounds. I walk aimlessly, with no purpose and realise I have forgotten what to do on my own.

The other people in the streets hurry on their way somewhere. Me, I just drift through the city in a bubble. Bopping up and down in the sun.

I end up by the river. I stay there till the

evening and the light turns orange. I like the orange glow of sunset more than the rosy pale of dawn. It is warm, not cold, like glowing rich honey next to brisk hibiscus tea.

Or something.

Five Days Later

I live in a cheap hotel now.

I am starting to remember what people do in the city, when they are alone. I go to the cinema, sit in cafés, read. Idle. I make sure to eat well and start to feel my body shape changing, my cheeks a little fuller, my breasts a little heavier. I spend Master's money carefully and with thought.

I find a bar for girls and spend the evenings there, not drinking but looking, savouring.

There are boys in the bar too, but I only see the girls. They are so beautiful.

One night I meet one. Her name is Anna. She is sweet and funny. She takes me back to her place and we make love. It is a giggly girly thing. She asks for my mobile number and I tell her I don't have one. She writes down her number and gives it to me. I write it on the inside of my lower left arm in black ballpoint, like a tattoo.

Viktor

Some days later, I see the girl again.

She comes out of a gay bar with another woman. I feel a sting of jealousy and one of disappointment. I can't believe she's a lesbo. I'm still intrigued, though.

I follow them from a distance and see them go into an apartment block. I wait for a while, but nobody comes back out. I don't know which one of them lives there, or if they live together, but I write down the address nevertheless.

The next day I visit the bar. I sit there all night but in vain. No one hits on me, my straight vibe keeping the fags at bay.

Two days later, I spot her again, this time in a café. She sits by a table near the window. Reading. I observe her for a while before I decide to approach. "I saw you in the alley the other day. You looked so peaceful in the sun."

She looks up and smiles at me. Her look drives a spear through my heart. Something deep and ancient awakens in me, prompted by that look.

She is an echo of something and she doesn't even know. Little girl. "Can I get you coffee?"

She nods and I order two, one for her and one for me. I sit down at the table. She looks dazed, not flustered. I wonder if she is drugged but decide she isn't.

I am. On her. "What are you reading?"

She holds the book out so I can see it. Henry Miller. I have never read Henry Miller. In fact I don't read much. I ask if it is good and she nods enigmatically. Her eyes glow.

The coffee arrives.

I make conversation for a while. Her name is Haima, she says. It is a Hindi name. Or Greek. Otherwise, she is quiet, but her eyes speak volumes.

I'm falling for her so fast I'm getting dizzy. I spot the tattoo on the inside of her arm and jealousy flares like a snake hidden in my sleeve whose head I have to clutch and beat against the table before it bites. Who is Anna demands the snake before it passes out. There is a moment before I realise it is writing on her arm, not a tattoo.

I ask her who Anna is and she smiles and shakes her head. It doesn't matter. I relax again.

We have a sort of conversation. I want to take her home with me, but that is not afforded by convention at this stage. I ask if I can see her again, and my heart pounds while I'm saying this, but she nods and suddenly I am ecstatic. I write down my number and give it to her on a piece of paper. Call me, I say and then get up to leave.

She nods. I think she will.

Over

The man leaves after the conversation and I hold his number in my hand. He is nice and interesting. His body is male. I had forgotten about male. Later, I write his number on my right arm, opposite that of Anna. It is hard because I have to use my left hand. His name is Viktor, which I write in block letters. I have two friends now. One on each arm.

Hold me for a while
Still against the night
Feeling the universe breathe

Synchronicity

The city is a long lost place. An artificial place, not natural. There are too many people here.

Things happen too often and too quick. Coincidences. I already have two friends and I am getting dizzy. Complexity. Sweetness. I say the word Love but it comes out wrong. I realise that I no longer know what it means and that maybe I never have. It makes me sad at first but then I think of the textures. The colours, the sounds. The city is an orchestra, a concert in perpetual motion. Symphonycity.

Chapter 2: Pain is Free

Anna and Viktor

I see Anna and Viktor every day now. They are both in love with me, which makes me feel warm and cosy. Anna is light and bubbly. She calls me her dreamygirl and says I am the most ethereal she has ever met. She likes to tickle me before we kiss, says it gets my attention, brings me into the present. I think it makes me forget about the colours for a while. I love her lips and hands.

Viktor is dark and gloomy. There is a lot of pain in him. I feel it and stroke him gently to make it better. I make love with Anna often but not with Viktor. Not yet.

The Mural

I walk across the city. I find a wall near the river where someone has written in large block letters: PAIN IS FREEDOM. It is not written with a spray can but with a brush, as if someone was painting their house and had a bit of paint left over.

296

I look around for a newly painted house but all the buildings look abandoned, and the only new paint here is the block letters.

The next day I take Viktor to see it. He disagrees, says it is all wrong. The day after we return with our own bucket of paint and erase the last three letters. PAIN IS FREE it says when we are done.

I have never seen Viktor so happy. He looks at the wall proudly. I dance around in front all bubbly, and then I kiss him on the mouth and he kisses me back and suddenly we are making out against the wall. It is very passionate, has been a long time in the waiting.

Viktor slips a hand under my t-shirt and all the senses in my skin explode. The feeling of male is overpowering, intoxicating. I want him to take me right there and then, against the wall, against the mural, right now. I tell him this. He hesitates for a moment but then it is okay.

I unbutton his jeans, then turn to face the mural while I flick my own jeans open. Slide them off, I whisper, and Viktor pulls my jeans and knickers down over my hips, baring my buttocks. He lets out a sigh as he does this.

I reach back to find his sex and guide it to mine. I hesitate for a split second when I touch him; I had forgotten how large male is. But it will be okay. I relax and guide. When he is in position, I bite my lip and nod. He then penetrates me all the way in one long motion.

Something releases into my blood stream and my whole body goes limp. I stretch my arms out and embrace the wall before me. Its surface is rough, its texture full of cracks and edges. Viktor withdraws and enters me again, pinning my body flat against the craggy surface. I see part of a letter near my face, but can't tell if it's pain or freedom. Fuck me, I whisper, as if he wasn't doing it already. It doesn't take long but the time stretches into eternity.

After
Viktor and I make love often after that. I also keep making love with Anna often. The two are so different.

When I meet Anna next, she asks about the scratches on my arms and body. I tell her they were from a wall and then she looks a little worried.

Are you okay, she asks, her eyes big and dark and her whole body like a question mark.

I nod. I wanted it, I say. I asked him to. I don't know if she understands, but she is calm. I kiss her fingers gently for a bit and then I place them between my legs.

It takes a second before she touches me back, but then she does and together we begin the long slow journey into ecstasy. It is so tender.

Return
I am happy in the city now. I alternate between Viktor and Anna, my two lovers. I feel like a child spending time with one parent, then with the other, getting the best of both worlds, getting double-spoiled.

One evening I walk home with Anna, hand in

hand along the river, when I spot a dark familiar figure on the quay.

Master.

It was only a glimpse but I know it was him. Absent for so long, but now he's here. He wants me, I know. I can feel it in my skin and in my bones. It is a deep tug, deeper than pain, deeper than love. Inescapable, physical, like gravity. Anna and I walk across the bridge, leaving Master behind us. I feel his pull across the river, like the moon pulling the tide. If he wants me, I will come. But he lets me go. He watches.

In Anna's home, we make love. I realise my time here may be ending, so I relish Anna's body like it was our final night together. She is so beautiful, so exquisite, my Anna. We savour each other.

It is only when we are finished that I hear the calling. He is in the hallway, outside Anna's apartment. Master.

Anna is asleep on her bed, on top of the duvet. I pull it over her, kiss her on the cheek and go.

In the hallway, he is waiting for me. Dark and pale and immeasurable. All shadow. I feel like I've always known him, always known his presence, yet I don't know if I have ever heard his voice.

"Welcome, Master," I say and cast my eyes down. "I heard you calling."

He smiles. I feel him surveying me and I know that he is pleased. I have been eating well, my body is rounder, my colour healthy. I realise I am undressed, naked in the hallway. But it doesn't matter.

Master opens his arms and draws me into his cape or between his wings. The blackness envelops me, and I disappear from sight. He is cool to the touch and carries the smell of exotic herbs. Cinnamon. Cloves. A hint of garlic.

He embraces me, and I instantly feel at home, at ease. This is heaven. Refuge from the colours, the sounds, the cacophony of the city. Here is only darkness, silence, peace.

He kisses me, and I vanish.

Morning

I wake up by Anna shaking me violently. Wake up, Haima, wake up! She is shouting, frantic.

I open my eyes a little bit. My head feels heavy. Very heavy. Strange dreams. Remnants. What is it, I ask groggily. Stop shaking me.

Thank god you're alive, says Anna. I was afraid you were dead. God, you look awful.

I get up and stagger to the bathroom, dizzy. It is a gigantic effort, like a marathon. When I reach the mirror, I am short of breath and my heart is pounding in my chest. My face is pale and my eyes are sunken. I examine the lining in my mouth and my vagina. Pale. There is a clock in the bathroom. It is nearly noon.

Anna is with me now, demanding to know what is going on.

I take a deep breath. This happens to me sometimes, I say. It is okay. I look at Anna's reflection in the mirror next to mine. There is worry in her face, fear almost. I sway a little in the mirror and have to catch my balance on the sink.

300

You are not okay, she says and helps me keep my balance.

I drink water from the tap and stagger back to the bed. I know what it is, I tell her. I can deal with it.

I want you to see a doctor, she says.

There is no need, I say and shake my head.

You were fine yesterday, she says, and now this. I shake my head again. No doctor, please. She looks at me, unsure of what to do.

Do you really want to help, I ask.

She nods and there are tears in her eyes. Get me some beef liver, I say, and cook it with parsley. And a glass of water. She gets me the water straight away. Then she goes out to shop.

Afternoon

Anna prepares a meal for me. It is a big meal. Her whole apartment smells like fried liver with parsley and it is only lunchtime.

I am not very hungry but I force myself to eat it all.

Anna watches me carefully and with amazement. Are you pregnant, she asks, and I have to laugh.

No I'm not, I say. I drink plenty of water with the meal.

Later, I find some supplements in Anna's bathroom, which I eat. Iron. Then I go back to sleep.

Days

It takes me a couple of days to recover. I phone

301

Viktor and tell him I can't see him for a bit. He hears the fatigue in my voice and asks if I'm okay. I have to assure him many times, but eventually he lets me go. I spend the days in Anna's apartment, relaxing, eating. Soon I am feeling better. I am getting good at this.

Next

When I meet Viktor next he asks me why I was away and why I still look a bit exhausted. It is a kind of condition I have, I say. It comes and goes. It's okay, I can deal with it. He looks sceptic. Anna helped me this time, I say. You can help me next. Viktor frowns but says nothing. I kiss him on the brow.

Next Week

The weather is changing in the city. It is less warm now. Less sun, more clouds. The evenings fall sooner and are a pale not rich orange. It is windy. I haven't seen Master since that night in the hallway, but I find money in an envelope in my hotel room, so he must be here. The thought of him makes me feel warm on the inside, means I'm doing all right.

Ki

Viktor is a pervert and I love him for it.

He confesses that he wants to tie me up and spank me. He is a little nervous about telling me this, doesn't know how I will react. I love the idea and say yes straightaway. I have done it before but

302

I don't tell him.

We go shopping for rope together and I show him how to do the knots. We also buy a flogger, a soft one made of suede. Viktor then ties me face down on his bed. It is a big brass thing and it takes the ropes easily.

He spanks me first with his bare hand and then with the flogger. He is tentative at first, keeps asking if I'm all right. Get on with it, I tell him from the pillows. Hit me baby.

He spanks me more and I get off on it. The long wide strokes put me in a soft and docile space where I can't speak, where there is no speech at all. When I am completely gone, he stops, then enters me from behind and fucks me senseless. It is exquisite.

Late

I come home late one night to my hotel. As soon as I insert the key in the lock, I know. Master is waiting for me, here in the hotel.

I open the door and enter my room. It is empty. I stand for a while, puzzled. Then he swoops down from out of nowhere and envelops me.

I giggle, did not expect this. He smiles at me inside the darkness, caresses my face. His thoughts, unspoken, form inside my head. Sweet Haima, they say as he sips gently from my neck. I smile and close my eyes in expectation. I flick my jeans open and wet a finger with my lips, then reach down between my legs. I know he likes it when I masturbate. But he stops me.

His thoughts appear in my mind again, now

serious. There is something I want you to do, they say.

Anything, I say. You know I will do anything.

He nods, then puts an image in my mind. I swallow. It is a big thing, difficult. But he is Master. I nod before I start touching myself again. He places his lips on my neck once more and I relax.

I will, Master, I whisper as I fade away into the darkness. I will.

Chapter 3: The Wish

Morning

I am less hung over this time. It is better when he takes me often and not so much. I now know what he wants. He likes the chemicals in my blood, the ones that come during sex, during orgasm. Endorphins. I should have known this a long time ago, when he first asked me to masturbate for him.

People think vampires are erotic and that they explode in sunlight. None of this is true; it is myths based on human obsession with sex and violence. Vampires care not for sex, it is not important to them, but they like the endorphins. Oh boy, do they like the endorphins. To them, the endorphins are like the honey on your pancakes, like the strawberries with your champagne. Sweet. Tasty. Exquisite.

And about the sunlight. A vampire in caught in the sun doesn't burn, it fades away slowly, shrinking like dry ice, until it's nothing but a thin spectral thing, catatonic and transparent, invisible to all but the most perceptive humans. Such a vampire becomes a torpid ghost, unable to move, caught forever in the daylight. So they stay in the dark.

I realise I'm talking about vampires as if there is more than one. I wonder if there is.

Preparations

I begin preparing for Master's wish. I buy a black scarf and plenty of incense sticks. I wonder if I will do this with Viktor or Anna and eventually decide on Viktor, simply because it will be easier. I ring Viktor. It is my turn to tie you up now, I say. Viktor hesitates. I don't want to spank you, I say. Just tie you up and feed you strawberries. You will like it. After that he agrees.

Viktor and I decide to do this on a Friday. I insist on doing it in my hotel room; it would be too weird to do it in his home. I am a little nervous, hope everything will be okay. I get the nicest strawberries I can find, big and red and ready to burst with juice. I don't know where they get them at this time of year. They are expensive, but it doesn't matter. I buy Champagne and two glasses also. Finally, I buy a corset for myself and a short black satin skirt. All the time, I feel Master lingering on the periphery of my senses. I feel his presence so strongly, and I know he is watching, but I never see him, no matter how hard I look. I don't have to tell him about the plan. He already knows.

Friday

In the afternoon I am a nervous wreck. I feel like my skin is inside out, like all my nerves are suddenly on the surface, unprotected. I am startled by the wind in the trees and by dogs barking two streets away. Hypersensitive. I go home and draw the curtains in the hotel and sit in the darkened room for a bit. It calms me a little. Then I start preparing for the evening. I set out candles and incense sticks, put the Champagne on ice and wash and dry the strawberries. They are gorgeous, the best I have ever seen. I try one and it explodes on my tongue in a mad crazy rainbow of a thousand billion colours jumbled up. Sensory fireworks. Sweet delicious. I suddenly remember that I haven't eaten all day.

Viktor arrives at 8pm. It is starting to get dark already. Autumn. I asked him to bring the ropes, which he has. He also brings the flogger. You're going to think I am a total pervert, I tell him. I already know, he says and smiles. I blush, a little embarrassed and very turned on. His presence makes me calmer. Maybe things will be all right. We talk for a spell, while we sip the Champagne. I am so turned on and so nervous that I have to touch him all the time, his chest and arms and face. I want you so much, I tell him and he smiles. I know he wants me too.

After a while, I give him a brief kiss, then disappear to change. When I emerge, I am wearing the skirt and the corset that I got yesterday. The skirt is very short and the corset silver with black print and lace. It is slutty and sophisticated, makes me feel like an expensive hooker. I can see in Viktor's eyes he loves it. I'm wearing elbow-length velvet gloves and have the flogger in my hand.

Look, don't touch, I say and eye him sternly. Now undress. He strips slowly while I watch. I'm not wearing knickers but he doesn't know that yet. When he is naked, I get him to lie down on the bed on his back. I then tie him to the bedposts, spread-eagled. I tie him the best I can, which is pretty good, better than he knows.

Next, I light the incense sticks and candles. The candles flood the room in a warm, orange light and the sticks create a heavy, complex smell. I picked many different sticks on purpose to create something complex and confusing. Viktor watches me from the bed as I walk the room with the matches. I cast occasional flirtatious looks in his direction but I take my time. When everything is finally lit, I walk over to the bed and survey Viktor's body. He glows.

Viktor

Haima stands beside the bed, flogger in her hand. She looks stunning. Like a dream, not a woman. I have never loved her more than this, think I would die if I did. The candles make her eyes glow, drunk with desire, tipsy with Champagne. She caresses my body slowly with the flogger. Legs, arms, chest. It tickles and I writhe. She smiles and tickles me more. I love her, love her, love her. Little girl. Goddess.

Haima climbs on top of me, sits across my chest, a leg on either side and her gloved hands against my chest. I have a surprise for you, she says and leans forward over me. Please, I say. I want you so much. She smiles, satisfied at my pain. She reaches down beside the bed and pulls up a black scarf. What's this, I ask, what are you going to do. She smiles enigmatically, then folds the scarf over and over till it becomes a thin strip. Blindfold. No please, I say, I want to see you. She hushes me and ties the blindfold around my head. Everything goes dark. Please Haima, I want to see. She hushes me again and puts something in my mouth. A strawberry, a large one. I feel her face close to mine. Suck it, she whispers, don't chew. Keep it in your mouth, whole. She caresses my face with her lips, licks me with her tongue. Her breath is heavy, turned on. The juices from the strawberry hit my tongue and the back of my mouth. There is another taste there also. Champagne. Sweetness.

Entry / Shadow and Pale

I kiss Viktor for a little while. He is mute now, the berry in his mouth. It is a special one, the best of the lot, which I have soaked in Champagne. I slide back to sit on the mattress between his legs, so I can see his body.

I stroke his thighs. He has a huge erection. I stroke it with my hand, then bend forward and take it in my mouth. I suck it for a while, caress it with my tongue and with my teeth. Viktor shivers and groans behind the strawberry. It makes me smile and turns me on even more. I masturbate myself while I suck him. It is delicious.

Perhaps it is a flickering of the candles that makes me notice. And even then it takes a second before I recognise his presence in the room. But

308

then he is there, all cinnamon and cloves and shadow. Absolute. All-encompassing. Master.

I let go of Viktor and turn around to face the darkness.

He smiles when our eyes meet, enigmatic, impossible to fathom. Shadow and pale. The moon in the pitch black sky. I see everything is ready, say his thoughts in my mind, and I nod in response. Let us begin, then.

I don't have to ask; I know what he wants.

I climb on top of Viktor and straddle him. I take his erection in my hand and caress it, play with it for a bit. Viktor's presence is so strange now, so foreign. I am not used to having two lovers in the room.

Suddenly it seems like I have always been alone. With Master.

Viktor moves, senses something is wrong, even past the ropes and through blindfold and the strawberry. I bend forward and kiss him on his neck and face. It takes an effort, doesn't come naturally now. Sweet baby, I whisper in his ear. I hope you're minding that strawberry for me. He relaxes a little. I kiss him more, then begin to caress his sex again. The scent of cinnamon is heavy in the room. Cloves.

I sit up straight. Viktor's erection is behind me now, and I press it into the crevice between my buttocks. It turns me on to feel him there. I raise my body up and guide him into me, then I lower myself and feel him sliding in all the way. Viktor moans on the bed and I let out a deep sigh. I stay still for a little while, relishing the feeling of him inside me. Then I start moving.

Sensation exquisite. I relax into the rhythm. The awkwardness from a moment ago is gone.

Viktor is breathing heavily, moaning behind the strawberry. This is good. I feel Master's hands and fingers on my shoulders now, long and pale and cool. He caresses my neck and shoulder bones, then takes good hold. I lean forward and place my palms on Viktor's chest.

Ready.

Bite

Master sinks his teeth into my neck and I go limp. He is on top of me now, on my upper back and on my shoulders.

I don't know which form he has but I'm sure it isn't human. He feels heavy, the extra weight pushing me down. My knees sink further into the mattress and Viktor sinks further into my womb.

He pushes gently against my cervix, and I ought to have flexed but I can't. In Master's grip I am limp, immobile, barely able to breathe. Viktor groans beneath me, from the weight or from pleasure, I don't know. So deep.

Master spreads his wings from my shoulders. They are wide, seem to fill the room from wall to wall. Darkness. Cloves. He beats them once, gently, and I feel my body rise, suddenly weightless, and then sink again.

I sense the candles in the room flicker and some blow out. I sense the slowly swirling odours of the incense scatter in sudden turbulence. Viktor lies below me, my hands on his chest, thinking it is I

310

who move so deeply. He moans behind the strawberry, his senses deprived and misled. I sense everything, without will, without effort.

Master beats his wings again, and I rise and fall once more. I feel the rhythm and realise it is a heartbeat. My heart. Master is moving me to its beat, slowly. Rise and fall. He drinks from me carefully to the beat, to the motion.

It is like a trance or a dream, like a slow, cautious dance. I give in, let myself go, drift away. To the beat, to the motion. To the dance.

Viktor

Haima fucks me slowly and with great care. I don't know how she manages to push me so deep inside her. I don't think I have ever been this deep inside any woman. But it's good.

Painful. I clench my teeth and the strawberry gets squeezed in my mouth, releases more juices. The sense of liquid in my mouth feels good. Erotic. I want her with my entire body, I want to be inside her and to envelop her at the same time, I want to hold her in my arms into eternity. Sweet Haima.

I feel the gust of wind next and then I hear something falling from the table at the other end of the room.

A survival instinct awakens in a corner of my mind, a primal fear of fire and an urge to see. What was that? A candle? Why did it fall? I wonder if we left the windows open, if there is a storm outside. Haima moves unaffected.

I wonder if she's noticed. Haima, I mumble through the strawberry. The candle, Haima, the

311

fire.

There is no response, not even a change of rhythm, and now I realise something is wrong.

She moves no longer like a lover but like a machine. Mechanically. I mash the strawberry with one movement of my jaw and swallow the bits to clear my mouth. Haima, I say, what is happening.

No answer, only the same movement up and down. Too heavy, too light. I think of a corpse swinging from the gallows in the wind and instantly lose my erection.

Cold sweat breaks on my body. Haima keeps moving, rhythm unchanged. I am scared now. I try to twist my hands out of the rope, but it is difficult and I have to struggle. Eventually I manage. She is still moving. I tear the blindfold off and see.

See

I stare into the face of my beautiful Haima. It is hanging there, her face, slumped in front of me, eyes and mouth open in a deathly grimace, hands limp on my chest.

Next, I see the face next to hers. A pale face with the black piercing eyes and long teeth like nails buried in my lover's neck.

Behind the face are wings, big black wings like leather or suede. The wings heave, bringing sweet Haima and that terrible face away from me and then back down again in that endless deadening motion that until so recently was love.

I scream into the face, into the faces of my sweet dead girl and the terrible nightmare on her

312

shoulders.

The nightmare reacts, moves, finally realises it is over. Then it pulls back, taking Haima with it in its claws, dragging her off the bed and towards the window.

I struggle to free my other hand and then my feet, but it's taking too long, too long, too long.

I glance up and see the nightmare opening the window and carefully edging my lover's body through it head first. We are on the second floor. It is more of a man and less of a beast now, the wings nearly folded on its back.

I tear at the ropes, and finally they give, but it is too late. The nightmare gently slips out through the window, unfolds its wings and grabs Haima's body in its claws, all in one fluid motion.

I run toward the window, but she is already out, hanging limply from the claws of whatever it is that has taken her.

The nightmare hovers for a moment outside the window, outside my reach, my sweet dead girl hanging from its claws, in the shadow of its wings. I see its face clearly now, pale against the night sky, with black piercing eyes. And then the nightmare meets my gaze.

I freeze.

There is nothing on the surface of these eyes, no emotions, no hatred, no compassion, none of these human things.

But underneath the surface, I sense something deeper, something older and more terrifying than anything I know. This nightmare is ancient. It has existed longer than I can know, longer than this city, longer than the city that was here before it.

But, to my surprise, it is none the wiser for all its years. It has not changed, has not moved on for all this time. It lives off the land, off the people, in the same way that it has done for millennia.

The realisation is terrifying and hopeful at the same time. I don't know how long I stand transfixed, gazing into these ancient eyes. But finally, with one heave of its wings, the nightmare turns in the air, and I watch with a profound sense of loss as it carries my sweet dead girl away across the city.

Epilogue: Viktor

I stand naked at the window for a long time, alone and cold in that empty hotel room. The candles that Haima bought and lit lie scattered across the room, extinguished, the unmade bed now a murder scene, not a love nest. But there is no blood. I shiver. What had happened?

I don't call the police, in the end. For what would be the point? I could tell them my lover was murdered in her hotel room while she and I were making love. Then her dead body was pulled from the bed, dragged through the window and flown across the city by something with large shadowy wings and a pale face. Oh, and I was in the room all the time. Saw everything. Yes, officer.

I consider contacting Anna, but I don't have her number (it was written on Haima's arm), and although I know where she lives, we have never actually met, and it is doubtful she would believe me.

Instead, I collect Haima's things and clean up the room a little. She doesn't have much, and everything fits neatly in a travel bag I find in one of the wardrobes, even the Champagne bottle and the two glasses.

It is 4am when I walk through the hotel lobby with the bag over my shoulder. No one is there, so I drop off the key in the deposit box and let myself out.

On the street, I snap into a brisk walk, and after a few minutes, I start to feel better. The cool morning air is doing me good.

When I reach the river, I pause on the quay for a minute. The city is quiet, sleeping. I look at the sky and I see the moon setting. It is full or near full, I can't tell.

But the sky is slightly rosy in the east. The sun is going to rise in a few hours. There will be life in the city again soon.

The End

Ezekiel M. Zachs is a scholar and researcher who hails from the icy islands of the Arctic Ocean. Dr. Zachs is currently working on a manuscript about his study of ghosts. Visit his website at www.ezekielzachs.com.

It's hard enough to protect the ones you love from danger when you know what the danger is and you know that they are, in fact, the ones you love. But when you know no such thing. . . .

The Wakings
by Alexis Brooks de Vita

I knew the man should not have tried to kiss me because the woman lingered in the window between kitchen and living room, silently watching. *She must be his wife*, I decided.

Yes, a whisper agreed inside my mind. *His wife.*

Then why did he keep his bright, dark-lashed eyes fixed on mine, confused and pleading as if the woman in the window—carefully turning her profile to us together on the couch—didn't matter? Didn't exist?

I wished she would say something to him to break his focus on me. *Would he bother*, I wondered, *to respond to her, if she did?* He didn't look like it.

I can't have been this man's lover, I fretted, with growing discomfort. *Tell me I haven't done that to this poor woman.*

The whisper came again. *No. But get away from him right now.*

I pulled out of his arms, off his chest, and rose.

He reached for me as though he were a child abandoned in a theme park. Yearning like a chained prisoner pickaxing a city street.

316

He said a word. His voice was exquisite, warm and inflected with crisp enunciation, something foreign tugging that single sound into a sharp slant against my ear. The beauty of his accent startled me and caught me up so that I missed the actual word itself.

Had he said my name? *I wish I hadn't missed it.*

I tried to think back, to figure out who I was, why I was here, what was happening. But it wouldn't come.

"Don't go up," he said carefully, as though aware of my confusion. "You don't want to go to him. Let me hold you."

His wife turned away from us into the depths of the kitchen, out of sight through the window. And, for no reason that I could think of, it struck me that she was surely an attorney. She could hurt him for his betrayal. She probably didn't want to. Yet.

Her name flitted through my sieve-like mind and was gone before I could catch it and call her to join us. Did I actually know these people?

Up, the man said. Whoever I was, whatever I was doing here, my place in this house and away from this couple—whatever *they* were doing here; did we all live together?—must be upstairs somewhere.

I looked around and saw a dark stairway that disappeared into blacker shadows, odd in this blank beige box of a—what was this place? An apartment? A townhouse? A split-level suburban?

I fled toward the darkened dirty carpet of the stairway and began to climb.

317

At first, blind fumbling at the loose railing. At the cramped landing, a thick sculpted door barely blocked out the thunderous sounds of a rapidly descending storm outside. Then, still climbing, just as I cleared the top stair, along with the thin yellow light of a low-watt incandescent bulb came the sharp faint wail of a child. "Mommy?"

Desperate, hushed. Furtive.

I headed for the closed door among many where the light trickled out beneath. I seized the knob and shoved.

A breakably slender little waif sat up in a welter of tear-wet pillows on a narrow child's bed. Her huge faun eyes glowed red from crying. *Oh, she can't be mine,* I thought at the sight of her straggling blonde-streaked tangles. *Can she?*

But the storm of relief that washed the terror from her in a flood of happy tears and opened arms said that, yes, I was the mother she'd been calling.

I rushed to the bed, breaching her little barricade of dolls and stuffed toys, and wrapped my bronze-gold arms around her.

I didn't need to be able to think up a name for her. She trusted my presence and my tight embrace and burbled wetly into my neck some tale of weird scary noises and don't go please stay with me tonight and hurry Mommy, close the door.

That last sent a shiver racing down my spine. I turned quickly as if to catch something out there in the hallway, beyond the brave little spill of light.

She pulled her fragile fingers out of the tight curls of my boy-cut Natural and pushed me away with her thin arms so I could get up. "Now,

318

Mommy," she insisted, her voice high and anxious, no longer whimpering as if afraid of being overheard. "Shut the door before it comes back. I think it's—"

She didn't have time to finish before I'd thrown myself at the door, shoved it shut, and heard the flimsy doorknob lock click with a wobbly turn. What good would that do us?

But someone had attached to this weathered solid wood door an old-fashioned deadbolt. On a little girl's bedroom door?

I wrenched the deadbolt knob, felt the hard resistance, and then the tumblers slipped sweetly into place. And we were safe.

I turned to the frightened little girl with a smile. "Snug as a bug in a rug, Cupcake," I repeated after the whispery voice in my head.

The little girl pointed toward me. Just as she did, I turned to the window next to me and saw its thin slatted blinds sling open. Had the storm ripped them wide apart?

She screamed, and beyond the shutters, something shrieked, not wind but a voice like steel claws gouging concrete.

I scrambled to grab at the shutters and slam them together, flat against the window frame. Something—white, ghastly, too quick to catch sight of—got caught between them for just the seconds I needed to snatch and yank the frail wood back into place. The something that broke through left me with a blood-trickling gash and a mind numbed by incomprehension and bemused, false calm, in its wake.

Do I have a cell phone? Call 911. Police have guns. They can shoot. What is this thing? What's out there?

I turned, panting, to the little girl. She clung to a pillow, bunched and buried against her tummy. All the while she sobbed, open-faced and leaning forward to stare at me after my battle with the thing in the dark outside.

I called to her firmly but softly, "Honey, you have to hide. In there." I motioned with my eyes toward what I hoped was her room's closed closet door.

She shook her head with mute horror.

Then the thing outside banged, and the shutters jumped in against my hands. I jammed my fingers into the slats and sank with all my body weight, to anchor them shut. The thing outside snarled and screeched with rage as I pulled the thin shutters against it.

Could I really keep it out with nothing but these flimsy shutters? That seemed impossible to me. It would smash my fingers, eat my hands or tear them off. . . . Oh, how to shut off my terrified images? I whimpered, resisting the scream that would undo me.

I had no idea if I had a cell phone. In the short time I'd come to in this awful place, it hadn't rung. I couldn't feel one anywhere between me and my jeans and the door as I braced my rear end there and pulled against the shutters. Nor could I take my eyes off the shutters or let go of them to check.

But the thing seemed to have stopped. For now. I looked at the shutters and my twisted fingers, numb. Dared I work them out of the slats and away from around the little wooden knob to try to flip that flimsy gold-tone latch shut?

Better not to risk it.

I looked toward the little girl again. Her wide tawny eyes were the same size and roundness as her opened mouth soundlessly breathing, "Oh."

"Honey," I whispered again.

She shifted her eyes from the shutters to my face.

"Get under your bed for me, please."

She stared at me as though the words made no sense.

"Please, darling," I insisted, this time holding her eyes and willing her to see me, and only me. Not the shutters. Not the door. "It's all right, honey. Mommy's here. I'll hold the shutters. I've locked the door. I want you to get in the closet or get under the bed. Do that for Mommy, Cupcake. Now, while. . . ." But I could think of no way to finish that sentence that would not spring fresh terror into the little girl's mind.

I wished I could ask her if she knew what the thing clawing and hammering to get in was. But how could I do that to this terrified little girl, when her "Mommy" didn't even know who *she* was?

As I watched, wondering what else to say, or at least how to say better the few things I'd said already, she eased the bunched pillow from her middle and cleared a path at her side. Then she obediently slid like a trickle of creamy skin laced with honey hair over the edge of her bed to pool beneath it.

When I no longer saw her large eyes glinting at me in the weak light I murmured, "Good, good girl. Everything's going to be all right now. Get some sleep, little one. Mommy loves you." I didn't know who else was in her life, as my internal informant seemed to have fled me. And I couldn't risk guessing who else to mention as loving the little girl and possibly end up raising her suspicions that I was not, in fact, her Mommy. Or, worse yet, that something was disastrously wrong with her Mommy at the worst possible moment, when any Mommy worth her salt should have had all her wits about her.

So I hung there and licked at the trickles of blood that oozed from the gash the white thing had given me on its way out.

While I watched, hoping for my whisperer to tell me the little girl's name, her slender arm slipped up the side of her bed. Her clawed hand snagged the first thing it reached—an old-fashioned naked teddy bear—and dragged the loveable prisoner down to the little girl's dark safe place.

"You rest now, angel," I called softly. *Angel will just have to do for a name tonight. Unless I'm going to get some help here.* "Mommy's watching out. Everything's going to be all right."

I hung there because I couldn't untangle my numb fingers from the slats and knobs of the shutters without risking letting go, and I couldn't let go without risking that the shutters would once again fly open. That rampaging thing outside might be waiting soundlessly for just such an opportunity.

But had no one else heard what was going on in

here? Why hadn't other people in the house rushed to help us? Not that I wanted anyone else to be outside the door or the window with that thing, whatever it was. But where was the man downstairs with the pleading eyes? Surely he and his wife must hear that whoever was upstairs was in terrible danger.

He knew I had come up here. He'd begged me not to go to "him." I'd assumed a husband or boyfriend. But could he have meant this savage thing outside the little girl's room?

That deadbolt on her door.

Would sane people deadbolt a little girl's door instead of getting her out of this house, altogether?

I looked over toward the bed and thought of calling good night to the little girl but decided against it. What if the thing outside heard and renewed its attack?

How long would I have to wait to move?

I thought of the man downstairs, his wordlessly staring wife, and the terrified little girl who called me Mommy, and tried to get that whisper of a voice to tell me anything. Give me pictures of our past together. Tell me why we were all in this house together under assault.

And what is the thing outside?

Silence. From the little girl under the bed. From the whisperer in my head. And from the thing at the shutters.

I was still wondering what I should call it to myself—*a force? a creature? a beast?*—when I opened my eyes to full sunlight pouring through the wide-open shutters.

I found myself huddled in the corner between the door and the window. My fingers had worked themselves out of the shutter slats but now clung uselessly to the windowsill, my arms cramped and tingling. My tight jeans must have cut off my circulation as I slept, because my legs and feet pulsed and prickled as if pins were stuck into them.

The little girl had jammed her teddy bear between my knees and my cheek as I slept. Its button eyes stared into the side of my head.

I looked around in panic. "Cupcake? Little princess? Honey?" I called.

"Mommy?"

The voice came from outside the window.

I scrambled up, clutching the window ledge. My legs wobbled and gave out from under me so that I knelt at the window and peered through the opening.

"What, Mommy?"

It took a moment for me to understand what I was seeing. The window of the little girl's bedroom opened onto a kind of balcony that stretched between several rooms on this floor above the ground. Right across from me, the little girl I'd worked so hard to protect and comfort looked back at me through a window to some kind of laundry room.

She was in the throes of dress-up, her face painted with red lipstick and shockingly vivid eye shadow, a golden drapery slung over one shoulder and tucked under the opposite armpit.

She seemed gloriously annoyed at being disturbed. "I left you Crumbles, Mommy," she pointed out, as if to say, "What does it take to satisfy you, woman?"

I suppressed my astonishment. Had she so soon forgotten the thing battering down her shutters to get at her—or at someone, at something, or just to get in—last night?

"Yes, I have Crumbles right here, Cupcake." I fished around down by my knees to produce the teddy bear and flourished him in the window beside my face, all without losing eye contact. "Come here and join us, okay? We're awake now."

"Why, Mommy? I'm playing. And Crumbles has been up since I got up. He's Mommy-sitting so I can play."

I was stunned. Was this child talking back to me when our lives were in danger, and I was trying to save her?

I knew when I met that little girl last night that she couldn't possibly be my child. I'm unsuited for this situation. How did one handle other people's stubborn children in an emergency?

"You look very pretty, little one," I cooed. "You can go right back to playing as soon as we find everybody and tell them what happened last night." *And get them all out of here.*

She puckered her face, obviously working up to give me her best rhetorical defense for more playtime.

But another voice called.

"Cassie? Are you in there?"

It was a man's voice, cautious and unhappy. The little girl's eyes shot past me, as if searching for someone else in her room. She didn't answer. *So maybe Cassie is not her name,* I calculated.

She must have unbolted the door when she left, for it swung in now against me. A paunchy man with watery grey eyes and hair like rivulets of new-fallen snow worked his way into the room just past the door and peered uneasily around.

"Cassie?" he said again when he found me crouched in the corner.

I looked up at him and waited. Evidently, my name was Cassie. For he said, "What are you doing in here? Did you sleep here last night? Manny and Jennifer told me you came up, but—"

He stopped himself. I was just realizing, to my distress, that there were matching silver-colored runic wedding bands on our ring fingers. This completely alien man, whom I was dead certain I never would have picked out of a crowd of strangers to have anything in common with me, was my husband.

He let go of the door and drew himself up. "Not another one," he said ominously. "Not now."

"Not another what?" I asked him carefully.

"Another one of your Wakings. Admit it, Cassie. I see that hazy look in your eyes. You're lost. You don't have a clue where you are or what's going on, do you?"

He leaned in closer and stared into my face. I tried not to pull back from him in revulsion.

My relief that someone here knew what was happening to me was stillborn.

I wished I could ask him to tell me about these "Wakings," as he called them. If he could. About the thing battering at the shutters last night, if I

326

dared ask. About how we could get everyone to safety, if he had any idea.

But he didn't seem at all receptive. He put his fists to his hips and said, "I bet you don't even know who I am, do you, this time?"

Whatever my Wakings were, he was obviously hostile to them and unconcerned about—*or ignorant of?*—the distress they caused me. He seemed to assume I had some measure of control over this situation. *Do I?*

I echoed that cowardly little whisper in my head, newly returned to me just in the nick of time: "You're my husband, Rob," I informed him and added on my own, "Why are you so upset with me?"

He flushed and turned away.

I could stand now with my finger pads still dug into the windowsill. I rose and called out to the little girl, "Honey, please. Come back in here, and let's get you dressed."

She popped back into view in the laundry room's window frame. "I am dressed, Mommy. See?" She spread her blood-reddened lips in a smeary grin and flung her arms wide. "Do I look pretty?" The golden drapery fell from one tiny shoulder and brought the whole toga down with it.

Dismayed, the girl dropped from sight to retrieve her wrap.

And Rob seized that moment to murmur, "Look, will you come out of Mazie's room, goddamn it?" He clamped a hand like a manacle on my wrist and dragged me out through the doorway.

I was propelled too quickly across the hallway

327

to another room to have a chance to get my bearings. What struck me was that this next room, apparently Rob's and his wife's (*which miserable woman couldn't possibly be me*), was even smaller than Mazie's (*so that's the little girl's name*) and painted neon white to give the illusion of space. It was empty except for the unmade bed that filled it wall-to-wall and a cheap plywood chest of drawers jammed in at the bed's foot.

We couldn't get far into the room without crawling across the bed. So Rob just reached behind me with his free hand to slam the door shut. "You didn't come to bed. I thought maybe, with Manny here and all—" But he shook his head and looked away from me. Waiting. Seething. Apparently hoping for something from me that his real wife never managed to deliver.

He wasn't going to finish his thought. Evidently, he couldn't. Not out loud, at least.

I wanted to retort, "So you thought what, exactly, about your wife and Manny, Rob?" But that would make no sense. That would be buying into the whole nightmare that this really was my life, that I really was married to this upset stranger, and that I really had given birth to that little girl out there playing dress-up in such terrible danger and thoroughly oblivious to it.

But wasn't there really a monster of some kind, something supremely ferocious and unimaginable, trying to break in last night? How could I get this petulant stranger to put aside his personal issues and get to that point?

I said abruptly, "I slept in Mazie's room, right

328

in the spot where you found me, Rob. I was with Mazie all night." I barely missed saying, "Your wife" for the second sentence, but I made it safely, giving him no further cause for upset. *Maybe this will calm him down and pave the way for some crucial conversation about our survival.*

Now Rob's face ran through that spurt of relief, quickly suppressed by caution and the smoldering resentment of his loneliness and vulnerability that I myself had just experienced in Mazie's bright yellow bedroom. Hope followed too soon by fear of trust about to be betrayed. *I know how he feels. I pity him.*

But why couldn't we talk about what I needed? No, here we were with demons clawing at the door while we paused to allay Rob's fears. *Never mind my loneliness, or if perhaps Manny tries harder than Rob to be appealing to me, and I just went down there for some pleasant company. Some innocent pleasant company, for heaven's sake!*

I stopped my internal tirade with a groan. What was I doing? Buying into this charade?

I grimaced at the thought of my intensely emotional response to Rob's pique. *As if all this is real.* As if the entanglements between these two couples—whoever they were—mattered more than the terror in the night that tried to get in and destroy us all.

I put out my free hand and touched the arm that imprisoned mine with hesitant fingertips, as a stranger might have done. *Or a lover. Be kind. After all,* I reasoned with myself, *can anything he says matter? I have, in reality, only been married to this man for about five minutes.*

"Why?" Rob asked miserably, interrupting my resolution. He had apparently taken my groan and my grimace as communications of some sort.

Or was it my touch? I thought, startled, just as, gathering courage, "Why didn't you just come to bed, Cassie?" Rob finished wretchedly.

At last! Here was my chance to tell him my unbelievable story of the monster raking at the little girl's window.

He didn't believe me.

As relieved as he looked when I described leaving Jennifer and Manny "in the living room" to go up and "check on Mazie," Rob cut me off as soon as I got to the flung-open shutters and the screeching thing that clawed my arm.

"Where is the wound?" he demanded and jerked the arm he still held up to my eye level.

Surely enough, there was nothing to be seen but my unblemished, sinew-sculpted, burnished-gold skin. With nothing more out-of-the-ordinary than tan lines from some favorite sweater.

Mouth open, I stared at it. "But—" I stammered.

Rob flung my arm away from him as if in disgust. "I knew it," he pronounced. "You're having another one of your goddamned Wakings, Cassie. Why did you lie to me?"

He is determined to find himself lied to, I seethed, confused and humiliated now.

"I—" I'd had every intention of answering all his questions and asking a few of my own. I wanted badly to confide in any adult and get some understanding of what I was going through, why I was here and what was real and therefore must be dealt with, and I would even work with Rob, if he was my only hope.

But he refused to be.

"I don't want to hear it," he declared and waved an affronted hand as if to fend me off. "What else have you lied to me about?" Apparently this was an oblique reference to Manny downstairs.

As if he poses a greater threat to all of us than the monster at Mazie's window! "I—" I started again.

But once again the palm of Rob's hand warded me off as if I were a talisman of evil.

"Never mind, Cassie," he snapped at me. "Monsters and goblins and gobbledy-gook," he muttered and raised his head as if with the vigor of his renewed contempt. "Get out front." He jerked his head, perhaps in the direction where I might find the front door. "Your Black Panthers are there, waiting for you. Those are the only monsters around here, if you ask me. They'll probably kill us all in our sleep some night while you're fantasizing."

Apparently, "Black Panthers" was a code name between Rob and his real wife, which unfortunate person I was, by now, convinced I could not possibly be. And it must have been an insulting code name that his wife was meant to bristle at and argue about. Clearly, I was going to disappoint Rob at every turn.

For, now, I deprived him of his right to a good fight.

In three long steps, I sprinted through the cramped hallway to the top of the filthy stairway, where I paused to grasp the handrail and realized that Rob lumbered morosely behind me. *In all decency, I shouldn't just dash away from him to beg these "Black Panthers" to listen to me and rescue us.* But that's exactly what I intended to do.

I hollered over my shoulder to Mazie to get into her room and put on regular clothes before I vaulted several steps down, swinging from my arms like an ape, to get to the tight little landing where the thick door leading outside stood ajar.

How long had my friends—or whatever they really were to me—been waiting? All the while that Rob and I bickered?

I emerged onto a phone booth-sized porch that blocked the welcome sunlight and bracingly cool air of the world outside and then leaped out of the dark wooden prison to get to the people who looked wonderfully familiar to me.

I felt my face beam sunny smiles at them. *I know these people!* Names and memories flooded my mind at the sight of each dear, consternated face.

Manny hung back at the edge of the small crowd of men, obviously uncertain of his welcome but determined to prove that he fit in. Jennifer had forced herself, frowning, onto a group of women and girls laughing at the edge of the handkerchief-sized front lawn, so tiny that there was no way to avoid hanging one's toes over the curb.

Overwhelmed by relief, I went to throw my arms around one black-bereted man who I was sure was a cousin of mine. "Rodney," I enthused.

From the corner of my eye, I saw Manny edge closer.

"You sure in a good mood, Cassandra," Rodney observed as he swept me against his muscular chest and put me firmly aside with one arm before he'd quite finished speaking.

"Rob musta done something right," another cousin of mine opined from across the cedar picnic table where they had some kind of diagrams or sketches spread out. "For a change," he added after a significant pause.

Manny looked down at the crabgrass at his feet and shoved his hands into his black khaki pockets.

I smiled at this cousin, too. "Hank the Hunk," I gushed. "So good to see you, cuz."

"Maybe that's what took her so long to get out here," a third man, an old family friend, rejoined. He didn't bother to look up or lift his finger from where he had pinpointed a strategic place on the makeshift map.

"Jamal, I love how you always come through," I praised him.

Manny turned his back on the men around the table and faced the street.

"Here's where the rally can start," Jamal went on without missing a beat. "It's legal to congregate at the outside of the courthouse. They can't get rid of us when they'll let reporters and other citizens wait for the defendants to come out."

"But how do we get the signs there before the march?" Hank wanted to know.

"I told you we can carry the signs. What can

they do about it?" Rodney insisted, impatient now.

"Target us for troublemakers before we can even start the rally," Hank shot back, "and break it up."

"How, man?"

"They can arrest us, fool. I'm out on parole, motherfucker. I can't take no arrest before I even—"

But Jamal interrupted. "Hey, don't say it out loud. Everybody who needs to know already knows."

The men closed in as Hank wailed, "Then it would all be for nothing, man. My life—"

"Hey," more cousins and friends chorused, and "Take it easy, man," Jamal advised, laying a heavy hand on Hank's shoulder.

Hank shrugged it off like a bullied child. I drew close to him again and touched him, too. He let my hand stay.

There was real anger here. It occurred to me that these men were not above resorting to fists, when they were desperate to resolve a matter.

But as crucial as memory told me this rally was today, I believed I had a greater emergency. And I knew, just *knew*, that these men would take my mindless fear seriously, if not my story. They would undertake to get Mazie and whoever else was in the house out of there. "Hank?" I began. "You guys?"

But a woman screamed and collapsed onto the strip of grass and sidewalk at the curb.

"Cassandra," Jennifer called to me. "Come help."

The men and I all whirled around. I raced them to the fallen woman and lifted her head onto my lap.

"What happened?" one of the men whispered. "She faint?"

"Something hit her," said another woman, her voice and face so heartbreakingly familiar, I knew these two must be my own flesh and blood.

But, "It's starting," Jennifer warned.

What is starting? drifted through my mind and was seared away like mist before the rising sun because the very young woman on the ground, her head now on my knee, and the equally young woman who had just spoken, weren't these my real daughters? *Not that frightened little girl under siege in a yellow bedroom upstairs.* Memory screamed to be heard.

Suddenly my only need was not to lose these two women, not to let them disappear with these men, my cousins and childhood friends.

Several of the men bent to help me raise my grown daughter to her feet. She swayed and fell into one of the men's arms again. "We need to get her inside," I pointed out reasonably enough, "out of this cold and away from the traffic and exhaust. Let's go in, everyone. You can finish your plans inside the house, while she recovers." *Don't go, everyone. Please stay and hear me out and help me get out of this penny-dreadful alien life.*

I rose and headed across the patch of bad grass to the ugly enclosed porch. One of the men jeered behind me, "Rob'll let us in, you think? Something changed?"

I couldn't tell who'd said that, but I turned in

time to see that it was Rodney who answered, "He'll let us in long enough to call the pigs and get us hauled off."

"Police," I corrected Rodney.

The men were not bringing the fallen young woman to the porch, behind me. One of them had hefted her into his arms, and they'd turned and were heading down the street, to where a couple of vans were parked.

"Buncha niggers up in his pad plotting the revolution? You know that crazy ex-banker honky ain't goin' for that, Cass," pointed out Jerome, who'd been the one who spoke a moment ago. I recognized his voice, now that I faced him.

"A bunch of African Americans and a crazy ex-banker European American," I corrected Jerome lamely.

"Yeah," Jerome chuckled, "you said it." He turned away from me, dug into his pocket to collect his keys, and then loped after the disappearing men and women.

Trailing them, Jennifer and Manny argued about getting into their car or crowding into the jammed vans. Manny no longer slid surreptitious glances at me.

So I started after them all, but my arm was caught up by someone behind me on the porch. I whirled to face whoever held me.

The other young woman who must be my real daughter had been waiting for me there. Roiling silver and slate clouds tumbled earthward down the only swatch of blue sky visible behind her.

She drew me into her arms, murmuring, "Don't

336

worry, Mommy. Sis'll be okay. I'll stay in the van with her while they do their rally and their march and whatever their big surprise event is. She's just over-tired. Maybe nothing struck her." Then, with a kiss on my cheek and a reassuring smile, she tried to move away.

"No, don't go!" I reached for her, but she was already retreating. "Honey, something's wrong in this house, with these people. Call everyone back. They need to help us get out of here. I'm desperate, but there was no chance to ask them—"

She shook her head, walking backward, still smiling as one does with a fractious child who doesn't want to be left at daycare. "Mommy, it's okay. Just bring everybody to the revolution in your own car, and we'll take care of everyone from there. We'll be at the courthouse waiting for you. I'll tell them you're coming, and they'll wait the big event for you."

I stared after her as she turned and ran nimbly to the van where her sister was briefly visible, lying on a bench seat. She swung herself onto the seat in back near her sister, slid the door closed behind her, and the vans and Manny and Jennifer's car all pulled away in a flurry of rickety metal and familiar faces.

Beyond them, out over the street, the bright sunshine of only a few moments ago was completely obscured in a tumult of wind-driven swirls of cloud and jagged lightning that hurtled down the sky.

The air was suddenly suffocating. No one could stay out here, in front of this house, and breathe. *What's happening?*

It's coming back! the whisper warned me. *You have minutes to get them out of here.*

My real daughter's words drove me on like a whip at my back. *They'll wait the big event for you.* I flung open the thick door to the flimsy house and leapt the stairs two and three at a time, calling out as I ran, "Mazie! Come on. Time to get out of here!" *Are there other children in this house? Elderly people?*

Within seconds, I slammed to a stop in Mazie's room in front of the open shutters at her window. I craned frantically across at the laundry window, at the toy-strewn balcony patio under a weirdly still bright sky, as if the storm at the front door were in another city altogether, at the ribbon of grassy backyard beyond.

There, three boys laughed and hosed each other more than the car they'd thoroughly soaped down. *So many people to get out of here.*

No time to waste.

"Mommy?"

I whirled on Mazie, petulantly crossing her arms over her dress-up golden drape, determined to play, no matter what I said. "Where are your clothes?" I demanded.

"I don't want to get dressed. Aren't I pretty?"

"Yes. Pretty enough to come as you are." I seized her bodily, slung her across my hip, and was at the door in one stride.

Mazie cried out, "Crumbles!"

Rob blocked my way. He frowned. "What do you—"

338

"Get out of my way." My tone shocked even me. I hadn't meant to communicate the utter disgust I felt for him.

I tried to reason with him in sixty seconds or less. "Everyone in this house is in danger, Rob. Stay if you insist. I'm getting the children out of here. We can park at a safe distance and watch what will happen. If you come, I'll explain it when we're safe."

"My clothes," Mazie wailed, and I thought bitterly, *She really needs to get away from her father before his whiny behavior solidifies in her plastic little character.* "Give me the car keys and get out of my way, Rob. Mazie wouldn't dress. So we're going as is. There's no time."

Apparently Rob only pushed when he knew he could get away with it. He fished a bundle of keys out of his rumpled khaki shorts pocket and ducked around me. "I'll get her clothes."

"She can dress in the car. Are you coming with us?"

"Cassie—"

"We're going! Help me get the boys in the car, even if you want to stay."

I felt Rob grasp the back of my arm only long enough to tuck a soft bundle alongside the suddenly limp Mazie. "Come on, Crumbles," she sobbed. And a burbled, "Daddy says Mommy got the Wakings. Don't let's make her mad," as I bounced her down the steps one at a time, slung sideways across my hip.

I was descending the stairs more slowly than I wanted to out of fear of tripping and falling with her. I'd only just now reached the landing. To my left, I could hear the boys laughing out back, beyond a sliding glass door left open.

Outside past the heavy door on my right, I heard a horrible howl and roar, as if a locomotive were barreling down on the house. *Wind? A tornado?*

Rob paused beside me on the landing as I bounced Mazie up to a sitting position to get a better grip. "Let me take her," he said. And then, "Is that someone banging on the door?"

How could he have heard anything?

Because it wanted him to hear.

Now even I could hear something pounding as if it had a medieval mace in its fist. "Rob, don't open that door," I pleaded.

"Don't be ridiculous, Cassie. If someone's caught out in that storm—"

The door exploded inward.

Splinters of wood and metal shot ahead of the heaviest part of the door as it swung. It slammed into the wall and stuck there, nailed by its own doorknob.

Rob, still beside me on the landing, turned back to the gaping door, mouth open, and stared at the two creatures that stood there.

A child-sized colorless thing looked with its blank off-white pupils straight ahead, toward the open glass door and the laughing boys I needed to save. Slightly behind the fake child, a twisted old man—white from head to toe as if bleached and bent double as if from osteoporosis—strained to peer upward at Rob.

340

Rob had been startled when the door exploded open. Within seconds, at sight of the old man, his relief preceded an immediate invitation to, "Come in, come in. Get out of the storm," as I begged, "Slam the door!"

I clutched the now silent Mazie tighter and bolted the last steps, past Rob.

As I passed him, I felt something hard and cold slip around his body, between us, and snatch him out past the opened door.

Horrible bellows of rage or pain followed me as I breached the sliding glass door's threshold and kicked it shut. No time to try to figure out how to latch and brace it.

"What's going on?" The three boys came loping, varying degrees of anxiety on their faces. "Was that Dad? What happened?"

"In the car," I demanded. *No time to ask the whispery voice their names.* "Dad's going to catch up with us when we get out of here." *I'll explain the lie to them someday when they are all safe.*

"What happened to him?" the oldest asked and headed purposefully toward the glass door.

"No!" I slid Mazie to her feet, commanding, "Get in the car, Mazie, and stay there." I straightened with Rob's keys dangling from my hand. "If you get in the car and stay there, and hold onto Mazie and anyone else we need to keep safe in there till we can go, you get to drive."

Do I know teenage boys, or what? I thought triumphantly as he wavered.

The teenager's questions—whatever his name was—died on his lips. He snatched the keys before

I could change my mind, took firm hold of Mazie's arm and her teddy bear, and dragged her to the car, grabbing up a scraggly striped kitten and a snuffling puppy as they marched.

I turned to the other two boys, who lingered, confused, on this side of the glass. "Get away from there and get in the car," I said levelly, backing away. "Dad wants you to get in the car and get out of here." *He would if he were alive.*

"Where is he?" the middle boy asked, edging after me, uncertain.

"Dad left another way. He's already gone." I'd faked them out. Now I lunged and seized each boy by an arm. "There's no time. Let's go. They're coming!"

The boys hadn't seen the vague white blurs behind them on the other side, small on the stairs and suddenly surging larger, right up to the glass.

"Run!" I screamed, and we raced all linked together toward the open driver's door where the teen gunned the engine.

True to his side of our bargain, he'd strapped down Mazie in the back, where she held the wriggling puppy and kitten to the car's floor with her hands and feet, and seat-belted himself in.

The other two boys tumbled in and scooted around to find seats. I leapt in next to them, behind the driver, crowding Mazie because I was afraid to run around the car to the passenger side, near the sliding glass door.

The middle brother dove over the top of the front passenger seat and twisted around to sit down. Past him, visible through the passenger windows, the garden hose writhed and spurted a fountain of spray.

And beyond the spray, the mannequin white-gray child emerged from the house, staring blankly somewhere, not quite at us.

"Go!" I urged the teenager. "Get us out of here."

He floored the gas pedal and revved the engine. "I don't know how to back off the grass down the driveway," he admitted, a bit sheepishly for an emergency.

A tall straight manlike shape that even the boys in their anxiety for their father didn't recognize as a remnant of some aspect of Rob moved into the glass doorway, turned its oddly melting face toward us, and looked at us.

I shouted to be heard above Mazie's crying and the other boys' questions. "Then get us out of here any way you can!"

The teenager slammed the soapy boxy clunker into drive, and it hurtled like a missile toward the splintery backyard fence.

The End

Alexis Brooks de Vita is the author of LEFT HAND OF THE MOON *and the trilogy* THE BOOKS OF JOY, including BURNING STREAMS, BLOOD OF ANGELS *and* CHAIN DANCE, *all published by Double Dragon/Blood Moon. She has also published a translation of* DANTE'S INFERNO: A WANDERER IN HELL *with Double Dragon/Blood Moon. Alexis's scholarly books include an exploration of the historical murder mystery,* THE 1855 MURDER CASE OF *MISSOURI VERSUS CELIA, and* MYTHATYPES: SIGNATURES AND SIGNS OF AFRICAN/DIASPORA AND BLACK GODDESSES. *Visit her YouTube Channel at* http://www.youtube.com/user/ABrooksdeVita *to follow the* BOOKS OF JOY *podcasts and book trailers, and her website at* www.alexisbrooksdevita.com *to read her characters' secret stories and journals and get to know your own inner protagonist.*